KNIGHT GAMES BOOK 2

USA TODAY BESTSELLING AUTHOR

GENEVIEVE JACK

Candle burn and cauldron bubble, Grateful Knight is in some trouble!

Commitment phobic Grateful Knight has her hands full. While she struggles to understand her new role as Monk's Hill Witch, evil isn't waiting for her to come up to speed. Not only is there an increase in supernatural activity in her ward, she's being evicted from her home, breaking in a snarky new familiar, and trying to sort out her feelings for her metaphysically connected and immortal boyfriend, Rick.

When Grateful foils a murder at a fae bordello, she uncovers a plot by a local vampire coven to obtain a secret weapon with the power to control both the living and the dead. History is threatening to repeat itself. And if Grateful doesn't give herself over to her role completely, it could cost her everything.

A FAMILIAR TALE

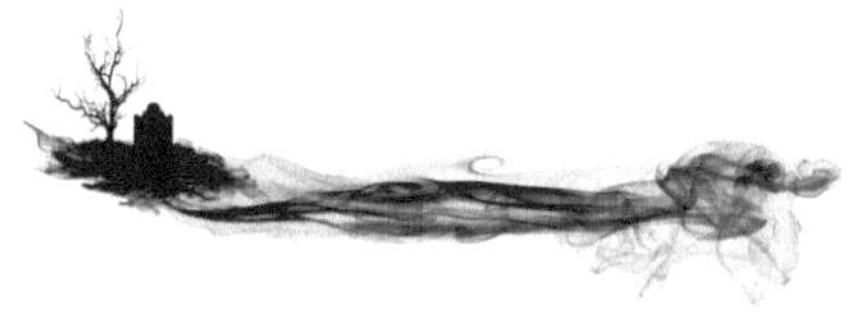

"Hey, Grateful, why are zombies entered under Wayward Magic instead of Supernaturals?" Absent-mindedly, Michelle leaned back from the computer monitor, hands cradling the base of her head.

"Because they're animated dead bodies," I explained to my friend. "The body itself is natural, as opposed to ghouls or fairies who were born and raised Supers." I flipped to the next page in *The Book of Light,* which featured an eavesdropping spell that enchanted a bee to listen in and relay information to the spell caster. *Sigh.* As if a vampire wouldn't be suspicious of a bumblebee persistently circling its head. Still, an earlier reincarnation of myself thought this spell was important enough to put in the daddy of all grimoires. My book of magic had been with me for multiple lifetimes; I needed to trust in its wisdom. With a tap of the return key, I started a new database entry.

Michelle lifted her cup of coffee from the desk and took a deep swig. "But what about vampires and shifters? They were human once. Why are they under Supernatural?"

I stopped typing and gave it some thought. I'd only been

the Monk's Hill Witch for two months. Magic and supernatural monsters were new to me too, even if I was a Hecate, aka sorceress of the dead.

"I think it's because with zombies, someone else is pulling the strings. Whoever animates them controls them. They're soulless, for lack of a better word. Vampires and shifters can make their own decisions—well, as long as it meshes with the orders of their coven or pack leader."

"Hmm. Who controls the ones you've imprisoned in the cemetery?" She stood and walked to the window overlooking my front yard. The glass still sported the Anderson Windows sticker from when Rick replaced it two months ago after the vampire Marcus shattered it while escaping us.

"The zombies? They're possessed by a type of vaporous demon from the underworld. In my last life, I sentenced them to hell for possessing humans. Of course, the demons were expunged from the human bodies, so…ah…they possess corpses to come out at night. They can't come out of the underworld without one. The fresh air is toxic to them."

"Oh."

I didn't want to be a bitch or anything, but I wished she'd get back to work. I'd slayed Marcus, but Julius was still out there. As vamps went, Marcus was child's play compared to Julius. I'd only met the vamp once, but once was enough. Julius was ancient, insidious, and had a following. I suspected Julius was behind the murder of my last incarnation, and now was growing his free coven to dangerous sizes in hopes history would repeat itself. The spells in *The Book of Light* offered my best hope for protecting myself against Julius, and this database promised fast and easy access on the move. The book itself wasn't going anywhere. The tome weighed hundreds of pounds.

I truly appreciated Michelle volunteering to help me with data entry, but when she got like this, questioning, it really slowed us down. We'd only put in about four hours. I wanted to get another hundred entries done before sunset and all the witchy responsibilities that came with nightfall. Thankfully, she walked back to my MacBook Pro and sat down. "At least we can work during the day now. Real, honest-to-goodness desks," she said, knocking on the wood.

I shrugged. I'd found two big desks at Elmer Bishop's estate sale for next to nothing, which was everything in my checking account. I butted them against each other and networked my new computer, a birthday gift from my dad, with my old laptop. We could both make entries to the same database. Plus, *The Book of Light* was large enough that if we opened it across the two desks, Michelle could enter one spell while I entered another. It was a nice setup.

"Not that your magic isn't totally cool, Grateful. I mean, conjuring shit out of the ether is wicked awesome, but you have to admit, it's nice not to have them disappear when the sun comes up."

"Yeah." Unfortunately, the magic of my attic was tied to the night air, and everything I conjured disappeared when the sun rose. It sucked, but I suppose everything has to have limits. Otherwise, I'd be conjuring myself a million dollars up here.

The soothing rhythm of vigorous typing filled the air between us...for all of thirty seconds.

"Did you hear about Logan?" Michelle asked, blowing away any delusions I'd had about her getting back to work.

"Hear what? I saw him at physical therapy yesterday. He's walking pretty well with a cane. Put some weight on too."

"He's starting back at Valentine's. Just a few days per week at first, but he's planning to work up to full time."

Valentine's was Logan's pride and joy. He'd started the restaurant from scratch, and it was one of Carlton City's best rated. In my opinion, Logan was lucky his assistant manager had kept the wheels on while he was missing. Another employee might have closed shop.

"That's good news," I said. "Logan needs somewhere to focus his energy."

"You mean on something other than you."

"No," I said defensively. "I mean on something other than the pain of his recovery." Logan had been in a coma for almost a month after a truck plowed into him on his bike. He'd been damaged badly enough to knock his soul out of his body and leave him unrecognizable to his rescuers. It was sheer coincidence he ended up in the hospital where I worked as a nurse, and serendipity that I was the one who could put his soul back into his body. His recovery had been a long, hard journey.

"So, you're saying that Logan hasn't tried to rekindle those old romantic feelings now that he has a body?"

"What Logan felt when he was a ghost was just a misunderstood metaphysical attraction to me as his soul sorter."

"Nice story. How do you explain what you felt for him?"

"Logan knows I'm with Rick now."

"Yeah," she drawled. Her eyes drilled into me.

I wasn't sure what she wanted me to say. Rick was part of my job description. He was my caretaker, the immortal vessel for my soul between lifetimes. Hundreds of years ago, the first me, Isabella Lockhart, had made Rick her caretaker. At the moment of her death, she stored a piece of her soul inside him, which he'd returned to her when she was reincarnated. I was a reincarnation of that same witch, and I'd taken back the immortal part of my soul from Rick in a ceremony that included blood, magic, and sex.

Pursuing anything with Logan didn't make sense for a number of reasons. Aside from the superhuman level of understanding it would require of him to allow me to continue to be the witch and have sex with Rick as needed, my feelings for Logan had changed since he was reunited with his body. As far as I was concerned, the night we shared when he was a ghost had been an accident. I was seeking comfort, and he'd accidentally slipped inside my body and given me an orgasm. Ancient history.

"Logan's my friend. That's all." To signal I was done with this particular avenue of conversation, I flattened my page with my palm and returned to typing vigorously on my laptop.

Michelle raised an eyebrow and pursed her lips inquisitively. "How is Caretaker Rick, anyway? You guys still trying to start a fire by rubbing your crotches together?"

I fought a smile but only half of my mouth obeyed my command. "Nice, Michelle. You know, it's not like it's tawdry or anything. We *have* to do it. It strengthens our powers."

"Power sex. Right. He gets all charged up and you get..."

"Multiple orgasms and sometimes his blood."

"Yum." She grimaced.

"It heals me. Last week, we were bringing in a vamp we caught feeding on a human at a strip club in the city. The thing practically bit though my arm before I sentenced it to hell. A little sip of Rick and the wound healed right up. It's nothing short of miraculous."

Michelle shook her head and took another gulp of coffee, as if she could rinse the taste of blood from her mouth. The TMI convo was enough to make her turn back to her work. She focused on the page closest to her and poised her fingers over the keyboard.

"Hey, here's something interesting," she said.

"What?"

"It's a spell to call a familiar."

"A what?"

Michelle scooted closer to the book and read to me. *"Familiar, Spell to Call. A familiar can be summoned to amplify*

Hecate's power by performing the following spell. A willing spirit will arrive in the form of an animal possessing those traits the current incarnation is deficient in and supporting optimum natural balance. Through mutual respect and bonding, a familiar can become a trusted and powerful companion."

"Cool. Like a black cat or whatnot."

"Or maybe you'll get an owl like Harry Potter!"

"Oh yeah, those things are wicked awesome." I stood and leaned over the book to get a good look at the spell.

Michelle tapped the yellowing page. "Hey, there are some notes here in the margin. *Tabitha 1721, Abraham 1823, Gertrude 1898.* Grateful, I think this is a list of past familiars. Is that how many times you've lived?"

I shrugged.

"Well? Are you going to do it?"

"Maybe. Does the spell look difficult?" I tried to read it through myself, but Michelle's head was in the way. She was practically crawling into the page. My friend seriously needed glasses.

"You tell me. It says you have to meditate. Once your mind is clear, you make an offering in your silver bowl and a willing spirit will come to you."

"What kind of offering?"

"It doesn't specify."

"As long as it's not blood." I'd learned the hard way that blood—my own—was required to sort a human soul to the afterlife. When I'd put Logan back into his body, I had to slice my arm and bleed into my silver bowl to make his soul "stick." The cut itself healed magically, but the blood loss on top of the mystical effort involved left me exhausted.

"I guess it can be anything that's valuable to you," she said.

I nudged her out of the way and read through the spell myself. "Look, this symbol in the corner means I can do it during the day." I pointed to a yellow circle next to the title.

Michelle nodded and looked at me expectantly.

"It might be nice to have a pet," I said.

"Grateful, this isn't just a pet. This is a *familiar*, the perfect pet to balance you. It's like petmatch.com but better. This little guy will make you more powerful. Hell, all I've got at home is a pug with flatulence."

"You love Bosco."

She giggled. "He was an impulse buy that grew on me."

I sighed and plopped back into my chair. "I don't know, Michelle. Do we have time for this? I really wanted to get more done today."

Tipping her head to the side, my friend folded her arms across her chest. "Really? The pages aren't numbered, but this thing has to be five thousand long. We've been at it all month and have barely made a dent."

With attitude, I combed my fingers through my hair and rolled my eyes. "All the more reason to buckle down and get to work."

She jabbed her open hands toward the mammoth book. "Hello? It's going to take us a year to enter all these spells. It's not like we don't both have full-time jobs. This is like moving a bucket of water with an eyedropper."

"Now you're exaggerating."

She folded her arms across her chest. "What's the rush?"

Crossing the attic, I leaned against the window frame and watched the naked branches of the oak tree in my front yard twist in the late November wind. Less than six weeks until Christmas. I was sure Michelle had better things to do with her day off than enter spells into my database. My chest sank thinking about the burden I'd been to her the last several months. I was the reason she'd been possessed by a vampire.

But I *was* in a hurry. Besides the danger of Julius's growing coven, and the fact that he probably wanted me dead, Julius said that Rick had lied to me, that I didn't need a caretaker to regain my power. Julius was a vampire and almost certainly deceiving me. I had no reason to trust him. But ever since he'd said the words, I'd questioned my connection to Rick and the boundaries of my power. In my gut, I had the tiniest needling that Rick was keeping something from me. I'd tried time and time again to put the feeling aside, but it wouldn't leave me alone.

My past incarnation had the wherewithal to name a guardian of my magical attic, Prudence. She'd helped me learn about what I was. Unfortunately, when I accepted my role, Prudence moved on to her eternal reward. With her gone, if I couldn't trust Rick, the only source of power, protection, and information I had was *The Book of Light*. I was sure all the answers I needed were within its pages.

I didn't want to trouble Michelle with all the details. She'd done enough to support me already. This was my boat to row. Besides, I was willing to bet obsessing about it was exactly what Julius wanted me to do.

"It could save my life, Michelle. The book weighs hundreds of pounds. This is the only way I can take it with me while I'm learning. I may need one of these spells in an emergency."

"Really?" She leaned across the book. "An eavesdropping bee is going to protect you against a vampire attack on the fly?"

"You've got a point," I mumbled. "But it's still my best hope."

Michelle rubbed her palms together. "I'm not saying the database isn't important, but it isn't everything. It's going to take time. No matter what you do, you're going to have to learn how to use this magic. There are no shortcuts."

I sighed. "You're right. This is just the workaholic in me coming out."

"Exactly. It will all get done eventually. A little a day and by the time you're thirty, you'll be done." With one arm, she hugged my shoulders playfully.

I suddenly felt compelled to entertain her. She'd earned it. "You wanna watch me summon a familiar, or what?"

"That's the spirit."

We jogged downstairs to look for something to offer the familiar's spirit. Unlike when Logan lived here, the house was a mess and there was nothing in my pantry but coffee grounds. I opened the refrigerator to check if food had mysteriously appeared there while I was in the attic. It hadn't. The contents consisted of a box of baking soda, a half-empty bottle of ketchup, and the remains of Valentine's takeout from two weeks ago with dodgy-looking fuzz growing under the lid. I tossed the takeout but grabbed the coffee grounds. Michelle appeared in front of me with a bottle of wine from the cellar.

"This should work," she said.

"Wine? Is that necessary?" I asked, not thrilled about wasting a bottle.

"The book said you needed an offering. The connotation is that you sacrifice something important to you. You don't want to use blood, and there's nothing more important to you in this house than wine and coffee, except maybe me, and I'm not sitting in that bowl."

"Wine and coffee it is."

We returned to the attic, and I pulled out the wooden trunk containing my magical paraphernalia. On top was my blade, Nightshade. Made from the femur of the patron saint of cemetery workers, Nightshade could only be wielded by me. I set her aside to dig beneath her space in the trunk. Under her was a silver bowl, salt, candles, a few shrouds, and a bell. My predecessor had left the witchy toolkit, and I was becoming more comfortable with it day by day. I selected the bowl.

Cross-legged on the floor next to the wine and coffee, I closed my eyes and tried to clear my mind. I flexed my shoulders toward my ears, inhaled, then released the breath, slumping forward. I tried to relax as much as possible, concentrating on the flow of breath at the back of my throat. When a thought threatened at the corner of my consciousness, I pushed it aside.

They say when you enter deep meditation that you visualize a light of some sort moving toward you. I did. A green light that seemed flat at first until I reached it and then expanded into a tunnel. The light branched out and formed leaves. And then, in my clear mind, I was in a garden. Even though I logically knew my body was sitting in my attic meditating, I *was* physically there, nestled in blades of cool dewy grass with my bowl and offering beside me. The sun was warm upon my face, and the leaves of the plants rustled in the sweet-smelling breeze.

From a grove of trees, a naked woman stepped toward me. Large dark eyes and silky black hair contrasted sharply against the light that shone behind her head. She stopped just short of my bowl.

"Hecate," she said. "Welcome to my garden. Make your offering."

I wanted to know more about this woman and this place, but my intuition warned this was not the time to ask. Maybe it was the way her skin glowed like it was radioactive and the light broke around her torso. Reflexively, I reached for the wine and poured half of it into the bowl. I sprinkled coffee over the top.

The woman laughed, a sound as pure and clear as a choir of bells. My eyes started to hurt so I looked away from her, back at the bowl. It was empty.

"Yes, I know who you seek, and I send him to you with

my blessing. He is yours and will teach you what you need to know."

The woman opened her hand. A black butterfly bobbed toward me, growing fast and spreading out until it barreled into me. I somersaulted backward from the impact, eyes closed against the onslaught. Everything—the garden, the woman—disappeared in a wash of darkness.

"Grateful!" A hand slapped my cheek. "Grateful, snap out of it!"

I opened my eyes to see Michelle hovering over me.

"D-Did it work?" I stammered.

The corner of Michelle's mouth tugged upward. "Um, yeah. It worked."

"So what is it? A cat? An owl?"

"Maybe you should see for yourself," she said.

She helped me up to a sitting position. Behind my silver bowl was a huge black ball of feathers. I reached for it and a pair of beady black eyes popped open to peer at me. A large hooked beak snapped the air and two shiny black wings stretched on either side of a lissome black body.

"It's a crow," I said with distaste. On the spectrum of magical creatures, I hadn't expected a yard rat. The thing looked like something I'd shoo off the garbage cans.

Michelle took a step back. "That's not a crow, Grateful; it's a *raven*. And I think it just pooped on your floor."

2

ALL CHARGED UP

Eww. My familiar had, in fact, pooped on the floor, and defecating appeared to be the extent of his talents. I spent a solid minute staring into his beady black eyes, but no shooting stars or magical tingles came to pass.

"What are you going to name it?" Michelle asked.

"Hmm, what do you name the creepy, hooked-beak bird of death? I'm not sure."

Michelle lowered her voice to an Alfred Hitchcock bass. "Quoth the raven, nevermore."

"Nevermore is too long and too obvious." I snapped my fingers. "Of course, Poe! I'll name him Poe."

"Stellar. Now that you've named him, what will you do with him?"

My shoulders sagged, the magic hangover hitting me hard. I hugged my knees to my chest and closed my eyes.

"Drained you, huh?"

"To the porcelain bottom." I rubbed my eyes. "Do you know what ravens eat?"

"Not a clue, but that's why I have my old friend Mrs.

Google." From her back pocket, she removed her phone and typed a few words into the search bar. "Ugh."

"What?"

"Listen to this: Ravens are omnivores eating whatever is easiest to catch, including the dead bodies of other animals, small living rodents, reptiles, other birds, and occasionally grains and berries. They will also eat maggots and animal poo."

"Eww," I said. "That's disgusting."

"I prefer baby goat, but don't knock maggots until you've tried them," Poe said, ignoring the way Michelle and I gaped in surprise at the deep tenor voice coming out of his throat. "They are surprisingly sweet and nutritious."

"The bird just spoke," I said.

"Yes. The big, scary bird just spoke to us in a muddled European accent."

"Do you have a problem with my accent? Because the East Coast Jersey Shore lilt you've acquired isn't exactly prizeworthy."

I snorted, covering my mouth with my hand.

"Oh, that's rich," Poe said, laughing low and dark. "Not exactly an aristocratic giggle you have. Did you snort like that before you became a witch, or was the cause a spell gone bad? Because if it was the second, my condolences for the loss of your femininity."

Michelle wrapped an arm around my shoulders and helped me to my feet. "Um, Grateful, your familiar is a total ass."

"Yeah. I don't get it. The woman in the spell said he would be what I needed. I don't think I needed another smart-ass in my life. I have you."

"I'll take that as a compliment."

I nodded.

"So, about that young goat. I am feeling quite hungry. It

doesn't have to be freshly born. A few days old is fine. If you open the window, I can find one myself."

I glanced toward the window, noticing the gray-toned sunset. Looked like a winter's storm was coming. Someone needed to tell Mother Nature it was still November. "Are you sure you can take care of yourself if I let you outside?" I turned toward the big black bird.

"Of course, dear witch. I may be new to you, but I am no spring chicken." He cackled at his own joke, breaking into caws that didn't match his low, humanlike voice.

"Do you think it's a good idea to set him loose on Red Grove, Grateful?" Michelle asked. "We hardly know him."

I pointed a hand toward the pressing night. "I've got to go see Rick," I said.

She groaned. "Right. You've got a job to do. You let Poe out. I'll get some paper towels to clean up the mess."

"You're the best."

"Sorry about the state of things," Poe said, tilting his head toward his excrement. "Blackberries. They're a habit really. Once you eat one…" His low laugh trailed off.

Michelle scrunched her eyes and stuck out her tongue in my direction.

"Sorry," I said, opening the window. Poe burst past me, taking to the cool November twilight like it was a long-lost friend.

"Never mind. Go to work. I'll take care of it," Michelle said.

I could always count on Michelle. I closed the window and coasted down the stairs, lifting my black wool coat from the rack near the door. Down my driveway I raced, spilling out into the street. At a jog, I crossed the stone bridge, but before I even reached the door to Rick's cottage, his shirtless form moved from his porch. He could feel me coming, just as I could feel his need for me pulsing in the twilight. Eyes as black as his ebony waves, their natural gray was drowned out, a sign that his beast was close to the surface. The scar on his chest, the scar I had caused in my past life when I made him my eternal soul's vessel, was the only mar on the smooth, golden expanse of his skin.

The storm I'd seen coming arrived. Downy white flakes dumped from the gray sky and swirled between us. If Rick felt the sting of the icy wind on his bare flesh, he didn't show it. In a flash, he met me where I was, in the street. He scooped his hands under my bottom and lifted me to him. *Bliss.* My arms instinctively wrapped around his neck, and my legs locked at the ankle behind his hips.

With super speed, he whirled me inside his place, our mouths melding together and his tongue working adeptly at kindling the fire within me. He pulled back long enough to unbutton my coat and hung it on the brass hook near the door. I'd threatened that I'd withhold myself if he tore any more of my clothes, so he was extra careful as he unbuttoned my blouse. The silky material was a deep lapis blue, a color I'd discovered made his eyes flash wider than any other in my wardrobe. I'd never admit I liked that reaction. With Rick, the specter of losing myself always nipped at the cuffs of our relationship. I had to be careful. I had to have boundaries.

While his fingers worked nimbly on the last button, his mouth found my pulse on the left side of my neck, his teeth raking over the taut flesh. Rick pushed the shirt off my shoulders and laid it carefully across the back of the couch. I slipped off my own shoes and socks, backing toward his bedroom. The fabric of his cotton pants peaked, teasing me. He blew into me like a dark wind. My bra was off and draped across the dresser in a heartbeat, nimbly undone while I was distracted with the way his thumb caressed my bottom rib. And then his hand cupped my breast and his hot mouth drew in my nipple, rolling it across his tongue and sending an exquisite cascade of electrical sparks straight to my nether regions.

I buried my fingers in his hair, arching my back. He didn't deny me. Finding my other breast, he kneaded the flesh with his fingers before playfully flicking his tongue across the nipple. In return, I bit his earlobe and kissed my way down to the well of skin between his neck and chest. My fingers reached for the waistband of his pants and pulled the cord like a ribbon on a birthday present I desperately wanted. The blessed cotton fell away without any effort on my part. I promptly wrapped him in my palm.

"*Mi cielo*," he moaned, closing his eyes. "I have missed you." His lips slanted across mine, his tongue stroking while his hands got busy down below.

"You saw me last night," I said lightly into his mouth.

He pulled back. "Exactly. An eternity." His brilliant smile lit up the room, and then his fingers found my zipper. In no time, my pants and underthings were off and carefully folded on his dresser.

Naked, I moved toward the bed and sat down on his duvet. I leaned back and allowed my knees to drift apart slightly, giving him full view of what was between them. "Why, Caretaker, you act as though I'm a sure thing."

"You are naked on my bed. Do you intend to tell me no?" He eyed me from head to toe and licked his lips.

I rolled back and flipped up onto my toes, feeling the power of the sexual energy between us swirl thick and musky in the bedroom. "I intend to make you work for it."

With a lithe leap, he landed in front of me, his body between my crouching knees. "What would you have me do?"

I leaned forward until my lips hovered in front of his. "You can have me when I say your name."

"Then I will make you scream it," he said before spreading my lips with his own and exploring my mouth once more.

The kiss turned my muscles into Jell-O, and I collapsed to my knees on the mattress. He held me up, straddling him chest to chest. One of his hands gripped the base of my skull while the other trailed down the outside of my breast, over my navel, and plunged between my thighs. His fingers worked, darting in and out of me. I closed my eyes, tipped my head back, and moaned. He pivoted, sinking to the bed, and slid his head between my knees. His tongue replaced his fingers.

Pleasure racked my body. I tipped forward, taking him into my mouth as well. The echo of ecstasy that coursed through our connection brought me to the crest of the first peak.

I tossed my head back. "Rick," I screamed. Manipulated by his able hands, he lowered me onto my back, cradled me in his arms against the mattress. Face to face, he entered me, slowly, gently. The heat and throb blasted me straight into oblivion, the first of many launches into the beyond that filled the room with golden energy.

When I thought I couldn't possibly take any more, his teeth found my neck. A soft nip and warm blood oozed over my skin. His partially shifted hand worked between our chests and a talon sliced a clean cut over his collarbone. I accepted what he offered, sealing my lips around the wound and gulping his blood. Vitality dripped down my throat until my head spun—that free dizzy feeling like running downhill as fast as my legs could carry me.

For a moment, I gave myself over to it, always knowing deep inside that this feeling was dangerous. Too close to an addiction. I'd messed up every relationship I'd ever been in; drove men away by moving too fast. My last boyfriend, Gary, had abandoned me and become a vampire. The guy before said I was too clingy. The one before that cheated on me. I wasn't ready to open myself up again.

Rick and I needed each other to stay strong and fight the bad guys. What would happen if this relationship went sour? Could I even survive without him? Better I didn't get too close. But that didn't mean I couldn't enjoy what we had together physically. I forced my thoughts to stop and simply relished the pleasure, the smell of him, the close, filling warmth.

Sometime later, we rolled apart. The wound from his bite healed immediately. It hadn't hurt at all. A side effect of our connection was that my flesh moved aside to give him access to my blood. The sexual energy bled from the room, and only then did I notice the storm had ended with the setting sun. The moon, through his bedroom window, cast the muscles of his chest in a pale light. Face to face, his eyes conveyed soft, awe-filled wonder. The expression was an ocean to my puddle of vacillating feelings.

"I love you, Grateful," he whispered. "Marry me."

I rolled onto my back and stared up at the ceiling. "No."

Silence. I listened to the snow blow against the window, the tick of my watch the only other sound. *Tick, tick, tick.* The bed sheets rustled. I looked at my watch.

"Looks like it's time to go to work," I murmured.

An awkward moment passed where I wondered if he was going to push the subject like he had in the past. Rick wanted to marry me. I wasn't ready for marriage. End of discussion.

"I'll get the mirror." He rolled off the bed and headed for the closet. I blew out a relieved breath.

Rick had been teaching me about our duties over the last couple of months, duties he'd been performing on his own in my absence. Our job was to police the supernaturals within our ward—the state of New Hampshire. It was a small ward in terms of square miles but had the third highest rate of supernatural activity. The highest was Arizona, followed by Maine. I'd learned that most supers were attracted to natural energy—forests, deserts, wide-open prairie. Trouble arose when they lived too close to humans. New Hampshire was the fifth least populated state in the country, which attracted the supers, but the small cities were spreading, putting humans closer and closer to overpopulated super territory. That's what was happening with the Carlton City vamp coven we'd discovered in September. That group was getting dangerously large and living in the city—a recipe for disaster.

The mirror in Rick's hands was a misshapen stretch of polished silver I'd enchanted during my second lifetime. It didn't exactly tell the future, but it did zero in on supers who were thinking about making bad choices. Nine times out of ten, they'd act on those impulses and Rick and I would catch them in the act. Rick placed it flat on the floor where it looked like a puddle on the hardwood.

I sat down across from him, not bothering with my clothes. It was better this way. Nature had the strongest connection with magic, and clothing only complicated the clarity of the vision.

"Ready?" I asked.

He nodded and placed his fingers at the edge of the mirror. I did the same. Instantly the magic awakened, the silver bubbling to a boil and swirling like liquid mercury.

"Mirror, mirror, on the floor—" I began.

"I do not know why you insist on starting that way," Rick said, giving me a sour glare.

"It's funny," I said. "It's from *Snow White*."

He rolled his eyes. "*Mi cielo*, please."

I straightened up. "Fine, but you could benefit from more humor in your life. You take yourself way too seriously."

He cocked his head to the side and raised his eyebrows.

"Okay, okay." I stared at the swirling silver and said in a cool, strong voice, "Reveal."

The bubbles rose to form buildings, a 3-D model of an area I recognized immediately.

"It's the edge of Carlton." I pointed at a blinking silver sign at the center of the cityscape. "See, it's the Mill Wheel nightclub."

"You know this place?"

"Everybody knows this place. It's where all the college kids go because they don't enforce the drinking age."

A male figure boiled up in the back alley, watching silver-skinned girls filter past him to smoke near the dumpster. I frowned.

"I believe a certain vamp would like to take advantage of the most impressionable guests." Rick's brows knit.

I passed my hand over the mirror and the scene melted into a pool of swirling silver.

"Reveal," I repeated. Another scene boiled to the surface. Another man, another alley.

"I know this place," he said. "Maison des Étoiles. It's a fae bordello."

"Should I ask why you are familiar with a bordello?" Rick told me he'd never been with anyone but me.

"These fae are friendly to our cause and often have information about creatures of the night due to their profession."

"So, you use them for information?"

"Yes."

"Ah." A wayward pang of jealousy sliced through me at the thought of Rick in a bordello. Had he really saved himself for me? And if he had, why did that mean so much to me now? Hell, why did the thought of Rick in a bordello fill me with green-eyed rage? I shoved the feeling down deep. I had no right to that emotion, not while I refused to commit.

I turned my attention back toward the mirror and

watched the voluptuous silhouette of a shiny-winged fae meet the man in the alley. He grabbed her shoulders and she writhed in pain, dissolving between his hands.

"That's not a vampire. What is this, Rick? He just eviscerated her with a simple touch."

"I'm not sure. The fae are filled with light and warmth. Whatever he is must possess the opposite to have that effect."

I blinked at the silvery scene, an ominous sinking feeling in my belly. Then I passed my hand over the top and said, "Reveal."

The scene changed again. This was going to be a busy night.

3

A ROUGH NIGHT AT THE OFFICE

"I sentence you to ten years in Monk's Hill Cemetery." I pressed the tip of Nightshade's razor-sharp bone blade into the vampire's neck, drawing the tiniest drop of blood. What once was a labored process was now something I could do as easily as breathing. Unlike sorting human souls, judging supernaturals only required the offender's own sacrifice, not mine. I watched his eyes grow wide before he poofed to the confines of the graveyard.

Ten years was a light sentence, but honestly, this time the victim asked for it. Literally.

"What have you done to him?" the brunette sorority girl screamed in my face, turning in circles as if I'd performed a magic trick with smoke and mirrors.

I pulled a tissue from the pocket of my long wool coat and mopped the blood from her neck. "Um, you must know he was a vampire. You were attacked. You're safe now."

"I *know* he was a vampire. Why do you think I come here?" She pointed at the door to Mill Wheel.

Stupid *Twilight*. These young girls actually wanted to be vamp fodder. "He could have killed you," I stated firmly.

She popped her hip out and placed her hand on it. "Or turned me," she said wistfully. She grinned like the thought warmed her soul.

I slapped my forehead in frustration.

Rick placed an arm around the girl's shoulders and turned her body to face him. Their eyes locked. "Vampires don't exist. You are going to collect your things and go straight home. Forget this ever happened."

Her face blanked for a moment. She smiled. "I've gotta go home. Nice to meet you." She disappeared through the door, leaving us alone in the alley.

"Nice," I said. Rick could channel the powers of the baddies we faced, which meant he could compel people, just like a vampire.

"I hate to do it. Taking away someone's free will is against everything I believe in."

I shook my head. "You had no choice. She needed it, she really did. Her free will was going to get her dead or turned."

He nodded and reached for my hand. "We have more work to do."

Next stop was Maison des Étoiles. We arrived minutes before midnight and found a shadowed place behind a dumpster to stake out the alley. The temperature had dropped. A chill breeze made me shiver. Thoughtfully, Rick wrapped his arms around me. I was dressed in a pair of stretchy black wool blend pants, boots with heels I'd enchanted to be comfortable (thank you, *The Book of Light*), and a gray sweater that was more librarian than soul sorter. I'd wrapped it all up in a black wool overcoat that could have been described as badass if it weren't for the J. Peterman embroidered pockets and cuffs. Still, it was cold when the wind blew, so I appreciated Rick's physical closeness for more than the immediate pleasure of his touch.

"What does Maison des Étoiles mean?" I asked Rick.

"Mansion of the stars. The fae here have a close relationship to the celestial."

"Like they're into astrology or something?"

He licked his lips and hummed like he was thinking. "Fae are born from and attach to natural things. For example, the forest fae who dwell behind my house are tied metaphysically to the trees. With a steady breath, they can make a sapling grow. Kill the tree; kill the fae. Maison's fae are tied to the stars, the moon, the planets, and so forth. It's said that they came from the heavens originally."

I had no idea there were forest fae behind Rick's house. I wondered what they looked like. I wondered if any of them had ever come on to Rick. My stomach twisted. Why did I do this to myself? I shook away the uninvited thought and tried to concentrate on my work.

Every day as the witch was a learning experience. Rick said these fae were celestial. I tried to imagine the implications of such a thing. Did they change with the course of the moon? If the forest fae could make a plant grow with a steady breath, what could celestial fae do?

"Have you noticed that there's no snow in this alley? It's been snowing since early evening and before we left, it was already accumulating in your yard. What happened to the snow?"

Rick didn't have to answer my question. Just then, a woman exited the Maison and click-clacked her way into the circle of light cast by the lamppost near the door. Her strappy silver stiletto heels made her legs look impossibly long, and her shimmering blue dress gave her dark red hair a purplish tint. Stunning.

With a deep cleansing breath, she tossed her head back and spread her arms wide, heart raised to the stars. Two gossamer wings unfurled from her back, stretching and flapping. Instantly, a wave of tropical heat blew through the alley, warming the skin of my face and sending a trickle of joy through me.

"Oh," I whispered. I pulled out my phone and started recording. "For my new database."

Rick brought his lips to my ear. "Shhh."

I was afraid to blink, that I might miss the beauty of the fae's connection with her roots. The air around her shimmered as if the stars were sprinkling her with their magic.

"Hello, Stella." A man moved into the alleyway, bald, with unusually large dark eyes and a tight mouth. Something about the duster he wore bothered me, but I couldn't put my finger on it. I reached for Nightshade. Rick placed a hand over mine. I paused.

Stella's wings retracted so quickly even I questioned whether they'd been there. She turned to face the man. "I'm sorry, sir, but as I mentioned inside, it's my break. If you want a girl, you need to go in the front door. Someone else will be provided for you." Her silvery voice chimed like a bell against his dark presence.

"What I want, I can't get inside." He extended his hands toward her shoulders.

Crap. With a thrust of encouragement from Rick, I bounded into the alley, Nightshade heralding my arrival with the blue glow of her blade. "Hold it right there," I yelled, using his startled composure as opportunity to slide in front of Stella. "Identify yourself."

The man took a step back, and the angle of the light gave me a good look at his coat. Sealskin. Bastard. With a strange hand gesture that I assumed was a foreign version of giving me the finger, the stranger turned to run. I wasn't sure what I was dealing with, but he wasn't human, not if he'd popped up in our silver mirror, so I leaped forward and swung Nightshade. I wasn't trying to kill him, only to maim him so that I could find out more and pass judgment. But I missed because at that moment Poe came shrieking at my face, talons bared.

"What the fuck?" I yelled as I dove sideways to avoid him. My shoulder smacked on the concrete but not hard enough for me to miss the enormous barbed club that whistled through the air over me. My momentum rolled me to my back.

A smoky black column blew through the alley. Rick! He materialized in front of the stranger in the seal coat, blocking the man's escape. "Grateful, move!"

The barbed club came crashing down toward my head. I barrel-rolled out of the way, getting my first glimpse of a meaty stump of a leg and a furry bare foot as large as my torso. Flipping to my feet, my eyes followed the leg to a fur toga-wearing creature, big as a house, with a pushed-in pig face complete with lower tusks that protruded in hideous arcs on either side of its snout. Poe was circling its head, trying to distract it, but the creature kept coming.

This time when the club fell, I darted between the beast's legs, stabbing toward the Achilles tendon on the back of the ankle. I missed. The force of the club upended the section of concrete I stood on, sending me flying into the opposite wall. I bounced off the bricks and landed on my feet. Thanks to the magic of my role and Rick's blood, I was stronger than an ordinary human. Good thing. That last blow to the head would've been fatal.

I raced forward before the beast had a chance to turn around and stabbed where I knew it would be most effective —the balls. Sure enough, as Nightshade sank through fur and soft flesh, the club dropped and the creature listed to the side, hands cupping between its legs. I wasted no time with formalities; this thing had tried to kill me. Using its knee and hip as leverage, I propelled myself over the massive pig creature and in one lithe stroke, decapitated it. Blood erupted from the kill, a geyser of red that showered the alleyway.

Once the spray of blood settled, I pivoted toward Rick and the creepy stranger he restrained at the front of the alley. Soft sobs reached my ears, Stella crying in the arms of another fae in the doorway to Maison des Étoiles.

"I'm sorry you had to see that," I said to her, then stomped up to Mr. Evil-Seal-Coat-Wearer and pressed the tip of my bloody blade into his neck. "Who the hell are you? And what the hell are you?"

The man started to laugh so hard it sounded like a low bark. With a movement like a backward shrug, he doffed the sealskin, slipped from Rick's arms, and fell to the pavement, writhing and foaming at the mouth.

"What's happening?" I asked Rick as the man flip-flopped. He coughed up a spew of liquid and gasped repeatedly. "Does he need CPR?"

Rick looked at the pig creature I'd slain behind me and then at the coat in his hand. I was so busy analyzing his expression that I didn't see the seizing man reach out and grab my ankle.

I hit the pavement so hard my teeth clacked together.

I CAME AWAKE WITH A GASP, STRETCHED OUT ON MY SIDE IN A Victoria's Secret ad—cherry red silk sheets, a plush velvet comforter. Rick leaned over me, blotting the back of my head with a rag. I grabbed his wrist.

"Where am I?"

"Inside Maison des Étoiles," he said, placing the rag on the nightstand.

I tried to look around the red-on-red decorated room but

my head was throbbing. I closed my eyes and leaned into the pillows. "What happened?"

"The finfolk caught you off guard. You hit your head. He's dead."

"You killed him?"

"No. He committed suicide. When he shed his skin, he reverted to his water form. He suffocated."

"Finfolk? So he was a type of shifter, like a mermaid? A sea creature that turns into a human."

"Yes, but usually they must return to the sea within a few days or they die. I've never seen one this far inland."

I thought about the coat the man wore. Rick's explanation sank in. That wasn't sealskin; it was *his* skin, the finfolk's. I shivered at the thought of wearing my own skin as a coat. Eww.

"And what was that thing with him?" I asked.

"An Appalachian troll."

"Of course it was. Seriously, can my life get any weirder? You know, a few months ago, I'd never have believed any of this existed."

Rick sighed and resumed cleaning my head wound. "Would you like some of my blood?"

His blood would heal me. As the vessel of my soul, my caretaker was mystically designed to maintain my life. Vitamin caretaker. But I balked. Not that I didn't want it. His blood was liquid orgasm, but something was bothering me about the finfolk attack and my injury was making it difficult to concentrate. I couldn't get distracted.

"Even though it's strange for finfolk to be this far inland, the troll bothers me more. We are a hundred miles from the Appalachians. Is that a misnomer?"

"No, it is not. I have never seen one in the city before."

"It's not like he could've taken a bus," I mumbled. "What was a troll doing here?"

"I am not sure, *mi cielo,* but the bodies are still in the alley and an investigator is on his way."

I sat up abruptly. "The police are coming? We need to hide the bodies!"

"Don't worry. This investigator is familiar with supernatural activity. He is a detective, but he's sympathetic to our cause."

I flopped back on the pillow, head pounding.

Rick scooped an arm under my shoulders, pulled one leg across his lap so I was straddling him, and tipped his head to expose his neck. "Come, *mi cielo.* Take of me."

His voice in my ear was as deep and soft as the velvet I'd been nestled in. Warm breath stroked my cheek. He adjusted the neck of his shirt to expose more skin. I nuzzled the smooth expanse over his artery. At the same time, his hand massaged behind my knee and began drifting up my outer thigh. When his hardened member grazed between my legs, even the fabric of my pants couldn't stop the pulse of need that jetted through me.

I bit down hard on the web of flesh between his neck and shoulder, his gasp an appetizer for the meal I was about to indulge in. The first drops spread across my tongue, salty and warm, enticing a deeper bite that proved prolific. I swallowed greedily, heat blossoming where he rubbed in just the right spot between my legs. I writhed in his lap. His fingers at the base of my skull massaged my neck, pulling slightly at the roots of my hair.

Rick's blood was a drug, building within me, coaxing me toward orgasm with every swallow. As I neared the brink, I had a vivid hallucination of a man's chest pressed up against my back, sandwiching me against Rick, and his hands sliding around my rib cage to roll my nipples between his fingers. That did it. I came so hard, only Rick's arms kept me from falling off his lap.

When I was capable of thought again, I sat up, feeling Rick's hands all over me. Looking down myself, Rick's hands were literally all over me! Or more accurately the hands of his two twins. One knelt by my side and one stood near my head.

"Holy crow! What the hell is going on?"

Rick cleared his throat and muttered a spell under his breath, sending the other two into oblivion. "It is the fae enchantment on this room. The magic picks up on your fantasies and provides, what you might call, virtual reality. They're not real and they can't hurt you, but the experience is very...intense. You can imagine why the Maison is so popular."

"Uh, yeah." I smoothed imaginary wrinkles from my shirt. "We are definitely coming back here," I mumbled under my breath.

A low rumble vibrated against me, Rick's laugh. Of course, he'd heard me. He had super hearing and eyesight. I stood and straightened my clothes again.

"Well, I guess it's no secret that I'd like to stay here and continue to test the room's charms, but I want to meet this investigator and see if he has any idea why a finfolk and troll would be willing to risk their lives to travel this far into the city."

Rick nodded his head and held open the door.

4

CALLING IN THE DOGS

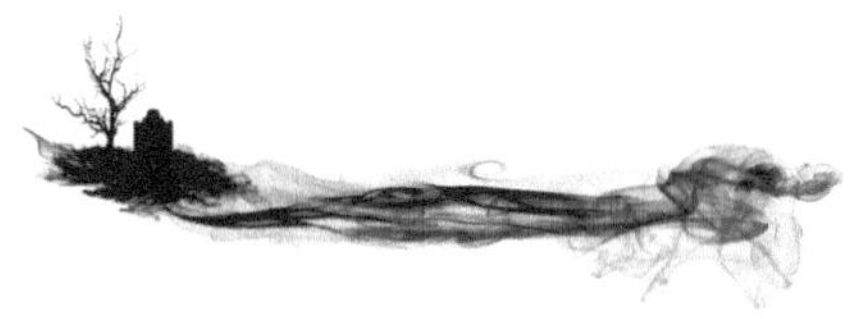

Detective Silas Flynn had a firm handshake and an intense, focused gaze that made my intuition do a swing step on my gut. With a toothy grin, he brought my hand to his face, presumably to kiss the back of it. Instead, at the last second, he flipped my forearm over and ran his nose up the inside of my wrist, smelling me. I laughed a little, more from the strangeness than the tickle of his breath.

"It's a pleasure to meet you, Hecate."

"Please, call me Grateful." I never did like being called by the name the supernaturals had for my station. Hecate was the goddess of the dead. I was not her, but as rumor had it, a piece of my soul, the eternal piece, was related to her. You might call me a chip off the old block…er…deity. I preferred to think of myself as a witch. Although, strictly speaking, normal witches couldn't judge the dead or the damned like I could.

"Only if you call me Silas." His green eyes twinkled from beneath bushy caramel-colored eyebrows.

I nodded as we progressed into the alley. Rick had stayed inside to interview the madam about the incident. Appar-

31

ently, she was an old friend. I ignored the pang of jealousy that bit of news cost me.

Police tape stretched across the mouth of the alley, and I noticed human faces ogling the scene from the sidewalk. I frowned.

"Don't worry. The *Do Not Cross* tape has been enchanted. All they're seeing is a typical murder scene, grisly by the looks on their faces." He chuckled.

"Peachy." A man passing by clutched his stomach and hurried across the street. "So, what do you make of Stella's uninvited visitors?"

He gestured with his head for me to follow him over to the body of the pig-faced troll and pointed his pen at the hammy wrist. "See that?

A massive bracelet of white stones was visible through the hair. On further inspection, they weren't stones. "Are those teeth?"

"Yes. These are the baby teeth of his children. This is an Appalachian mountain troll. They live in tight family units and never venture far from home. In fact, this is the first time I've seen one in the city."

The baby teeth of his children. I immediately felt guilty for slaying the troll, even though logically it would have killed me if I hadn't. "Why was it here?"

"That's a mystery, but a big clue has to do with this guy." He strolled over to the body of the finfolk. "How much do you know about finfolk?"

"Next to nothing."

"Good, then I won't feel bad about regurgitating the basics." He took a deep breath. "I hate to stereotype supers, but finfolk have a penchant for the dark side. They never live peaceably among humans like the fae or werewolves do." He pressed a hand into his chest when he said *werewolves*, and I finally had my question answered as to what he was. "They're known for luring humans to the water's edge and forcibly abducting them."

"Count themselves as baddies, do they?" I kicked the crumpled skin of the finfolk with my toe. It had already begun to stiffen to the consistency of beef jerky. When the stranger had shrugged out of his skin, he was, in fact, skinning himself. The flesh beneath where the coat had been was all muscle, fat, and tendon. Apparently, a finfolk's skin was a living thing until it was removed.

"Yeah. And we've noticed an increase in vampiric activity here the last couple of weeks, too. Streets have been swarming with them."

"Vampires also have a penchant for the dark side." This I knew from personal experience.

"Exactly. Something is luring them to come here and mix with humans."

"Rick and I found a vampire coven living in Carlton City a couple of months ago. They're organized, led by a vamp named—"

"Julius?" Silas rubbed his chin.

"Yeah. You've heard of him?"

"Yep. Our department has a long history with Julius and his coven. Seems like he's always on the fringes of the crimes we investigate. Can't pin anything on him, though. Slippery."

"The coven was feeding on animals. Had a whole vampire-style butcher shop for blood collection," I said.

"I don't trust him."

"Neither do I, but without any evidence, I can't judge or sentence him. Not unless I want to start a war with his coven."

Silas nodded in agreement. "So, Julius sets up shop in Carlton City and months later the streets are swarming with supernaturals who normally wouldn't set foot on pavement."

Silas nudged the finfolk body for good measure. "I can't prove it, but I think Julius is behind this."

"He had a demon with him named Padnon. Evil SOB."

Silas narrowed his eyes. "He's gathering allies. What the hell is he after?"

"I wish I knew."

At that moment, Rick and a fae woman I assumed was the madam entered the alley. I'd expected the bordello madam to be an older, less attractive, former working girl, but I was wrong. She was the model of sophistication, grace, and beauty. Tall, lanky, with silky honey-colored hair, her golden skin stretched flawlessly across her high cheekbones. A warm breeze blew off her and chased the winter chill from the alley. Thankfully, Rick seemed unaffected by her beauty, although a surge of unwanted possessiveness came over me anyway. Silas, on the other hand, was ogling her, lips parted slightly. *Oh, for crying out loud.*

I stepped over the body and extended my hand. "Hi, I'm Grateful Knight."

Graciously, she slid her manicured fingers into mine. "I am Soleil. I owe you a huge debt of gratitude, Grateful. Stella and Rick told me what happened. Thank you for saving us. Who knows how many fae he would have killed if you hadn't stopped him?"

"Did you know this man?" I used the term "man" loosely. It didn't seem to confuse her.

"No. We've never had any finfolk come here before. But, as I told Rick, there is a legend among our people that if one of their kind touches one of ours, they are capable of draining our life force and turning us to dust. The dust is said to have magical properties useful in black magic."

The term black magic made my skin itch. As far as I knew, all magic was neutral; it was the spell caster who had either good or evil intentions. But I'd have to ask Rick about it when we got home. Caretaker magic was a different practice with a different source of power than mine. Maybe there was such a thing as black magic.

A hand jutted between us. "Detective Silas Flynn, Soleil. It's a pleasure to make your acquaintance."

My eyes followed Silas's hand to his face, which was flushed bright red. At first, the nurse in me wondered if he was having a heart attack, but then the woman in me recognized the look in his eyes. He was blushing. With a half grin, I took a step back, allowing him to move in closer. He still hadn't released Soleil's hand.

Rick sidled up to me. "Her enchantment is especially effective on werewolves. Her connection is to the sun. It is said that a werewolf in her bed during the full moon won't shift."

"Oh," I said. "That makes sense." Damn. No wonder Silas was pouring it on thick. "Did you find out anything else?"

"Just that there have been an unusual number of supernatural visitors to the Maison the last several weeks."

"Silas said the same thing. Apparently, the city's overrun. He thinks the breadcrumbs lead back to Julius."

"I've thought the same thing, *mi cielo*, but we need proof. There are supernaturals in this city waiting for an excuse to organize against us. Sentencing an innocent vampire could cause an uprising."

"I agree we need proof, but we don't even know what they're looking for. What is Julius after? A secret weapon? Is he raising an army?"

Rick shrugged.

A flurry of black flapping wings circled our heads and landed on the lip of the dumpster. "Well, I'm sure standing there talking about what we *don't* know is going to be productive." Poe's beady black eyes rolled in his head.

"Hey, the sarcasm isn't helping, Poe," I said.

Rick grimaced. "Do you know this bird?"

"Rick, this is my new familiar, Poe. Poe, this is my caretaker, Rick."

"You called a familiar? Already?" Rick asked.

"Oh, sure, question my existence. Don't bother thanking me for saving her life or anything. If not for me, her head would be impaled on the end of the mountain troll's club." Poe flapped his glossy black wings.

"Thank you, Poe," I said. I didn't appreciate his attitude, but he had a point. He *had* saved my life.

"You're welcome. Now, tell me I can have some of the finfolk. I have a taste for fish."

I gagged a little. "You want to eat that?"

"Don't judge."

Silas must have overheard because he made eye contact and nodded his head.

"Guess it's okay, Poe. Enjoy."

Without hesitation, he soared down and attacked the carnage.

"*Mi cielo*, we should probably go. More to do tonight, and we are behind schedule," Rick prompted.

"Right." I approached Soleil and Silas, extending my hand. "Rick and I need to move on. It's been a pleasure."

Soleil gripped my fingers, her gaze meeting mine in the most intense way. "In gratitude for your help, I grant you one favor, Grateful Knight." Her body glowed, and I shielded my eyes. "Thank you for your service to the Celestial Fae."

The skin of my face felt warm, like I was lying in a tanning bed or on the beach. I released her hand and touched my cheek. "Uh, thanks."

She retreated inside, and Rick ushered me out of the alley.

"You are very fortunate, *mi cielo*."

"Yeah?"

"A fae favor is as good as a miracle. Use it wisely." Rick pressed his lips together, his gaze deadly serious.

Why did his explanation sound more like a warning? "What are you trying to say, Rick? You know what? Never mind. I'll look it up later in *The Book of Light*. My brain can't handle any more surprises."

He nodded curtly. Now if only fate would be as agreeable as Rick.

5

MR. NEKOMATA

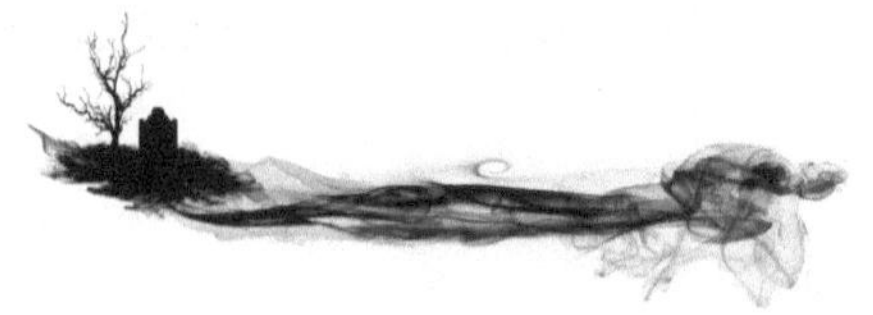

B ang. Bang.
     Pause.
Bang. Bang. Bang.

Monday morning. Someone was knocking on my front door. I opened one eye and groaned. My alarm clock said it was just after eight. I'd worked all day Sunday and then Rick and I had patrolled into the wee hours of the night, trying our best to keep up with the influx of supernatural activity. I'd clocked approximately three hours of sleep. Who the hell had come-a-callin' at this hour?

The metal on metal sound of a key turning in a lock had me bolt upright in bed. What the heck? The only other person with a key to my house was my dad and he... *Oh crap.*

"Please, come in Mr. Nekomata," my father's voice boomed from below me. *Oh crap, oh crap, oh crap.*

I bound out of bed and dressed like the house was on fire, not even bothering to brush my hair. Instead, I ran my fingers through it and tucked it behind my ears on the way down the stairs. In my foyer, an elderly Japanese man in an expensive-looking camel hair coat smiled at me from my father's side.

"Um, Dad? What's going on?" I said through a forced smile.

He cleared his throat and adjusted his briefcase in his hands. "We knocked, Grateful."

"I was sleeping."

With the professional demeanor worthy of a top real estate agent, Dad addressed his client. "Mr. Nekomata, will you excuse me for just a moment?" He grabbed my elbow and nudged me through the kitchen to the semi-private nook that led to the garage.

"What are you doing here?" I asked.

He leaned in close and whispered, "Grateful, I know you wanted to buy this place, and I turned aside Mr. Helleborine just as you asked, but it's been more than six weeks and you haven't made an offer."

Helleborine was the name of the herb used to kill me during my last lifetime. I'd called in a favor from my dad when a "Mr. Helleborine" wanted to buy my house. I was sure it was actually Julius threatening my seat of magic. At least this guy was human. There was a protective enchantment around the house that kept anything preternatural from entering without an invitation. "Why didn't you call?"

"Nekomata is a big spender. He's been snatching up property all over the state, paying above market price. I told him I'd taken the place off the market temporarily. He showed up at my office today and *paid* me to show it."

"He paid you to show him the house?" That was highly irregular.

"Two hundred dollars, Grateful. I'm showing it. If you'd like us to wait a moment for you to leave, we will."

"Leave? No, I'm not leaving."

"Okay then. Awkward or not, I'm carrying on." He straightened his suit jacket.

What could I do? I swallowed hard and marched back up the stairs. As my father began explaining the amenities in the kitchen, I cruised into the attic and roused Poe.

"Yes, My Supreme Witchiness," he said dryly.

"There's someone here looking at the house, like to *buy* it. We can't let that happen."

"I agree that would be unfortunate," the raven said.

"You've got to do something." I poked his black-feathered chest.

"*I've* got to do something? Seems like *you've* got to do something."

"Hey, you're my familiar. You're supposed to help me."

Poe sighed and ruffled his feathers. He yawned and his beak clacked a few times like he was trying to wake up. "Okay. What do you want me to do?"

"Maybe you could fly down the chimney and, like, flap your wings in his face or something."

The raven tilted his head and closed one eye as if to say the idea was pathetic. "How about if I transform into a rat and scurry down into your kitchen?"

"You can do that?"

"Honestly, woman, read the damn book." Promptly, he fluttered down to the floor, transformed into a huge black sewer rat, and scurried out the door. A few moments later I heard Dad scream like a girl and then the sound of the broom being smacked against the floor.

"Sorry, Poe," I whispered under my breath.

"Robert, do not worry. Where I come from, a rat in the kitchen is a sign of good fortune."

"Oh? Is that a Japanese thing?"

"No, a Nekomata family thing. Rat in the kitchen means there must be food in the kitchen." The men laughed. I heard my father lead the way into the basement.

"You've got to be kidding me," I said to Poe as he returned, transforming into his feathered self.

"Gave it my best shot," he said, returning to the spot next to *The Book of Light* where I'd found him sleeping.

"Noooo, we are not giving up that easily." I opened the book, forcing him to move from his perch to make room. "What can I do during the day?" I asked Poe. But it was the book that answered. Frantically, its pages flipped until they settled open near the middle.

"Damn! Did you know it could do that?"

The raven gave a rhythmic caw that sounded a lot like a laugh.

I peeked at the open page. "*Connecting to the Earth*," I read. Poe stretched his neck to see the spell. "*Although Hecate draws her power from the night air, it can be useful for her to connect to the Earth during the day. This is possible by drawing on her connection to her caretaker and his earthly bond. To do so, she need only concentrate on the bond and direct the resulting energy into the form she requires.*"

Poe fluffed his wings. "Sounds easy enough, even for you."

"Hey! Aren't you supposed to be more supportive?"

He shrugged.

I plopped down on the floor, opening my connection with Rick. Poe flapped down from his perch and crawled into my lap. "What're you doing?" I asked him.

"I'm your familiar; I'm amplifying your power," he drawled.

I sank my fingers into his feathers, reflexively massaging the muscles around his neck. Eyes closed, I pictured Rick and took a deep breath. Our connection opened. I saw him in the shower, rinsing his hair. He paused and looked directly at me, as if he could actually see me. Was my mind creating this, or was it real? Mentally, I shifted my attention to the house. I needed something to scare my father and Mr. Nekomata out. Focusing on the basement where they were, I channeled my will.

With a violent start, the house began to shake, foundation rumbling until the windows rattled. Three floors below, my dad cursed. Uh-oh. I forgot about the wine cellar. My eyes popped open. I hoped I hadn't cracked a bottle of Shiraz with the earthquake I caused.

The house gradually stopped shaking. "That should do it," I said to Poe.

He bobbed his head. "Well done, Spell-Casting Queen. My pleasure to have assisted you." His words carried more than a tinge of sarcasm. He flew up to his perch next to the book and tucked his head back under his wing.

That was all the help I was getting from Poe. "Thanks," I said impassively. I jogged down two flights of stairs and met the two men as they came up from the basement. Dad was whiter than the ghosts that used to live in my attic, but Mr. Nekomata seemed even more elated with the place.

"I guess you noticed the rumbling. It's been happening sporadically since I moved in. The residents of Red Grove tell me the house is built over a sinkhole. Could go at any time." There, that should do it.

Mr. Nekomata nodded and walked toward the door. Good, he was going. Only he didn't. He turned at the stairs. "Show me upstairs, Mr. Knight," he said.

"But… But, aren't you worried about the sinkhole?" I stammered.

"No. My company plans to demolish the place anyway. This town needs a modern bed and breakfast." He started up the stairs.

Holy mother of all clients who would not leave! This guy was killing me. I chased after my father who still looked like he might vomit but was forcing himself up the stairs. I still had one ace up my sleeve, and I was about to play it. I rushed past them to the curtains I kept drawn on the second floor landing.

"I'm so sorry to have wasted your time, Mr. Nekomata, but this property is all wrong for a bed and breakfast. No one would ever pay money to stay here."

My father gave me stink eye, but I didn't quit.

"Why do you think so, young lady?" Mr. Nekomata asked.

Dramatically, I threw back the curtains and pointed at the backyard. "The house backs right up to a graveyard. It will scare away the customers."

The old man approached the window, wrinkled hands moving gracefully to couple behind his back, gaze falling softly across the rows of snow-covered headstones. Seconds ticked by. Dad looked like his head might explode because he was so mad at me. His face was bright red, and he kept doing this clenching thing with his jaw. The bottom eyelid of his right eye twitched.

"I don't think so," Client From Hell said. "No backyard neighbors means no noise. Plus, paranormal investigations are very popular these days. We might be able to capitalize on the trend."

My jaw hinged open. Dad's face split into a told-you-he-was-serious smile. He raised eyebrows in my direction. I was speechless and completely out of magic.

"Robert, I will be in touch with my offer. Thank you for accommodating me on such short notice."

"You're welcome!" my dad said. "No problem whatsoever."

He didn't even bother with the bedrooms. The two men descended and Dad opened the door for his client. They exchanged a firm handshake and then Mr. Nekomata was gone.

With a slow thud, Dad closed the door and pivoted toward me. The look he gave me was one I hadn't seen since my teen years, a quiet anger that told me I was in big trouble.

"Don't you have to drive him back to your office?" I mumbled.

"Nope. He met me here."

"You promised me you'd let me buy this place."

He blinked slowly and shook his head. "Grateful…"

"You *promised* me."

He shook a finger at me. "There is no way you are going to raise $250,000! I said I'd give you six weeks; I gave you eight. Now get over it."

"All I have to do is qualify for a loan. I'm making good money now. If I pay off my debt, it could happen."

Dad put his hands on his hips and lowered his head. After a few moments, he gave an exasperated sigh. "I'm sorry, Grateful, but if Nekomata offers me above market price for this house, I'm selling."

"But—"

He placed his hands on my shoulders and rubbed. With a sigh, he met my eyes. I thought he'd cave, give me a month or something. But I was wrong. "You'll thank me someday. Your attachment to this place is unnatural. You belong in the city where you can have fun, meet people. We never intended this to be permanent, and frankly, with the way this house shook today, I'm not comfortable with you staying here much longer. It might not even be safe."

"But, Dad…" *Crap*. In hindsight, the earthquake was a bad idea.

Before I could say another word, he pulled me into his embrace. "You'll see. It'll be for the best."

At this point, what could I say? Yes, I want to live in a

house that will soon be swallowed by a sinkhole? I was so stupid. My ruse had been a double-edged sword. After the rat and the earthquake, there was no way Dad was going to do anything to help me stay here. I was lucky he hadn't insisted I move out immediately.

For the second time since I'd moved in, I thought about telling Dad the truth. Coming clean about the nature of the house and my role as the witch might solve the problem. But just like before, my conscience wouldn't let me. For me, learning about the supernatural was like waking up to find myself living in a nightmare. Before I'd accepted my role as witch, I'd been overwhelmed with helplessness. At least now I could defend myself. Dad would have no such luxury. In this case, ignorance truly was bliss.

I reassured myself that I could fix this without ruining my dad's life with the truth. Nekomata was only a man, and I had a book of magic on my side. Maybe I was getting ahead of myself, anyway. Mr. Nekomata might change his mind and not make an offer. Even if he did, buying a house took time. Likely, I'd have months before the closing to do what I needed to botch the sale. Perhaps his financing wouldn't go through or some other misfortunate event would render the sale impossible.

With a deep sigh, I took a step back. "What do you want to do about Thanksgiving?"

He glanced around my foyer as if he expected it to crumble around us at any moment. "I don't think we should have it here."

Stupid. Stupid. Why had I made this house seem danger-ous? I offered an olive branch. "Your place?"

"One o'clock?"

"Sure. A late lunch would be fine with me."

He shook his head. "Oh no. We'll be having dinner. I need you there at one to help me cook the bird. We're not ordering out this year. We're going to do this the traditional way or not at all."

I tried to remember the last time my father and I cooked together. Nothing. The part of my brain compartmentalized for cooking was empty and cobweb filled. "It's your stomach," I said cynically.

6

LOGAN

After an uneventful day at the hospital, I caught up on some badly needed sleep. Good thing because I had to get up early to help Logan through physical therapy. For the last six weeks, I'd been assisting with his outpatient recovery. My involvement was more than simply cheering him on. Every Tuesday and Thursday I met him at the rehab center, my special energy shake in hand.

Of course, the drink was actually a healing potion from *The Book of Light*. I hadn't exactly mentioned its magical properties to him, afraid he might forgo the benefits, but in this case the ends justified the means. I'd noticed a marked improvement during the last several weeks.

I filled a sports bottle with the elixir from a pitcher I kept in the refrigerator. The stuff was foul—hunter green and smelled like feet. I'd told Logan it was wheat grass. If he suspected anything, he'd never let on.

Warily, I backed down my driveway. There was only one way to get to Logan's physical therapy, and it required passing Rick's place. As expected, my caretaker was brooding in the middle of the road.

"You're going to see him," Rick accused. His breath fogged the glass of my window. I pressed the button to roll it down.

"We've been over this. I'm a nurse, and Logan's my friend. I'm helping with his recovery. That's all. I promised him I would, and I intend to see it through."

The line of Rick's jaw hardened and his eyes bled to black. "I don't like it. He wants you, Grateful. He always has."

I popped my chin into the air. Jeez. Rick's jealousy hadn't dulled at all during the last six weeks. Well, tough cookies. I wouldn't go back on my word. "Then I suppose you'll just have to trust me."

"It's him I don't trust. I take care of what's mine."

I rolled my eyes and leaned away from him. "You don't own me." I wanted to add that we weren't even exclusive, but I was afraid it would start an argument that would make me late. As it was, Rick looked like he wanted to punch something.

I rolled the window back up.

* * *

St. John's Rehabilitation Center is attached to the hospital, a state-of-the-art facility with physical therapy, massage, and acupuncture. When I walked in the front door, Logan was already in the waiting area, his cane propped against his leg. Thinner than he had been as a ghost, his physique had come a long way the last six weeks. The outline of long, lean muscle was visible under his clingy athletic shirt. He'd shaved the beard he'd grown while in the coma, but left his hair a little longer than it had been in his spectral state.

His smile was the same as always. "Grateful, you came."

"Wouldn't miss it." I handed him the drink. When he took it from me, he grabbed the bottle right above my hand, engulfing my fingers in his. He didn't immediately pull the goods away. I retracted my hand and placed it safely on my hip. "How are you feeling today?"

"Good. Right hip is still giving out on me occasionally. I think another couple of months of this, and I'll be able to resume some normal activities."

"Another couple of months?"

"Yeah." He tipped back the sports bottle, and I watched green liquid slosh into his mouth. He squeezed his eyes shut against the taste and chugged.

I popped out a hip, my bottom jaw jutting forward in an exaggerated pout. "That's funny because I heard you're going back to work at Valentine's this weekend."

He choked on a swallow. In a fit of coughing, his hand lashed out to cover his mouth and knocked over his cane. Face red, he set the sports bottle down on the side table and really poured on the steam, hacking like a machine gun.

I raised an eyebrow. "Oh, and I also heard there's a welcome back party next Saturday night that I wasn't invited to."

As if he could explain everything if only he could survive the siege on his lungs, he waved a hand dismissively. I noticed the eruptions from his throat becoming more controlled, even forced. The jig was up. I swiped his hand out of the air and leaned forward until our noses almost touched. He gave one last pitiful cough as my eyes dug into his. "Just admit it, Logan. You're better."

He dropped the charade. After checking over his shoulder to make sure none of the rehab staff were watching, he bounded from his chair and swept up his fallen cane before returning to his seat.

I gasped theatrically. "You little weasel!"

"Oh, please. You suspected as much all along. You've been playing the game as well as I have."

"What? Don't try to turn this around on me."

"No? You're innocent, eh? Just so you know, this energy shake tastes like ass." He picked up the green juice and poked a finger in my direction. "This ain't wheat grass, darlin'. You've been slipping me a potion against my will."

I pointed a finger back at him. "That was for your own good. And it wasn't against your will. You chose to drink it."

"I didn't know it was magic."

"Obviously you did, or we wouldn't be having this conversation."

"And obviously you suspected I was better because you've been pumping me up with healing juju the last six weeks. Jesus, I might never catch a cold again."

My jaw worked, opening and closing in a weak attempt to form a rebuttal. I composed myself, straightening up so I was looking down my nose at him. "You should be thanking me."

"Thanking you?"

At that moment, Miss Physical Therapist America passed by and gave me a harsh look. Really, who has a waist that long and thin without plastic surgery?

"Please, keep your voice down," she reprimanded me sternly.

Logan's eyes darted in her direction and he flashed her an overly charming smile followed by a short wave. His eyes twinkled. Was that a dimple in his chin?

She smiled back. "Just a few more minutes, Mr. Valentine."

"No problem, Sally. And please, call me Logan."

"Okay, Logan. See you soon. I hope you're ready to work." With one last warm, flirtatious smile for him and a death stare for me, she continued on her way. I thought my eyes might roll out of my head.

Logan leaned toward me and whispered, "Did it ever occur to you that I don't want to be better yet? Huh?"

"Why wouldn't you want to get better?" I asked incredulously.

He startled backward, lifting an eyebrow at me like I was insane. His wide eyes said it all. I was temporarily taken aback by the vulnerability I saw there. Michelle was right. He still had feelings for me.

"You're afraid...of losing me." I swallowed the lump that had formed in my throat. "That's not going to happen, Logan. We're still going to be friends, right?"

"Sure." With a sigh, he leaned forward, propping his elbows on his knees. He rubbed a toe on the floor.

"But?"

"It's not going to be the same. We won't have a reason."

"That's just silly. We—" I had to stop midsentence. He was right. Without the excuse of helping him through rehab, I wouldn't see him regularly. He'd be busy at the restaurant, and I'd have my nursing job and my responsibilities as the witch. Could we maintain a friendship? Probably. But I couldn't promise our relationship wouldn't change.

"Okay, Logan, I'm ready for you." Sally was back, her red curls bouncing over her perky shoulders.

He reached for my hand and used it, along with his cane, to shakily stand. It was very convincing.

"I'll bring your drink," I said, grabbing the sports bottle off the end table with my free hand. For the next hour, I needlessly assisted Logan through his therapy, while Sally cheerily guided us. When we were done, I pretended to help him to his truck.

"This is the last time I'm doing this," I said. "It's a lie. As much as I believe Sally enjoys working with you, it's practically insurance fraud."

"Yeah, I thought so." With speed and agility, he dropped my hand, pulled open the door to his black, half-ton pickup, and propelled himself into the driver's seat. He tossed me the cane. "So, ah, since I'm not going to see you for the next appointment, can you come to my welcome back party at Valentine's next Saturday?"

"Should I just forgive your dishonesty and unctuous secondhand invite?"

The charmer he beamed my way should've been illegal. It actually made my knees buckle. I had to use the cane. "Yes, you should, because if there's anyone in this world who understands the extenuating circumstances, it's you." One green eye winked at me. Jesus, he actually winked!

I groaned. "Okay, I'll see you then. But you owe me a drink."

"Excellent. See you then."

Before I could say anything else, he backed out of the parking space and was gone. I tossed his cane in the dumpster. Things needed to change. It was inevitable. What I needed to figure out was how much...and how fast.

7

STUPID GARY

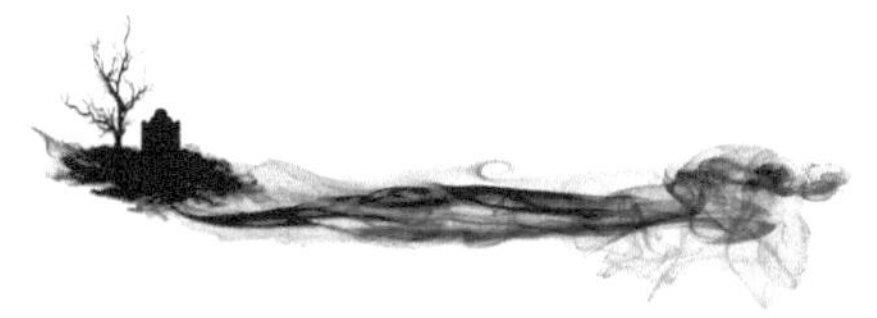

After a rough night of tossing and turning, I put in a twelve-hour shift at St. John's. I'd been transferred from the ICU to the ER, a move I liked because my day usually rushed by, allowing no time for my brain to taunt me with its unanswered questions. But today, even though I'd been off witchy duty the night before, I was dragging, and a cup of tar-thick cafeteria coffee didn't seem to help.

During my break, I texted Michelle.

Valentine's next Saturday. This isn't a request. You're going with me.

Like I'd miss the drama.

What drama?

Watching you interact with Logan should be interesting.

No doubt you plan to analyze my interactions and report back to me on my repressed feelings.

U bet.

Oy. Not repressing! I made a choice.

Hmm.

We can talk about this then.

Looking forward to it.

At the end of my shift, I drove home on autopilot. I had to get some sleep tonight. Besides worrying about the house, the dead finfolk in the alley, Rick, and Logan, tomorrow was Thanksgiving, just a month until Christmas. I didn't even have a tree to put up, let alone any shopping done.

The driveway was dark as I pulled in, the new moon doing nothing to help break the bleak night. Distracted as I was with my problems, I almost plowed into the silhouette of a man standing in front of my garage door. Luckily, the reflective glint of my headlights off his inhuman eyes came in time for me to slam on the brakes.

Vampire. Nightshade was in the attic, but I grabbed the shovel I kept in the back of the Jeep in case of snow emergencies. Faster than humanly possible, I was out of the car and had the vamp thrust against the garage door with the edge pressed into his jugular. That's when I saw who it was— my ex-boyfriend turned vampire.

"Gary."

"Uh, hi, Grateful."

I pressed a little harder on the shovel.

"What are you doing here?"

He held up a large duffle bag. "I have your money. With interest."

I searched his face for any sign of threat or insincerity but his fangs were retracted and his eyes, although slightly nocturnal looking, were without guile. I lowered the shovel and grabbed the bag. *Damn!* It was heavy. I unzipped the top and my heart started to pound. It was filled with bricks of twenty-dollar bills. The satchel thumped to the pavement and I investigated further, flipping the bills through my icy cold fingers. Each brick had ten bills, two hundred dollars, stacked twenty high and fifteen wide. Sixty thousand dollars. I licked my lips. This would get me out of debt and provide a small down payment; I might be able to qualify for a loan to buy my house.

"Are these real?" I asked Gary.

"Of course they're real! Do you think Julius would pull one over on you? Contrary to your apparent assumption, he enjoys having his head attached to his body."

"You only stole forty thousand. That's some pretty crazy interest."

Gary squatted down next to me in the driveway. "So young, so naïve."

All of my negative feelings toward him channeled into a look that could cut glass. He actually waddled back a step. "If you've got something to say, just say it."

"You're Hecate, acting goddess of the dead in this district. Julius is sucking up to you on behalf of the coven. We'd all like to stay on this side of the gate."

"Yeah." I wasn't buying for a minute that Julius was scared of me. I suspected he was behind the increase in supernaturals in the area and the money was his attempt to grease the scales of justice in his favor. I fully intended to keep the money, but refused to promise anything in return. But then, Gary hadn't asked for anything.

"Thanks for paying me back," I said. "I better go inside. My fingers are getting numb." I stood, lifted the heavy bag to my shoulder, and sidestepped to the front door so I could keep one eye on him.

"There's something else, Grateful. We need to talk."

Here it was. He was going to tell me what this bribe was for. I needed to hear it, to know what I was getting myself into by taking the money, but first, I needed to get warm. And there was no way in hell I was inviting him inside.

"Can you wait out here for fifteen minutes? I just got off work. I need to get out of these scrubs and take a bio break."

He glanced at the door, seeming to resign himself to not

being invited in and nodded. It wasn't a big deal for him. Undead bodies didn't get cold. As for me, I was inside before I could take my next breath.

* * *

Fifteen minutes later, I returned to my porch dressed for an Antarctic expedition, complete with snow pants, poofy jacket, hat, gloves, and boots. I turned on the porch light so I could see Gary better, and plopped down on a dining room chair I'd dragged out because I didn't have any patio furniture. Poe came out with me, circling Gary's head before taking off to do some hunting.

"Damned winged rat!" he said, swiping at the air Poe had just vacated.

"Hey! Don't badmouth my familiar. You're on borrowed time, so say what you came to say and get out of here."

"Got one for me?" he said, gesturing toward the chair.

I glanced at the door and the five other dining room chairs behind it. "No." I made myself comfortable.

He leaned against the railing, dressed only in a dress shirt and slacks. If he'd been human, he'd have frostbite by now. "I need to tell you something about the night I became this." He circled a hand through the air in front of his body.

All of the feelings around his abandonment of me came back like a recurring sore. I was over Gary but I wasn't over *it*. Why had he left? What was wrong with me? I needed answers. "Okay. I'll listen. But first, answer me this question. Did you leave me because you became a vampire, or did you become a vampire after you left me?"

Turning toward the road, he scanned my snow-covered yard with the interest of a nocturnal predator. I could picture him leaping over the banister in one lithe movement to capture a rabbit between his teeth.

"I wanted to open our bookstore. I really did. But then I met this woman," Gary began.

"Uh-huh." There was venom in my voice. So, he left me before becoming a vamp. For another woman. My ego curled up at the pit of my stomach.

"No, it wasn't like that. She'd heard my poetry and said she was a big fan. When I told her I was thinking about opening a bookstore, she insisted it was suicide. 'People don't buy paper books anymore,' she said. 'Everything's going electronic.' Instead, she convinced me to partner with her to open a coffeehouse designed around readers. We were going to call it Drink, Eat, Read. Free Wi-Fi. I was excited to tell you about it."

"Wait. Are you saying this happened while we were still together? You never told me about any of this!"

"No."

"Why not?"

"She was a vampire."

I narrowed my eyes, willing him to tell me more.

"She compelled me to empty your accounts and give her the money."

"Why? To open some lame café?"

"No. She never intended to follow through on that idea. She turned me the night I handed the money over." The last sentence came out so quietly I could barely hear it.

My thoughts raced, sifting through the details of his story. "Did you consent to being turned?" I demanded. My stare burrowed into the side of his head.

He pivoted to meet my eyes. "I'm not sure how to answer that question."

"How could you not be sure? You either did or you didn't."

"I left you for her, Grateful. How much of that was compulsion and how much was choice is impossible for me to say. What I do know is I was happy with you before I left, and after she turned me, she used me as slave labor."

"Forced you to make cappuccinos against your will, eh?"

"Like I said, she never opened a coffee shop. She owns a bar, had owned one for years, a nightclub called Mill Wheel. Deals in vamps for hire."

My memory flashed to the vamp I'd sentenced to a decade in the graveyard in Mill Wheel's alley. "Mill Wheel? I'm familiar with the establishment. What exactly do you mean by 'vamps for hire'?"

"Compulsion. Men pay her to have the vamps in the place compel young women to be interested in them. It's like a supernatural roofie. Only, sucks to be the vamp. No pun intended."

The hair on the back of my neck stood on end. "Wait. Human men? How do they even know about the vamps?"

"They don't, really. They think Mill Wheel is like an escort service. They pay for the girl. The girl gets compelled. The queen vamp gets her money, and the slave vamp gets drained."

Gross. How many girls had been taken advantage of? "What do you mean drained?"

"Compelling someone in a way that will last long enough for the men to, uh, get their money's worth, is extremely draining, and we weren't allowed to feed on the customers. Most of us subsisted on sewer rats and pig's blood from the butcher. But with the number of regulars she had, I was starving to death. If it wasn't for Julius, I'd probably have walked into the sunlight."

"You're lying. I caught a vamp feeding on a girl there last week."

"Some of the vamps try to take a sip when they're compelling the girls. It's like a waitress pilfering fries off her customers' plates."

I rubbed a hand over my face, disturbed with the analogy. "So, Julius saved you from the vampires who turned you?" Gary couldn't be trusted. I needed a way to verify if what he was saying was true. "What's this femme fatale's name, anyway? The one who turned you?"

"Anna Bathory."

"Bathory? Why does that name sound familiar?"

He didn't answer me but took a step closer. "There's one more thing I have to tell you. I don't want to, but Julius says I can't leave until I do."

"What is it?"

"Rick was there."

"Where? At Mill Wheel?" I had this horrific thought Gary was going to say Rick paid for sex by compulsion, but knowing how women looked at him, it seemed unlikely.

"No. He was there in the alley when Anna changed me. He knew who I was, and he could've stopped it, Grateful."

"What?" Suddenly, the cold night air seemed too thin for my lungs. I cocked my head to the side. "How would you even know what he looked like?"

"I didn't know who he was exactly, but he'd been following us for weeks. In hindsight, I'm sure he was checking in on you. Rick knew who you were long before you or I did. Anna turned me in the alley behind Mill Wheel. Drained me to the point of death, then fed me her blood. While she was...drinking...I saw him, the guy I'd seen at the grocery store and our favorite restaurant. He was perched on the roof, watching. He looked almost happy about it. I suppose it got me out of the way."

"You're saying he watched it happen and did nothing?"

"Nothing. After I was turned, I asked Anna who he was and she explained."

"Did he know what was happening? Does he know what's going on in Mill Wheel?" Inside my gloves, my hands were shaking. I told myself again that it probably wasn't true, just Gary up to his old tricks or Julius trying to get under my skin. But my stomach sank. One memory kept popping into my head, the night after Rick and I had slain Marcus at Tilt-World. I'd asked Rick if he knew Gary was a vampire and he'd denied it. But there was something about the way he said it. I'd always suspected he was lying. I'd just had this overwhelming feeling that night that Rick was keeping something from me.

Gary shrugged. "I'm not sure what Rick understood or didn't understand. He's been around a long time. Seems like he should know what someone being turned looks like."

The night pressed in around me and my shoulders slumped with exhaustion. I glanced at my watch. After ten. "I think you should go now, Gary," I said flatly. "Unless there's something else Julius wants you to tell me?"

"One more thing. It's true what Julius said. You didn't need Rick to become the witch, Grateful. You would have become who you are no matter what. Rick manipulated you into thinking you needed him. He tricked you into binding yourself to him again. The caretaker orchestrated his position at your side, and he did it at my expense."

I stared at him blankly, letting what he said sink in like a topical poison. "Just go."

To his credit, he left. Three steps into the yard, and he broke apart, melding with the darkness and blowing toward the city. I sat out there, staring at the spot where he'd last been, losing time to the insecurities that played out in my head. When I looked at my watch again, it was after eleven. I forced myself up, out of the chair, and stomped down the street and across the bridge.

Rick was standing in the road naked. I couldn't tell if he was getting ready to shift or had just shifted back. But he was staring in my direction. We shared a strong connection. He'd been waiting for me. He knew I was upset.

"Is it true?" I asked, shoving him in the chest with my gloved hand.

"Is what true, *mi cielo*?" His face took on a stony expression, eyes black, lips a straight line.

I ran through my memories of Gary and our conversation now that I knew Rick was paying attention. He could see my thoughts when he tried. It was easier than trying to explain the whole thing.

"He consented," Rick said flatly. "There was nothing I could do. Anna wasn't breaking the law."

"Why did you lie to me? That night, after TiltWorld, you said you didn't know Gary was a vampire."

"I didn't. Not for sure. More than half of attempted vampire conversions end in death. Either the vampire drinks too much or the human body rejects the change. It's true I saw Anna start the process, but I never saw Gary wake up. I didn't know for sure he'd been turned."

"Splitting hairs, Rick."

He straightened his spine. "I did not lie to you."

"Is it true that you'd been following me and knew that Gary and I were involved?"

"Yes, I've known you since you were born." Rick took a step toward me, his bare feet crunching on the snow.

"Then you must have known how upset I'd be when Gary didn't come home. I thought he'd abandoned me. How could you let that happen?"

"He consented."

"So now you're all about the rules."

"There are rules for a reason."

"All you had to do was interrupt her, jump down from your perch and say 'Hey, Anna, did this guy consent to this?'" I tossed up my hands in frustration. "You could have used your power to compel the truth out of Gary. You didn't have to fight Anna or start a supernatural war. All you had to do was your *job*! You should have made sure Gary was able to consent."

Rick looked toward the cemetery. "It didn't occur to me at the time."

"It didn't *occur* to you?" I gaped at him. "Can you honestly say that no part of you wanted him to die?"

He blinked at me and I got the strangest mix of emotions through our connection. I couldn't decipher all of them: defensiveness, possessiveness, guilt, and under the lot of it, love. I didn't want to feel that part at the moment. It was like finding a rose blossoming in the center of dog poop.

"I did not kill Gary," he said. "The boy consented. I heard Anna ask for his consent, and I heard him answer in the positive. I couldn't interfere without risking a backlash from her and her supporters. True, his response might have been compelled. I didn't think so."

"You didn't think so, but you didn't check."

"No."

I shook my head.

He rushed me, grabbing my shoulders and shaking. His black eyes met mine. "I would be dishonest if I said I was disappointed. He left you, stole your money. You deserved better."

Through my teeth, I let him know I wasn't buying it. "Gary said he was compelled by Anna to do those things. Why would you assume his consent wasn't compelled too? If you'd been following us, you had to know there was some compulsion going on. And if you suspected any compulsion at all, then you should have suspected she compelled his consent. You let him die—"

"It was meant to be!" he snapped. He paced away from

me, hands on his naked hips. I was reminded again how cold it was outside.

"Julius says you manipulated me to get what you wanted, to secure your place as my caretaker."

Rick whirled on me, finger pointing at my nose. "You can't believe that."

"I don't know what to believe." I spread my hands. "I'm supposed to be this all-powerful witch, but it's *you* who are immortal. It doesn't make logical sense. If I was as powerful as you say I was, why did I need you?"

His face paled, then contorted as if he was at a loss for words. "I can't explain to you why. The magic wasn't my doing."

I shook my head. "You are keeping something from me. You may not have lied to me outright, but you didn't tell me the entire truth. This is a pattern with you. Just like when we first met. You have to be upfront with me. I want to know the truth. The whole truth."

He brought his face close to mine. "The truth is, I died every day I saw you with Gary. I'd waited so long to have you back." Closing his eyes, he said, "I was happy the day she turned him. I knew our meeting was close. When I finally had you, I delayed telling you because I knew it would be difficult for you to believe. I wanted you to have time to enjoy the unfolding of who you are." His eyes opened again and they were black as death. "But I am your caretaker. *You* chose me for this role. I didn't lie to you about that or anything else. You needed me. Julius is deceiving you."

What could I say to that? Everything he said was plausible, even if not entirely logical. And as I searched our connection, he seemed to be telling the truth. Still, one thought ate at me. If he knew what Gary had meant to me, how could he let him die, knowing how it would hurt me?

"I floundered for months," I whispered. "I contemplated

suicide. Do you remember, Rick, how I had to see a therapist because I thought I was unlovable. Your inaction left me destitute. I barely avoided bankruptcy for God's sake!" The memories of that time in my life left my chest heavy with anger and betrayal. At that moment, I wanted to hurt Rick like he'd allowed me to be hurt.

"I'm sorry," he murmured. He did not sound sorry. "I wish it could have been different, but things happen for a reason."

Whether or not Rick realized it, he'd injured me. I knew I should ask him more about Mill Wheel and if what Gary said went on there was true, but I couldn't get past the personal stuff. Gary's abandonment had caused major issues in every aspect of my life, and he had the nerve to stare at me with that icy expression and say everything unfolded like it was supposed to? Fuck that. Fuck him.

"You know what I wish? I wish I'd had a *choice*! I wish I'd never made *you* my caretaker. Magic may bind me to you, but make no mistake, Rick, if I had a *choice*, I'd walk away right now. You had no right to fuck with my life like that."

He took a step back like I'd physically punched him. "I'll fix this, *mi cielo*. I'll find a way to prove to you—"

"Save it. I wish I'd never met you. Just stay away from me. I can't even look at you right now."

I pulled away, began walking home. He started after me. I stopped, glared at him until his feet halted at the force of my will. When I was sure he understood exactly how serious I was, I headed home.

8

MY CONFIDANT

By the time I reached my house, it was after midnight, but there was no way I was going to be able to sleep. Poe, who must have been watching from a distance, met me at the door and flew in to perch on the banister.

"He's right, you know. The caretaker is not allowed to interfere with vampire activity if the human consents."

I placed a hand on my hip. "But if vampires can compel humans, how do we know what's legitimate consent?"

He fluffed his wings in response and turned away from me.

"Exactly. Keep your beak shut if you don't know what you're talking about."

At that, he turned completely around, his back to me. Raven cold shoulder.

My brain flipped Rick's side of the story over in my head, searching for the seams, then mused over everything Julius and Gary had said. I needed to talk it through and not with a snarky familiar. I tried to call Michelle's cell phone, but the call went straight to voicemail. If she'd been working tonight, I'd call the hospital, but Wednesdays were her day off, and I couldn't call her home number without waking the baby. A best friend never, ever wakes another friend's baby.

I paced the floor. The whole situation made my skin crawl. If Julius was telling the truth, then I was literally in bed with the enemy. He had to be lying. Why would I believe a vampire over my caretaker? So then, why was I still thinking about this? On impulse, I grabbed my keys.

"Not a good idea," Poe said over his shoulder.

I gave him the finger and slammed the door behind me.

* * *

Logan's apartment was on the top floor of a secured building ten minutes from Valentine's. I stormed through the front door, still worked up over my argument with Rick. A white-haired man in a uniform eyed me suspiciously from behind a large circular desk in the atrium.

"I'm here to see Logan Valentine," I said.

The old man frowned. "It's after hours. Can't call up." His liver-spotted jowls flapped with his objection.

"Uh, it's kind of an emergency."

With an adjustment of his bifocals, the guard looked me up and down. He gave a low, throaty laugh. "What kind of emergency brings a girl like you to a man's house in the middle of the night?"

"Hey! I don't appreciate the conjecture." I poked the tip of one finger into the desk in front of him. "We're *friends*, practically family!"

"Family, eh?" The man rubbed his stubbled cheek. "What's your name?"

"Grateful Knight."

The guard started typing, the glow of a computer screen coming to life beyond the counter. I couldn't see what he was doing because the monitor was the type that sank into the desk, but the expression on the man's face told me I was one bug he'd like to squash. I pulled out my phone. "If you won't call up, I will," I said.

"Hold your horses, missy. Your booty call has been approved."

"Booty call? Wha—" The door to the foyer opened automatically with a soft buzz.

"Don't make me change my mind." The guard's bushy eyebrows descended and then he let out a deep laugh.

I scurried through and into the elevator, chin up and ego bruised. When I reached the top floor, the doors opened. Logan stood waiting for me with his phone in hand—all bed head and wrinkled T-shirt.

"Sorry," I said. "Didn't mean to wake you."

"What's happened? Are you okay?" His voice sounded frantic.

"Uh, yeah. I just need to talk…if you are available…to do the talking thing."

He gaped at me. "When the doorman called, I thought you were engaged in some nighttime battle with the undead and needed my help."

"What, you thought I was like injured or something?"

"Yeah, like maybe bleeding from an artery? I've left instructions with the front desk to let you in any time, day or night, just in case you can't make it back to your house."

"Oh, really? Just for the record, your doorman is a complete asshat." This was my first time here, and Logan had never offered his home as a safe house to me before. Sweet gesture, but that info would have saved me some face downstairs. I guess he just assumed I would know I could count on him if I needed to.

"Yeah. Sorry about that. Fred is good at what he does, but he can be a little rough around the edges."

"He thought I was your booty call."

Logan raised eyebrows and whistled.

"I'm not."

He ran a hand through his hair and wiped his eyes with his fingers. "Well, now that we've cleared that up, come on in. You want something to drink? Hot cocoa?"

I remembered the comfort Logan's hot cocoa had given me when I was deciding if I should accept my role as the witch. I'd spent weeks detoxing from my addiction to his hot cocoa. I couldn't go back there. "Tea would be fine."

He nodded sleepily and led the way across the hall, into the foyer of an enormous apartment. The open floor plan showcased a wall of windows overlooking Carlton City. A balcony extended behind the sliding glass doors. Logan's furniture was neutral leather, the floors mahogany, and the décor, craftsman. Clean lines, warm wood tones, and splashes of red, yellow, and purple reminded me of Frank Lloyd Wright's designs. It was masculine but comfortable, unmistakably Logan.

"You have an eye for decorating," I said.

He glanced at me over the granite countertop of the kitchen island as he filled a copper kettle with water. "Actually, I had it decorated. I didn't do it myself."

"Someone in town?"

"Not anymore. An ex-girlfriend."

"Oh." I was beginning to melt inside my arctic outerwear, so I did the cold weather striptease. I shed hat, gloves, coat, boots, and snow pants, piling the outerwear on the back of his sofa, and took a seat on the barstool in front of the island. "At least something good came of the relationship." I shrugged.

"Said like a jaded lover."

"Maybe. Speaking of, I saw Gary tonight."

Logan almost dropped the canister he was holding. "Gary, as in your missing ex-boyfriend, Gary?"

"The one and only. Didn't I tell you? He's a vampire now."

Logan set down the canister and opened a cabinet across the kitchen. "You're going to need something stronger than tea." He pulled out a bottle of my favorite Shiraz and popped the cork. A moment later, I had a full glass in front of me.

"Did you have to kill him?" Logan asked softly.

"Oddly, no. He paid me back. All the money he owed me plus interest. Just showed up at my door with a big leather bag full of cash."

"What's he want?" Logan narrowed his eyes and pressed his lips into a flat line.

"He said he didn't want anything, that it was in the coven's best interest to keep me happy and Julius insisted."

With a long swig of wine, he drank that explanation in and rolled it in his mouth. "I smell bullshit."

"I know, but then he told me something else…"

"The reason you're here?"

I nodded. "Turns out Rick has been following me around my whole life. He knew about Gary and me. The night Gary was turned, Rick allowed it to happen. He was there."

"What the hell?"

"Yeah, he admitted it. Said Gary consented, so the vampire wasn't breaking any rules. But he knew, Logan. He knew it would break my heart, and he allowed it to happen because he wanted me for himself."

"Are you sure it's true?"

I took a sip of liquid courage. "He admitted it."

"Whoa."

"That's not even the worst part. Julius says that Rick manipulated me into thinking that I needed him to become the witch, when really I could've done it myself. Gary said that I bound myself to him needlessly. *I* would have become the witch anyway, but Rick might not have been my caretaker. The ceremony was for *his* sake, not mine."

Logan drained the rest of his glass and poured another. He lifted it to his mouth, but paused and gestured in my direction. "That last part has to be a lie. Prudence backed Rick up. She told both of us it had to be sex and blood. She said he was the vessel; you had to drink from the vessel."

"Yeah. Rick denies it, and I know in my heart that it's a lie, but it's under my skin. It's like my intuition is telling me that Rick is hiding something, and it's fucking with my head."

"I wonder where Prudence got her information?" Logan asked.

I became inordinately interested in my empty glass. "Me. In my last life, I'd shared what I was and given her the power to care for my seat of magic in my absence."

He cupped my face and rubbed my cheek with his thumb. "There you have it, hon. You wouldn't lie to you. Julius is lying. As much as I hate the gravedigger, I think Rick was telling you the truth."

"But what about this feeling I have?"

The remains of the bottle of Shiraz were emptied into my glass. "We're friends, right?"

"Right."

"Friends can be honest with each other."

"Of course."

"I think this feeling you have has more to do with you than with Rick."

I swung my hand through the air like the mere thought was ridiculous.

"You're afraid of commitment, Grateful. You told me as much when I was living in your attic. Rick represents the first permanent thing in your life besides your dad, and it terrifies you."

"Why are you standing up for Rick? I thought you hated—"

Logan's wineglass slipped from his hand, shattering on

the counter. Shards of glass skimmed along the granite. His face turned hospital sheet white, and he stared open mouthed over my shoulder into the living room. I followed his line of sight, thinking I'd see an ax murderer approaching from that direction, but there was nothing there.

"What's going on Logan?"

"Sh-She says you have to find it."

"She? She who?"

He pointed to a spot over my shoulder, but there was still no one there. "She says you can't see her because her soul has already crossed over to the other side. You need to find the book before they do, or the entire human race is in great danger."

"What book?" I shook my head. I could tell Logan was really shook up, but maybe he was hallucinating or something.

"*The Book of Flesh and Bone.*"

"Flesh and Bone?" I raised my eyebrows as I remembered where I'd heard that title before. Rick told me Reverend Monk had used *The Book of Flesh and Bone* to bind my spirit to my human body before he burned me alive—well, the first me. But the grimoire exacted a high price; Monk and all of his parishioners were struck dead. What happened to the book after that? Rick never said and who else could know?

"Who are you talking to, Logan?" I asked, softly.

He swallowed hard and turned to face me. Like a fish out of water, his mouth opened and closed, but nothing came out. I placed a hand on his and shook a little. "Who?" I repeated.

"My mother. Only, she's been dead for ten years."

9

MEDIUM

"You saw your mother's ghost?" I looked toward the empty space where he'd been staring but couldn't sense anything. Even when I focused with the part of me that was the witch, the living room was empty. "I don't see anything. Is she still there?"

His breath caught, and I noticed his fingers whiten as he caught himself on the countertop, fingers narrowly missing the shards of broken glass. Red wine dripped off the edge of the granite, but he didn't seem to notice. "No. She's gone. She just dissipated." Closing his lids, he released a shaky exhale.

I squinted in the direction of his sofa. "Are you sure it wasn't the wine?" When he didn't answer me, I glanced back in his direction.

He winced and shook his head. "I'm sure. I just saw the ghost of my dead mother, Grateful. This isn't a case of the spins."

I spread my hands. "I'm a goddess of the dead. If an apparition of your dead mother was really here, shouldn't I be able to sense her in some way?"

"You sort souls. She said hers was already sorted. Maybe you can only see those people who haven't moved on."

"I guess it's possible, but—"

"What's *The Book of Flesh and Bone*?" With his elbows replacing his hands on the granite, he bent at the waist until his forehead rested on his fists. He seemed too exhausted to hold his head up, let alone clean up the broken glass.

I sighed. Why had I unloaded this burden on Logan? And at this hour of the night? He should have been free of all this. Now I owed him an answer. "The first witch was a woman named Isabella Lockhart. In 1698, Reverend Monk and his Puritan parishioners used a spell from *The Book of Flesh and Bone*, a grimoire or book of magic given to him by a demon in the woods behind Rick's house. The spell bound Isabella to her body and allowed Monk to burn her at the stake. Her soul survived only because she stored it inside a living host, her caretaker, Rick. But Reverend Monk and every person who had chanted the spell from the book died instantly from using the dark magic. Their blood became a forced sacrifice to Beelzebub and opened the hellmouth in Monk's Hill Cemetery."

"So, it's the devil's own grimoire with recipes to control the living and the dead, flesh and bone. Nice. Definitely dangerous in the wrong hands."

"For sure."

"So where is it now?"

"I have no idea. As far as I know, it hasn't been seen since the day Monk used it on me."

Logan shivered. "You'd better find it, Grateful. What if that's what Julius wants? Based on your story about Isabella, the book contains some powerful magic. Maybe he wants to control you with it."

"But why would Julius give me the money tonight if he intended to hurt me?" I shook my head, folding my hands.

Logan straightened. "Maybe he thinks you know where the book is. Maybe he thinks if he gets close enough to you, you will lead him to it." He bent down to dig under his sink, emerging with a dustpan and hand broom.

I thought about that. "Why would he think I would know where it was? If anyone would know where *The Book of Flesh and Bone* was today, it would be Rick. He was there the day I died, and lived to tell the tale."

Positioning the dustpan, Logan methodically swept glass and spilled wine with the faraway expression of someone deep in thought. For a moment, I allowed my brain to blank, absorbed in watching his domestic task. I bounced down from the stool and grabbed a rag from the sink, crouching to wipe the spilled red liquid from the floor.

"Grateful, why am I seeing my dead mother?" Logan stopped sweeping and glared at me with the beginnings of dark circles under his eyes.

"What? She's back?"

"No. Not at the moment. But before?"

I shrugged. The rag was saturated, so I stood and wrung it in the sink. The red swirled the stainless steel drain like blood in my silver bowl, and an answer popped into my head from somewhere deep inside. "There's something of the ghost left in you. Your soul was as close to dead as anyone gets and lives to talk about. You've glimpsed the other side of the veil. It remains thin for you."

He wiped a hand over his face. "That sounded like the witch talking."

"I think it was."

"So, I'm a medium or something?"

"Or something." I gave him an empathetic frown over my shoulder. "I can do some research in *The Book of Light* if you want me to."

He nodded. The dustpan was full, and he nudged me

aside to empty it into the garbage can under the sink. Standing hip to hip, I noticed the scruff along his jaw and the fine lines at the corners of his eyes, features ghost Logan hadn't had. He was really human again.

"What else aren't you telling me?" he asked. Ghost or not, his green eyes blazed just as bright. I ignored the subtle pang of attraction his look elicited and turned away to finish wiping the counter.

"There's a guy trying to buy my house out from under me and a recent influx of supernatural baddies in Carlton City. Rick and I can hardly keep up."

Logan groaned.

"My sentiments exactly."

He returned the cleaning supplies to their place under the sink and stretched to open the little cabinet door over the fridge. When he returned, there was a bottle of Jack Daniels in his hand. "We're going to need something stronger than wine."

By the time I finished wiping, two shot glasses had appeared next to the bottle. He poured. "Do you think the two are related?"

I blinked once, twice.

He downed his shot and plunked the glass down on the counter. His lips pressed together for a moment, then he pointed a finger at me. "What if Julius isn't trying to woo you but distract you?"

I raised my eyebrows.

The pointed finger waved deliberately. "He needs to distract you while he searches for *The Book of Flesh and Bone*. He does this by sending someone to buy your house, then planting the seed of doubt in your head about Rick. Maybe returning the money wasn't about the money at all but about giving Gary the chance to drop that little emotional bomb on you. Meanwhile, he's calling in his buddies to help him look for Satan's grimoire while you reel from all the shit he's thrown your way."

For a moment, I tried to digest that, taking interest in the whiskey on the counter. "You may be right. I had the sense he was trying to stir the pot, but it doesn't change that what he said was true. Rick admitted as much. Unfortunately, if Julius wanted to shake me up, he did a good job. I can't let this go. I need to know the truth."

"Even if you can't change it? You can't go back. You've accepted your role, and Rick is your caretaker. Finding out that he manipulated you and had a hand in Gary's fate isn't going to change your dependence on each other. Believe me, I'd like to think that it could for my own selfish reasons, but it won't."

His eyes burned into me, and I looked toward the shot snuggled in my grip for release from the heat. The conversation was veering toward dangerous territory. Again, I'd let Logan in too deep without taking into consideration his feelings for me, feelings I knew in my heart I couldn't return. I nudged my full shot in his direction. "Sorry, I can't partake. Getting ridiculously drunk with you sounds magically delicious at this point, but I need to get home while I'm sober enough to drive. I have to work in the morning."

"Ah. Sick people don't stop coming to the hospital because a vampire is threatening to take over the city."

I laughed. "Unfortunately, no. Plus, if you're right about Julius, I've got to get to my attic and make a plan. Tainted or not, the money will help. I'll use it as a down payment and buy my house."

Collecting my arctic outfit from the sofa, I stepped into my snow pants.

"I know you have to go, Grateful, but we haven't had a chance to talk about us."

Intent on my coat zipper, I refused to meet his eyes. I

couldn't start this with him right now. I shook my head and reached for my gloves.

"This conversation isn't over," he murmured. "Maybe at my party?"

Reluctantly, I agreed. I guess I owed him that much. But for now, I was exhausted. I donned my winter layers and kissed him goodbye on the cheek. He escorted me to the elevator, and I stepped into the empty compartment.

"I meant what I said before. Fred downstairs knows to let you up here day or night. If you ever need anything…"

"Thanks, Logan." The doors closed between us. A wave of guilt passed through me. Why was I so careless with Logan's emotions? I knew he had feelings for me, feelings I couldn't return, yet like a sore tooth, I couldn't stop poking it where it ached. I had to be more careful with him.

I made a mental note to protect his apartment with an enchantment. The last thing I needed was some jagged-toothed supernatural nabbing Logan and using him against me. So far, I didn't think Julius knew about our friendship. I needed to keep it that way. Medium or not, Logan wasn't equipped to handle the life I could inflict on him.

THANKSGIVING

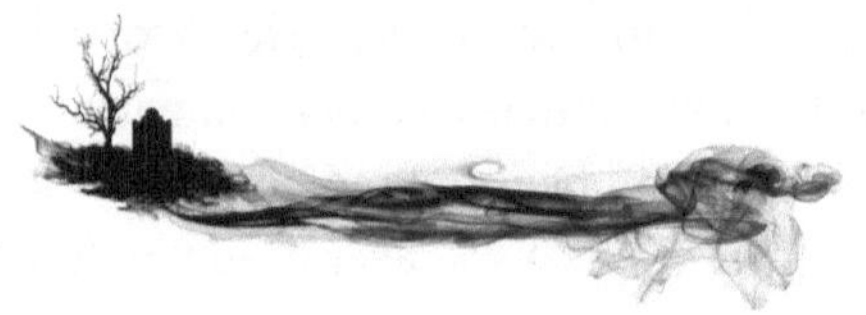

I arrived at Dad's brownstone in the city around a quarter to one, having already put in a half shift at the hospital. Dad wanted a traditional Thanksgiving, so I'd changed out of my scrubs and into a formfitting chocolate brown sweater with an ankle length skirt and tall boots. Since I'd promised to help him cook, I'd gathered my honey-blond waves into a messy bun.

Dad came to the door in a suit and tie. Geesh. He was really taking this seriously. Seemed like a lot of fuss for just the two of us. I returned his hug.

"You look great," he said, kissing me on my forehead.

"Well, I have good news."

He pulled back, raising his eyebrows. "Do tell."

"I have the money for the house. I'm going in for the loan as soon as possible."

He smiled stiffly. I expected him to argue that I shouldn't live there or ask me how I'd gotten the money. Instead, he seemed distracted. He shifted from foot to foot in front of his traditionally decorated living room. Since I'd moved out, my dad's house always looked "staged," as if he could put a "for sale" sign out front without so much as dusting. But then as the owner of one of the few historical buildings in the city, he was often asked to show the place for newspaper and magazine features. He took the privilege seriously. Usually, though, there was some hint of the man behind the décor. I instinctively looked toward the decorative cabinet on the far wall, the source of what I considered to be the house's dirty secret. The doors were closed. The TV wasn't on.

"Aren't you going to watch the game?" I couldn't remember a time he hadn't had the cabinet open for football on Thanksgiving.

He shrugged. I glanced across the foyer into the dining room. Flowers. My father had purchased centerpieces. "What the hell is going on, Dad? Are you going to tell me you have cancer? I don't think I can take a cancer diagnosis right now."

"I don't have cancer."

I breathed a sigh of relief. "Then what is all this?"

Hands on hips, he pressed his lips together. "You're going to find out sooner or later. I might as well just tell you now."

I bobbed my head emphatically.

He opened his mouth, but like a cartoon, the sound of the doorbell replaced his voice. Holding up one finger, he backed into the foyer and reached for the doorknob. Who the hell was visiting my dad on Thanksgiving? If it was a client, we'd have to have a serious talk about boundaries.

The bell ringer was a ballerina. Tall, lanky, graceful, and holding a casserole dish. Since when did ballerinas deliver Thanksgiving casseroles?

"Seraphina, you look lovely as always." Dad extended his hand, and she nestled her long fingers in his palm. He helped her over the threshold. Yeah, like that quarter-inch strip of wood was a hazard. Don't let her go, she might trip on the rug. Now his hand was on the small of her back, pressing into the graceful drape of her tailored black wool coat. I pressed my lips together to keep my mouth from falling open.

"Thank you again for inviting me, Robert." Her too-full lips planted on his cheek in slow motion, leaving a smear of red lipstick in her wake. Then she turned her sights on me. Her eyes were green with flecks of amber and gold around the pupil that brought out the highlights in her golden brown hair. And she was young. Really young.

"Dad, aren't you going to introduce us?" I muttered.

He cleared his throat. "Of course. Grateful, this is my girlfriend, Seraphina. Seraphina, my daughter, Grateful."

Girlfriend? "How old are you?" I sputtered. "Oh, hell, that was rude. I'm sorry." I pressed my thumb and forefinger into my temple.

My father held up his hands. "I should have told you…" His voice trailed off and his eyes rolled toward the ceiling.

Seraphina gave my father a harsh look and handed him the casserole.

"Sorry about that. Let's start again," I offered. "I'm Grateful."

"Seraphina." She extended her perfectly manicured hand.

I waited for a "nice to meet you" or some sort of greeting that would indicate she accepted my apology, but all I got was a retraction of her hand and a regal movement of her fingers, like she was waving our greeting out of the air before the smell could hit her. We all stood staring at each other. Dad made a sound like a cough. Seraphina rubbed the palms of her hands together. My lips parted. I was staring, definitely staring. She had no pores. Was she *my* age? She couldn't be much older.

"Can I take your coat?" Dad finally said. Seraphina nodded and shrugged it off into his hands, exposing a red wrap dress that showed off her ridiculously svelte figure.

I forced my lips to form words. "Can I get you a drink?"

"Don't you want to take off your coat, too?" Dad asked.

Crap. I unbuttoned and handed the heavy wool to my dad, flashing him a confused and accusatory look.

"Dad, can I talk to you in the kitchen for a moment?"

"Of course, honey. Seraphina, wine?"

"Please."

Dad led the way through the dining room and the swinging white door into the kitchen. I waited until there was a polite amount of space between us and the complete stranger he'd invited to our family gathering before I raised my eyebrows and pointed at the closed door.

He answered without me having to ask. "She was a client. We hit it off. We've been dating a couple of months."

"And it's already serious enough to bring her home to meet the family?"

From a cabinet behind me, he retrieved a wineglass. "Wine?"

"Ooooh yeah."

He pulled down two more and retrieved a bottle of red wine from a rack on the counter. "I've been lonely, Grateful. Your mom's been gone a long time. She's a beautiful, intelligent woman. Give her a chance."

All my annoyance drained out of me, replaced by guilt for not putting my father's happiness above my own. He had *never* introduced me to a woman before. Did I expect him to play the monk forever? It was one afternoon and it was *his* house. Was it too much for him to ask for me to put on my happy face and deal for one afternoon? No. And I was a complete bitch to even suggest it. "Oh…ah…I want you to be happy, Dad. Of course she's welcome. I just wish you had warned me. I'm shocked, that's all. I've never seen you with a woman before."

Popping the cork, he filled the glasses one by one. "Overdue, then. Wouldn't you say?" He shot me an accusatory glance, took a swig of his wine.

Okay. I deserved that. I hadn't reacted to Seraphina fairly.

"You're right. I'm so sorry. I should have handled that better. I was just caught off guard." I concentrated on the best way to make it up to him. "Hey, why don't you go out there and smooth things over while I start dinner? Make her feel at home. Once she's settled in, I'll come out and get to know her better."

"You can't cook." Dad stared at me blankly. It wasn't an insult. I'd admitted the truth of my inability to cook enough times that Dad was simply repeating the undeniable fact.

"I'm a grown woman with a smartphone. I'll figure it out."

Dad wrapped me in a too firm hug and kissed me on the forehead. "Excellent idea. She's wonderful. You'll see." He grabbed two glasses of the wine and shouldered his way into the dining room.

I lifted my glass from the pristine counter and paused. So, Dad had a girlfriend. An incredibly young, shamelessly beautiful girlfriend. *Wrap your head around it, Grateful!* I mentally shook my own shoulders. Well, one good thing, I'd be too busy cooking to have much time to visit.

I yanked open the door to the refrigerator, resigned to get started. No turkey. In horror, I opened the freezer. Yep. There it was: one frozen twelve-pound turkey. I pulled the ball of ice from the freezer and plopped it on the counter with a foreboding *thunk*. The icy sheen on the shrink-wrap frosted from the heat of the kitchen.

Wine in hand, I returned to the dining room to break the bad news. It was empty. I proceeded to the living room. Dad and Seraphina were shoulder to shoulder on the couch, carrying on an animated discussion. After a few moments, I cleared my throat to get their attention.

"Dad, the turkey is…" I trailed off when I saw his face fall.

For some reason, this was really important to him. He must have strong feelings for Seraphina to introduce her to me and I could see he wanted tonight to be special. I hated the thought of disappointing him.

"What is it, sweetheart?"

"The turkey is going to take a few hours. I don't mean to be rude, Seraphina, but I'm going to be working in the kitchen for a while."

"Grateful, I didn't mean to leave that all to you. Let me finish this drink and I'll be in to help." Dad scooted to the edge of his seat.

Seraphina gave me a pouty smile. "I'll help too. I trained as a chef at a prestigious school in France."

Was she kidding me? A chef? Over my dead body. I could only imagine what Seraphina would think of the frozen turkey on the counter, and there was no way I was suffering her critique of my lacking culinary skills for…as long as it took to cook a frozen turkey. It was a matter of pride. Maybe I hadn't attended a European culinary school, but I could cook dinner for my dad. "You know what? Why don't I get the turkey started while you guys enjoy your drinks, and then you can help with the salad a little closer to dinner?"

The two lovebirds didn't argue with me. In fact, my dad scooted closer to Seraphina as he nodded his head. Great. I was officially relegated to third wheel status. I shook it off and headed back into the kitchen where I dialed Logan. He answered on the first ring.

"How do you thaw a turkey?"

Logan cleared his throat. "Two days in the cooler."

"I've gotta cook this sucker this afternoon."

"How big?

"Twelve pounds."

"I've heard you can cook it from frozen but it takes five hours and the results are inconsistent."

"Inconsistent?"

"It might taste like rubber."

I groaned. "Six isn't too late to eat rubber turkey," I said hopefully. "So just throw it in a pan and pop it in the oven?"

"Melt some butter over the top, salt it inside and out. You and the bird will be golden."

"Thanks."

"You are still coming Saturday, right?" he asked.

"Wouldn't miss it."

"Good, because we need to talk about us. No interruptions. I need to know where I stand in your life." Metal clanked against metal in the background.

"Where are you?" I changed the subject, desperate to avoid the inevitable conversation, even though I was dying to invite him over to help cook dinner.

"Volunteering at the mission. My dad's coming into town later for a low-key dinner."

The mission! As if Logan could possibly be any more attractive, now he was backlit by a halo. But oddly, when I thought about seeing Logan on Saturday, I didn't tingle with excitement. I dreaded it. Every day he'd been out of my attic, my thoughts of him had gravitated more toward "planet friendship" than "over the moon." And it wasn't because of Rick or my commitment to him. Something had shifted between us. Maybe it was the loss of the connection we'd shared when I was sorting his soul. I wasn't sure. My feelings for him were garbled and confused. Random memories of our time under the same roof mixed with feelings at odds with each other.

"Thanks again, and happy Thanksgiving," I said in a voice more cheerful than my disposition.

"Grateful, one last thing."

"Yeah?"

"You could always bamboozle it."

"Bamboozle?"

"You know, bippidy boppity blip, perfect Thanksgiving dinner."

I huffed in offense. "Logan Valentine, I'll have you know I am woman enough to make a Thanksgiving dinner without the use of magic."

"That's my girl!" He wished me luck and said his goodbyes.

I found an apron in Dad's drawer that said *Realtors Do It in Every Room of the House.* Eww. A quick dig through the lower cabinets and I located the heavy-duty roasting pan we'd used when I was a kid. I tossed the frozen turkey inside. The icy flesh clanked against the metal. You could ice skate on this sucker. I hoped when Logan said I could cook the turkey frozen he meant Antarctic tundra style because no part of this bird was even partially thawed out. To combat the risk of rubberized meat, I microwaved a stick of butter and poured it over the top. Everything was better with butter, right? Into the oven it went.

I took a sip of wine to celebrate my accomplishment.

Then I got my Martha Stewart on, yanking veggies and potatoes from the fridge and selecting a blade from Dad's drawer. I had nothing if not knife skills. Like a culinary pro, I cubed potatoes and chopped broccoli with mechanical preci-sion. The taters went into a pot of water and the broccoli into the steamer. I pulled Dad's crystal salad bowl from its place under the counter, rinsed out a year's worth of dust, and positioned it on the butcher block island.

I drummed my fingers on the counter. Four hours to go. Seraphina and Dad had said they wanted to help with the salad. No putting this off, I needed to go socialize. Pushing the door open, I moseyed into the living room. Yes, moseyed, a slow drift rather than a beeline.

As I turned the corner, a tangle of arms and legs slapped

my visual cortex. *Gah!* They were making out on the couch. Hastily, I receded back into the kitchen. What the hell? How long had that been going on? Apparently, Dad and Seraphina were in the hot-and-heavy stage of their relationship. Could this possibly get any more awkward?

Resolved that help was not coming, I chopped the lettuce and some carrots, tomatoes, and peppers for the salad. When there was nothing left to do, I checked the turkey, hoping a time warp in the oven had magically cooked it for five hours instead of one and a half. No such luck. In fact, it was ice cold, as was the oven…which I'd forgot to turn on.

My head hit the counter with a thud. I could not hide in this kitchen for another five hours. I snatched my phone from my pocket and searched my new *The Book of Light* app for help. There wasn't a spell for instant Thanksgiving, but I could control the elements. Water—ice—was an element. Air was my element of choice, mine to control. I had an idea that maybe I could bamboozle Thanksgiving after all.

To start, I lit the burner under the potatoes, but I didn't wait for them to boil. I raised my flattened palm to my lips and blew gently across the top of the water. Instantly, the liquid came to a rolling boil. I pumped my fist. Being a witch had some definite perks.

The turkey was next. I preheated the oven while I set the roasting pan on the island. Again, I blew across my palm, using my power to ask the air to coax the water molecules inside the bird to heat up. The breeze hit the turkey. Steam billowed. The skin where my breath hit began to brown. Hot damn! I circled the island as I blew out breath after breath. When the turkey's skin had taken on an even, golden glow, and I was feeling a bit lightheaded, I stopped.

"Starting to smell good, Grateful!" I heard my Dad call from the family room.

At least I knew he was up for air. I dug out a meat

thermometer from the drawer next to the stove and slid it into the breast. One hundred eighty degrees! I slid the bird back into the now warm oven, and grabbed the salad out of the fridge. "Should be ready in a few minutes," I yelled.

I stomped through the door, loudly placing the bowl at the center of the dining table. When I dared to glance in their direction, they were on opposite sides of the couch, straightening their clothes.

"Already?" Dad said. "I meant to come in and help you, but I guess I lost track of time. Seraphina here does that to me."

She giggled.

"I see that." I supposed I should make conversation. "So, ah, Seraphina is a beautiful name. Is it a family name?" I plopped down in one of my father's leather chairs across from the sofa and crossed my legs, pumping my foot in the air nervously.

"Yes, it is. It means 'burning one.' In my family, most names have to do with the elements. My uncle's name is Kai. It means ocean. My mother's was Gaea."

"Earth. How interesting." Hippies. "And you're a chef?"

"No." She laughed. "I'm an art and antiques dealer."

"I thought you said you went to culinary school?"

"I did. Just for fun. My masters is in art history."

"No kidding?" Now I was dying to know how old she was.

"Seraphina interned at Christie's," Dad chimed in.

Christie's? "You're practically a child prodigy," I blurted. Damn, that came out catty, but I couldn't get over how young she looked and how much she'd accomplished.

She straightened her back and raised her chin. "I finished early. Discipline is the key. I've never shied away from hard work."

Was she looking down her nose at me? Blink. Blink. "I'm a nurse."

"Good for you," she sang in a patronizing tone.

Enough chat. This chick rubbed me the wrong way, and I really didn't think it was because she was the cradle my dad was robbing. There was something about her, an arrogance that made my chest tighten. She hadn't even asked about my name. Had my father told her the story behind Grateful, or was she too self-centered to care? By the smug look on her face, I was going with self-centered.

"Excuse me. I better check on the potatoes." I stood and moved toward the kitchen.

As I cut through the dining room, I heard my dad brag about my meager achievement of being first in my nursing class. But I didn't graduate early, and I didn't have my masters. Frankly, it was embarrassing, like he was showing off my participation awards to an Olympic medalist. Not to mention, this wasn't a competition. Sure felt like it though.

I repeated the mantra, "I will not be jealous of my father's girlfriend. I will not be jealous of my father's girlfriend."

A minute later, Dad swung through the door and joined me in the kitchen. "Isn't she great?"

I let my breath out all at once, smiled, and lied. "Yeah! Oh, she is charming, Dad." I bobbed my head.

"You don't like her?"

"Of course I do," I said in a pinched voice.

He looked at me skeptically. I changed the subject.

"Everything's done. Let's bring it out." Four o'clock and I had a fully cooked, golden brown turkey with all the fixings, which I had prepared myself. Take that, Seraphina.

Dad carried everything out while I whipped the potatoes. By the time I emerged with a pretty china bowl heaping with spuds, the table looked sponsored by Norman Rockwell.

"I, for one, am thankful to have a daughter who can cook. Thank you, Grateful. Everything looks perfect."

"You're welcome, Dad."

He stood, knife poised over the crispy golden skin, and smiled at Seraphina and then at me. Not so bad. Chances were this May/November romance of theirs wouldn't last. This was a beautiful moment. I decided to accept it for what it was.

The knife sliced the breast portion, a curl of steam rising gently toward the chandelier. Perfect.

Then Seraphina opened her mouth.

"What is that?" Her long, manicured finger pointed at my masterpiece. Near the neck cavity there was a tiny piece of paper poking out from under the flap of skin. Dad poked it with his fork, then gave it a good pull. A white bag flopped out onto the tablecloth.

Seraphina giggled. "The giblets. You forgot to take them out." She pressed three fingers over her lips and looked at me like I'd made a major faux pas.

Dad joined in the laughter, poking the neck gently with his knife. "Eh, your mom used to do the same thing. Meat will taste fine."

"My apologies, Grateful. This is my fault. I should have insisted I help you in the kitchen," Seraphina said, as if I were twelve and she'd overestimated my abilities.

I decided right then that I hated her. Sorry, Dad. She had to go. I started filling my plate. She passed me her stuffing casserole.

"Allergic," I said, casting aside the dish.

She frowned and locked eyes with me. Game on.

11

CRAZY

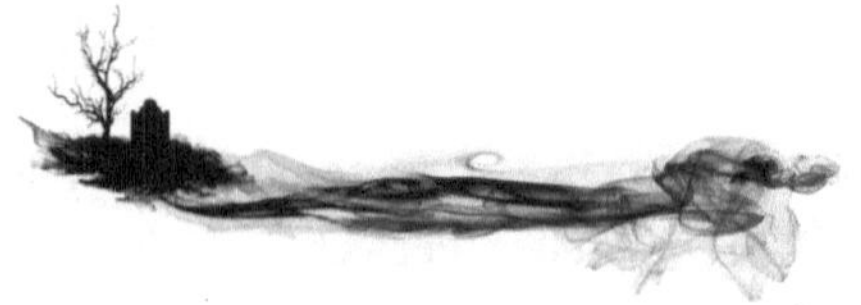

The next morning, the emergency room at St. John's was unusually quiet. Good thing because I was distracted by the horror of my father's new romantic interest. What did she want from him? Money? Probably not. She made her own. Attention? Maybe. I told myself for the fiftieth time that it wouldn't last. I wasn't going to worry about it. She'd realize he was all about his work and leave him the minute the novelty wore off.

Hours ticked by filled with average, run-of-the-mill illnesses and broken bones. I had a patient with appendicitis around ten and otherwise uneventful cases the rest of the day. Around six that night though, an ambulance phoned ahead, something paramedics do for the seriously ill and injured, and I was called in to respond.

"Dr. Anderson needs you in the trauma room, stat!" Julie, my charge nurse, pointed at the trauma room. "I'll take your beds."

My heart started racing from the adrenaline zing that flooded my system. It had been months since I helped in trauma. It wasn't my specialty. With my limited experience, I couldn't have been Julie or Dr. Anderson's first choice, but the day had been so slow she'd sent a few of my fellow nurses home, leaving us short-staffed. To call *me* in, the situation had to be desperate.

I shoved the door open with my shoulder and eyed my friend Jay with a sigh of relief. A certified trauma nurse specialist, nothing shook this guy. I'd seen him reach into a gunshot wound half the size of New Hampshire to clamp down on a nicked artery. Jay was made of fortified steel.

"What's coming?" I asked. "Julie didn't give me any specifics."

He glanced up from his work readying a table of supplies. "Female. Near drowning."

"Drowning?" There wasn't a natural body of water inside Carlton City limits, and the indoor pools were sticklers about safety. A drowning this time of year was highly unusual.

"Red Grove Lake."

"Red Grove Lake. My Red Grove? What the heck is anyone doing out there this time of year?" Aside from being frozen solid, Red Grove Lake was miles behind Rick's place at the heart of Monk's forest. The only access was by foot through unmarked footpaths. *I* wouldn't even know about the lake if not for Rick. He'd taken me back there a few weeks ago to show me where a rare form of holly grew.

"Not sure."

"Well, who found her?"

"Not sure."

"Jay! What do you know about this patient?"

"She was crazy enough to almost drown in a frozen lake in the middle of nowhere on the Friday after Thanksgiving."

The automatic doors flew open and a familiar paramedic rolled a woman in on a stretcher. "Unidentified female, abandoned at a Fuel Up station on the edge of town. Attendant was told by the man who dropped her off she was found crawling out of Red Grove Lake. We tried to get her cooking for you, but she's still below temp and unconscious. Heart's pumping but her breathing is erratic."

I took over her ventilation bag while Jay checked her vitals. Pulse was thready, and she was still cold as ice. She looked to be around forty with wavy brown hair and a round but muscular build that gave her a sturdy appearance. She'd been wrapped in a blanket with heat packs tucked in her armpits and groin.

"Grateful, warmed IV," Dr. Anderson ordered. "Jay, forced air blanket. Hopefully we can get her breathing on her own again." Dr. Anderson took over the bag and began assessing her airway, talking to the patient in an attempt to elicit a response.

I went to work. In a flash, I'd found a suitable vein, high on her shoulder, near her core. I ran the tips of my gloved fingers over the raised blue swell and pierced her skin with a large gauge needle. The warm fluids began to flow.

"Come on," Dr. Anderson said, removing the bag and shaking her shoulder. "Ma'am! Breathe."

The gasp the woman gave relieved us all.

Her lids flipped open, and she fixed me with a blood-tinged stare. "You!" the woman yelled. "Where is it?"

"Welcome back, miss," Dr. Anderson said, patting her shoulder. "You're in the emergency room at St. John's. You've had an accident."

The woman refused to look at him, but her eyes drilled into me, through me. I had an impulse to reach for Night-shade, but of course my blade wasn't on my back.

Overriding my panic impulse, I forced my voice to respond in a gentle, even tone. "Just relax. You're going to be fine." I patted her shoulder.

"Not fine," she rasped. A hand shot out from under the

blanket and grabbed my wrist, pulling me toward her. Before I could register what she was doing, a pillar of water exploded from her mouth, drenching me in icy cold vomit.

I jolted backward, the witchy part of me going all five-alarm tingly. Either this woman was possessed or someone had released a can of bees up my spine. Her voice echoed, a deep baritone hiss, and the smell of wet vermin filled my nostrils.

"You can't hide the book forever. We know you have it."

"What?" I whispered.

Dr. Anderson shot me a beware-the-crazy-patient look and helped me pry her fingers from my arm. "What's your name?" he asked.

The woman laughed, low and cruel. "I have a message for you, Hecate. The book is as good as ours. You can either cooperate or be eliminated."

With a confused glance in my direction, Dr. Anderson piped up. "Your name, ma'am? We need to know who you are. Can we call someone for you?"

She rolled her head on the table, finally training her eyes on the doctor. A wicked cackle turned into a rattling cough. I watched a dark mist escape her lips, waft to the ceiling, and disappear into the nearest vent. *Shit!* Instantly, the woman seized on the table and the steady tone of a flatlined heart monitor filled the room. I started CPR. Jay grabbed the paddles and we defibrillated the woman. But she never regained consciousness.

I didn't have to ask if Jay or Dr. Anderson had seen the mist; they couldn't see the supernatural and that wasn't indigestion oozing out from between her lips. The buzz of my power pressed against my skin. I itched to have Nightshade in my hand.

As soon as the woman's body was processed, I took a moment in the break room and consulted my *The Book of*

Light app. Yep. I'd seen this baddy before in a past life. The vaporous demon was called a Nightmare or Cauchemar. Usually, the black mist was relatively harmless. At night, the demons only became corporeal in the presence of a sleeping human. Named for their habit of weighing down people's chests while they slept, they fed on the resulting fear. As terrorizing as they could be, in their natural form they couldn't actually hurt anyone. The person affected would simply wake up and the nightmare would disappear. Obviously, this one had graduated to more sinister pursuits. Possession was a serious metaphysical felony and something the creature couldn't accomplish on its own. It would take a witch or other magical creature to facilitate the possession. I owed this thing judgment and prison time, along with whatever entity had enabled it. Worse, the grim vapor was asking about the book, which meant it was probably working with Julius and targeting me.

I needed to talk to Rick. As angry and confused as I was about his involvement in Gary's turning, he was the only one who could help me figure out a plan for dealing with this. Why did Julius think I had *The Book of Flesh and Bone?* I had no idea where the book was. But maybe Rick did. I needed answers.

One other question, was the nightmare that had emerged from my patient's body out for good, or could it infect someone else in the hospital? If the answer was in *The Book of Light,* I hadn't made it that far with populating my phone app. Until I knew for sure, I had to be careful to keep my witchy senses tuned in. The nightmare could be anywhere and look like anyone.

I slipped my phone back into my pocket and returned to the nurse's station. The paramedic who had brought the woman in was still hanging around, filling out paperwork at the desk.

I eyed his nametag. "Hey, Eric."

"Hey. Grateful, nice to see you again."

"Just wondering if the attendant at Fuel Up said anything about the guy who'd dropped off that patient? She died. Can't help but wonder why he waited so long to call for help."

He tore the first page off the form he was filling out and slipped it in the appropriate slot on the desk. "Yeah, he was still there when me and my partner arrived, but we must've scared him. He took off when he saw the lights."

"What did he look like?"

"Couldn't say. He was wearing a parka with the hood up."

"And you didn't think that was suspicious?"

"Actually, no. It's fifteen below out there today. Everyone should be wearing a hood."

"Red Grove Lake is in the middle of the woods; he didn't just trip over her in the street. I wonder if he had something to do with it." I narrowed my eyes.

"He told the attendant he went out for a walk and found her on the bank of the lake."

My breath caught in my throat. As far as I knew, there was only one house occupied in the area, only one owner who could have gone for a walk behind it. Rick. He had to be the one who found her. An icy ripple climbed my backbone and made my scalp tingle. He must have sensed the nightmare inside the woman. Rick didn't own a phone. Maybe he used the attendant to call 911 thinking I was her best bet for survival? But if so, why not drive her to the hospital? I didn't usually work trauma. I could have easily missed her.

Then again, maybe I wasn't meant to find her. What if Rick had been the one to drown her? An overzealous battle with the nightmare might have resulted in the woman's fate, and this was the way he covered it up. He'd covered up Gary. It was possible. My head spun with unanswered questions.

Eric said goodbye and headed for the exit to resume his shift. Mine was over. It was time for me to clock out and pay a visit to the caretaker.

* * *

SOME THINGS YOU JUST COME TO TAKE FOR GRANTED: THE SUN rising in the morning, taxes due on April fifteenth, dandelions in the lawn in summer. I had come to expect Rick's door to open for me any time that I should walk up to it, day or night. But tonight I waited in front of his stone cottage, even resorted to knocking on the door, to no avail. Furthermore, our connection had gone dead. Either he was far away, or he was blocking me.

"Why don't you try the door?" Poe said, landing with an inordinate amount of flapping above me. The cross beams of the porch roof housed dozens of wind chimes, and the disruption of the air by his large black wings sent the closest ones into a fit of musical clinking.

"How did you get out?" I asked. Christ, I was moody, but the strange woman's death weighed heavily on my mind.

"Attic window. I performed the most fabulous rendition of Bruce Willis in *Die Hard*. Even rolled through the air as the glass shattered around me." With a snap of his hooked beak, he slurped a wolf spider from the side of the house.

"You broke my window?" I fisted my hands on my hips and peered at him through narrowed eyes. "I just got that window fixed like a month ago!"

"You left a predatory bird in the attic for fourteen hours?" he singsonged back at me in a mimicked version of my voice. "Relax. I only broke one small pane. You can seal it with magic tonight and fix it tomorrow."

"Yeah, right. With all my advanced window-fixing skills! Damn it, Poe. I really didn't need this tonight."

He cawed in my face. "Really? Well, you know what I need? To eat every four to six hours. You'd know that if you'd taken the time to learn anything about ravens. And it's not like you left me a lot of options. Your pantry is a joke."

I huffed, feeling like my head might explode. When it was clear Poe didn't feel the slightest bit of remorse for his crime against my house, I rolled my eyes and reached for the doorknob. Not surprisingly, it swung open. Rick never locked his door; he didn't need to. I strode into the sparsely decorated living room. "Rick?" I called, but there was no way he was home. If he had been, I'd be naked and draped over the couch by now. I was at a loss.

Poe circled the small living room, then disappeared through the bedroom door, returning almost immediately. "He's not here."

"I'd surmised that much. Did you see anything strange tonight, Poe?"

"Strange how? One of the field mice I ate gave me heartburn but otherwise, no."

I gave him a quick rundown of what happened in the ER. He raised the muscle over his left eye that might count as an eyebrow. "You know, it had to be Rick. Who else would find her out here? Plus, there's this." He pointed his beak toward the linoleum kitchen floor.

A few steps closer and I could clearly make out a puddle. The door to the garage was slightly ajar. With two fingers, I nudged it the rest of the way open. Rick's car, a Tesla Roadster I quite admired, was missing. Wet floor, near drowning victim in Red Grove Lake, missing Rick. Hmm. How was he involved? Where had he gone? Why hadn't he contacted me for backup? I didn't like this. Not at all.

"You can't possibly blame him. After you went all craycray about the Gary incident, it's no wonder he wanted to give you some space."

Blink. Blink. "Cray-Cray?" I wiped a hand over my face to try to calm my burgeoning temper. "Rick knew I was in love with Gary and watched his heart stop beating under the fangs of Anna the Vampire."

"Anna the Vampire." Poe ruffled his feathers. "You wouldn't be talking about Anna Bathory, would you?"

"Yeah. I guess she owns the Mill Wheel. According to Gary, she runs a tight ship."

Poe bobbed his head. "Anna Bathory was daughter to Erzsébet Báthory, countess of Hungary in the late 1500s, also called the Blood Countess."

I knew I'd heard that name before! "That's right, Erzsébet killed hundreds of young girls before she was put to death. She was the most notable female serial killer in history." I'd seen her story on the History Channel as a possible origination of vampire lore, along with Vlad the Impaler.

"Anna was her daughter. Interesting thing about Anna, no one is sure when she was turned, or by whom, but many believed her mother was feeding her early appetite."

I hugged my stomach, suddenly feeling cold even though Rick's house was a comfortable temperature. "So, you are telling me that a five hundred-year-old vamp is running a bar in Carlton City and is responsible for turning my ex-boyfriend."

Poe bobbed his head again.

"Look, I get what you're saying. Anna is like this ancient, uber-evil vamp and Rick was at his weakest. Even if I could understand why Rick wouldn't be in a position to confront *her* at that point, that doesn't explain why he didn't do more to help *me*. Why not find a way to tell me? I was in *misery*, Poe. I cried for days. I lost my apartment." Tears formed in my eyes just thinking about that time in my life. "I couldn't even get out of bed. I felt abandoned, worthless. Those first weeks after I realized he wasn't coming back and the money was gone was the only time in my entire life I considered suicide. Rick may not have caused that low, but he allowed it to fester by not revealing himself to me sooner."

"Some things have to happen in their own time," Poe said softly, sounding eerily human…until he rotated his neck and started preening his feathers.

I searched the counter for a pad of paper, finding a promotional stack of sticky notes from Winshire Bank and Loan next to the fridge. Finding a pen next to it, I scratched Rick a note that I needed to talk to him pronto. Then, on a whim, I tore off a blank sheet from the bottom.

"What do you need that for?" Poe asked, hopping to my shoulder.

"Hey, watch the talons. New scrubs," I said. He loosened his grip. "As it so happens, I have some banking needs, like, for instance, a big leather satchel full of money, and if Rick uses Winshire, then I feel very safe placing my wad into their hands."

"Ah. Can we go home now?" he asked.

"Sure. We have a window to fix. And I haven't had dinner yet. Of course, depending on the mess you left, maybe I'll be having raven."

I was joking, of course, but when I opened the door, Poe disappeared into the night.

12

SOLD

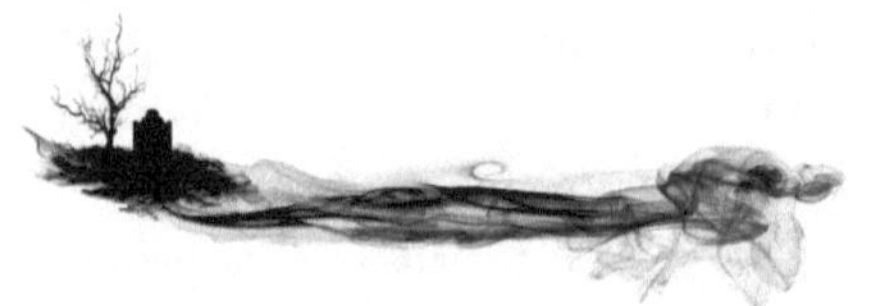

Clearly, bank teller Maggie thought I was either a drug dealer or a prostitute. She glared at me out of the corner of her eye as she counted and recounted the money from Gary's leather bag. While I'd hoped to get this out of the way earlier, it had taken me an entire week of working at the hospital during the day and taking up the slack for missing-in-action Rick at night to make it to Winshire Bank and Loan. I just hoped the process would be fast and easy. I hadn't heard from my father since Thanksgiving, but I didn't think he'd wait forever.

"Not many people come in here with this much cash," she said with an upswing in her tone that clearly indicated her desire for me to explain my situation.

I didn't. It was none of her blue eyeshadow-wearing, curly-headed business. Lips pressed together, I stared at her impatiently.

"And you would like to deposit the entire sixty thousand into your savings account?"

"Yes. And I need to talk to one of your loan officers about a possible mortgage loan."

"Oh, I see." A supervisor removed my bag of money, and Maggie handed me a receipt with my new savings account balance of $60,800. The extra eight hundred was the result of the closing transfer from my previous savings account, everything I had in the world. "Wait here and I'll see if a representative is available."

I nodded. Soon, a balding man in a tan oxford and striped brown tie was shaking my hand vigorously. His too-long mustache tickled the lip over his crooked teeth.

"Maggie says you'd like to talk about a loan. I'm Chuck. I can help you with that," he said excitedly. He released my hand and adjusted his square-framed glasses on his nose. The lenses were dirty. I had the strangest urge to remove them from his face and chamois the glass.

"Yes. I'm interested in buying the house I'm currently living in."

"Excellent. Step on down to my office, and let's get some info."

I followed him to the cubicle he called his "office" and took a seat in a springy chair across from his desk. For the next thirty minutes he grilled me about my income, expenses, debts, and the estimated value of my property. Thanks to my dad letting me stay in the house rent-free, my debt-to-income ratio was above average, and I'd kept up on my credit card payments, so my credit score was decent as well. The money was as good as mine; I could feel it.

"There's just one tiny fly in the honey," Chuck said, rubbing a knuckle across the tip of his nose. "Our bank requires twenty percent down. I see you have that in your account, but it was made with a large deposit of cash. We're going to need documentation on the source of that cash."

My jaw dropped. "Why do you need that?"

He fake laughed a low hardee-har-har. "Can't have any illegal funding going on. You're not a drug dealer, are you?"

I smiled. "Nope."

"Well then, we just need some documentation to prove you didn't come by the funds illegally. See, the twenty percent has to be from legitimate income sources. You couldn't, say, take out a loan against your credit card for the cash or even borrow the cash from a relative. Both of those activities would add debt to your portfolio." He pointed a finger gun in my general direction.

I nodded slowly, letting my eyes drift to the cubicle wall behind him.

"So…ah… Where did you get the sixty thousand dollars?" He leaned forward, giving me the sense that his question had as much to do with his curiosity as the loan requirements.

"I'd loaned it to a boyfriend and he just paid me back."

"Hmm. That could be a pickle. What we're going to need is some documented proof that you earned the money, gave it to him, and then he returned it to you. Account statements and the like. Will he vouch for you?"

I worked my jaw, my mind searching for a story that wouldn't come back to haunt me later. I could probably come up with documentation on the forty thousand, but part of those funds had been a cash advance against my credit card and the additional twenty thousand was a gift from Julius. Not to mention that the person who was supposed to "vouch" for me was technically dead and legally missing. "I'll have to get back to you on that," I said.

"Okey-dokey, artichokey." He grabbed an empty folder from his credenza and placed all of my paperwork inside. "Come back and see us when you figure it out." He stood, handing me the folder with his left hand while simultaneously offering his right. I recognized the move as the diploma handshake, meant to be quick and to give you a psychological nudge to move along and not hold up the line. Was there some form of training loan officers went through for this? Obviously, the practiced body language was meant to usher me out of the office as quickly as possible.

Like a good little customer, I left his cubicle and headed for the revolving door. Halfway around, I saw Chuck leaning up against Maggie's counter. *Drug dealer,* he mouthed. I knit my brow. Cell phone in hand, I scrolled through my database of spells. Who knew getting a loan would be this difficult, or that an itching pox was soon to befall the staff of Winshire Bank and Loan?

* * *

AS I APPROACHED RED GROVE, MY MOOD WAS ABOUT AS DARK as it had ever been. No loan. What were the chances my father would give me another extension? He couldn't put Mr. Nekomata off forever. Under better circumstances, I could ask Rick for the money. He'd mentioned he was loaded; he'd made some good investments in the 1940s, and it wasn't like he had many expenses.

The problem with that plan? I wasn't sure where Rick was. I hadn't heard from him since our fight. I was still angry and wasn't exactly counting the moments until our reunion, but I was beginning to get concerned. For one, I still didn't know what had happened with the drowned woman in the ER. Plus, it wasn't like Rick to go this long without a feeding. If we didn't get it on soon, he'd start to weaken, which wasn't a good idea for either of us with Julius turning up the steam on his search efforts.

Where was *The Book of Flesh and Bone,* anyway? And why did the baddies think *I* had it? My head pounded with questions. Crap, I needed a nap.

I pulled into my driveway, stabbing the button for my garage door on autopilot, then slammed on my brakes when a brightly colored poster in my front yard caught my eye. My father's smiling face stared back at me from one of his real estate signs, wire legs piercing the snow. That was new. Under his cat-who-ate-the-canary grin was a sliding panel. What I saw there made my blood run cold and my breath catch. This had to be a mistake.

With one shaking hand, I retrieved my phone from the cupholder and used my thumb to hit my dad's number. My foot wandered, and the Jeep lurched forward. I slammed on the brakes. Holding the ringing phone to my ear, I eased into the garage and parked. My dad and I were European mutts with heritage so blended we simply called ourselves American, but at that moment I was feeling full-on Soprano Italian. I needed both hands for this conversation.

"Robert Knight," my father's voice trickled out to me, brimming with real estate sunshine, even on this cold December day.

"You sold my house." The words were venomous. Quiet in a deadly way.

There was a pause, my father undoubtedly registering who I was. "Grateful, Mr. Nekomata offered me twice the market price. I don't know why he wants the place so bad, but that was an offer I couldn't refuse."

"You don't know what you've done." My voice cracked. I was trembling so hard I could barely grip the phone.

"Oh, Grateful, I know you liked the place but honestly, it's for the best. I'll help you buy a condo downtown with the proceeds. We'll be closer, and you won't have such a long commute to work. Seraphina always says how important it is to keep family close, and I think she's right. It will be good for us to see more of each other."

"Seraphina? Seraphina doesn't know jack, Dad. You promised me you'd give me time to buy this place."

"It's sold, Grateful. Get over it. If you don't want to move closer to us, fine, but you don't have to attack Seraphina for problems you brought upon yourself."

"Us? Is she living with you now?"

The exasperated sigh he let out gave him away. "I was going to tell you in person the next time I saw you."

Head spinning, I stared out the windshield, the engine still rumbling in the garage. Words tumbled out of my mouth faster than I could censor them. "I don't know if I can forgive you for selling my house."

Silence. Part of me wanted to take it back, but I was too devastated. I couldn't. Not yet.

"Grateful." One word, loaded with hurt and disappointment.

I poked the *end call* button. Never had I disrespected my father like this. He was my only family. But as I lowered my forehead to the steering wheel, and fat tears began to flow down my cheeks, the wrong I inflicted on him seemed justified by the terror that flooded me.

Somehow, I had to stop this sale or I'd be forced to move my seat of magic. Was that even possible? How could I manage the graveyard if I wasn't here? What about the portal in my attic? Would lost souls like Logan's know where to find me? I couldn't even begin to think about Rick and me; I had too many questions about our relationship already. At this point, every option seemed insurmountable, and I could almost feel my skin splitting from the weight piled on my shoulders.

I pulled the key from the ignition, threw open the door, and stomped into the snow-covered yard to rip the sign, wire frame and all, from its place. Once my dad's smiling face was safely beneath the Rubbermaid lid of my garbage can, I tried to comfort myself by saying things couldn't get any worse.

But they could.

Way worse.

13

ANCIENT HISTORY

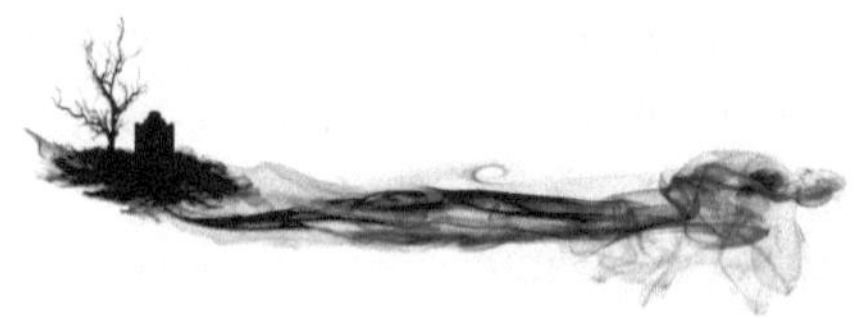

"What are we going to do?" I sat cross-legged in the middle of my attic floor, head in my hands, bundled against the daytime cold that coursed through the plastic wrap covering my broken window.

Poe's beady black eyes lacked their usual sharp luster. "I'm not sure." The flat words didn't hold the sarcasm or wit I'd come to expect from the raven, which meant my situation was all the more serious.

"What good are you?" I snapped. "The woman in my hallucination said you were exactly what I needed. Help me, now!"

The bird bowed his head. "You don't need to be hurtful. I'm sure we'll find a way. I have feathers in the game after all."

"Feathers in the game? You don't want to be associated with a washed-up witch?"

He jumped down to my level and looked me in the eye. "I have served you in various forms during your many lifetimes, Grateful, and by many different names. I die when you die."

"Oh."

"Here's what I know for sure: if you lose this attic, you can establish a new one—"

"I can?"

"—but it will leave you vulnerable. You'll need Rick."

"In case you hadn't noticed, Rick's not here," I snapped. "He's been gone for more than a week. I have no idea where he is or what he's doing. I'm not even sure I can trust him! This is the worst possible time for this to be happening. Who is this asshole anyway? Who buys an ancient house in rural Red Grove in the middle of winter?"

Poe's eye's widened and a shiver traveled the length of his feathers. "Oh, dear. What if it's not a coincidence?"

"Huh?"

With a flurry of flapping, he hopped up to the desk with the book. "Ask *The Book of Light* to tell you who Nekomata is."

My feet obeyed my command to stand, although ungracefully, and I approached Poe and the book. "Show me Nekomata," I said loud and clear toward my grimoire.

The pages flipped so fast a breeze caused my hair to blow off my shoulders. The book settled open on a page near the back. I leaned over, noting the sketch of a ferocious-looking cat-creature with a forked tail in the corner of the page.

"The nekomata is an ancient supernatural being first encountered in China in the year 589 A.D. Nekomata is a shapeshifter that can take any form, including human, but prefers to spend time in a natural state resembling a large cat with a forked tail. The nekomata tends toward allegiance with the Dark One as it is a necromancer, gaining power by using the dead. As such, it is extremely dangerous to Hecate as it preys on the gravesites that are conducive to her power." I slapped my hands over my face. "Oh shit, Poe.

"Looks like Nekomata knows exactly why this house is worth twice the market price."

I brushed back my bangs and ran my palms over my hair. "Wait, wait. Let's not get ahead of ourselves. Maybe the name is a coincidence. I've got a spell on this place. Nothing supernatural gets in without an invitation. Even Rick had to ask my permission."

Poe clacked his beak together. "Your father invited him in. He is the rightful owner of the property and is of your blood. Depending on how the spell was cast, that would be enough."

I moaned. "Wouldn't I know to restrict it to my own invitation?"

"If you had, Prudence wouldn't have been able to invite Rick in if she needed him. You were thinking ahead."

"Fuck. Fuck. Double fuck!" I stomped in a circle. "I'm such an imbecile. He even used his real name."

"Cocky SOB."

"What are we going to do?"

"Mmm, High Priestess of the Grave, I think I should point out that the timing seems noteworthy. *The Book of Flesh and Bone* is in such high demand that trolls and finfolk are dying for it, a possessed human says she thinks you have it, and a nekomata shows up to buy your house. If I was a betting bird, I'd say someone knows something about you that you don't."

"Like what?"

"Like maybe the book is hidden in this house."

I stared at him dumbly. "If it was, wouldn't you know? You said you've been with me in my past lives."

"Not all and not always. Plus, dear witch, there were things so important you kept them from me."

"Then how do I find out? I don't remember and there's no one left alive to ask."

Poe tipped his head to the side. "Why not ask yourself? The book holds your memories, remember?" He chuckled.

And that's when it dawned on me, I'd been so worried about learning what was written on the pages, I'd forgotten the magic of the book itself. *The Book of Light* held my memories. All I had to do was ask it to show them to me. I'd conveniently forgotten to use this particular ability because the last time I had, I relived my own tragic death, pain and all. In fact, it was the death that kicked me out of the memory. I wasn't entirely sure how to control how much I experienced of my former life. The idea of being a prisoner of my past frightened me, and I wasn't just speaking metaphorically.

"I don't want to do this."

"Your only other option is to ask Rick."

"I have no idea where he is."

"Then put on your big witch panties and get in there."

"You wouldn't possibly know how to put the brakes on a memory, would you?"

He shook his head. "I only know that the past can't hurt you. Not really."

"The past can totally hurt you. That's why people say 'don't live in the past.' People who suffer from PTSD are injured by their pasts on a regular basis."

Poe cleared his throat. "You won't physically die."

I rolled my eyes and gave him a sarcastic thumbs up. "Thanks for the pep talk."

"Just trying to help." He sighed.

I turned back to the book, resting my hands on either side of the crease. In a loud and clear voice, I said, "Show me what happened to *The Book of Flesh and Bone*."

Light poured out of the pages, filling the attic, blinding me. When I could see again, I was in another world.

* * *

THE SMELL OF DRIED HERBS AND SMOKE FILLED MY NOSTRILS. I was nestled in a wooden chair, watching the fire crackle under a cooking caldron. As before, I was living my memory from the inside out, along for the ride as my former self took the wheel and drove me through the events of her past. I was in a cozy cottage. Daylight shone through a small window near the door, and my stomach growled for the lunch warming in the pot.

There was a knock on the door. I made sure my lengthy black hair was braided and coiled neatly behind my head. With a surprisingly dark, russet-colored hand, I smoothed the fabric of my floor-length black skirt as I moved to answer it. I was covered in yards and yards of black material only broken by a wide lace collar.

Rick was on the other side of the door. Not the Rick I knew, but a softer, more innocent version. Human. He was dressed in the Puritan fashion—black suit, white collar. His dark hair fell in long waves to his shoulders.

"Good day, Enrique."

He smiled and a blush colored his cheeks. Breath caught in his throat, his eyes flicked away bashfully. "Miss Lockhart, you must excuse me, as I find your beauty arresting and forget myself even as I try to speak."

"If thy speaketh truth, then come partake of it, as you have before." I gave him a sultry smile, leading him inside by the hand and closing the door behind him.

Rick's voice broke when he answered me. "I pray a day will come when I can openly do so as your husband. But not today. I've come to warn you. Monk is convinced of your guilt and will not be undone. He comes now to take you to the stake."

I snickered. "Monk will not take me. The impertinent windbag hath not the strength."

"Please. I beg of you. Run. You must flee." Rick took my

hands in his, tears flowing openly down his face. "You cannot ask me to watch you burn. Though the flames not touch my flesh, the fire would consume me, eternally."

"Do not worry thyself, Enrique. I shall plead my case, and Monk's wrath shall pass over me." All I had to do was look Monk squarely in the eye and I could bend his thoughts to my will.

"Pass over you? When you have stew in your pot and still the hint of meat on your bones."

"I've kept stew in many pots." I lowered my voice to a whisper. "But even I have limits."

A gaunt cheek pressed against mine, and I could feel his bones under the thin blanket of his skin. He was starving. All of them were starving. And I had a pot of stew. "Would you share my lunch with me?"

"No, no, listen to me. It is different this time, my love. The entire town, aside from me, is *chanting* for your blood. Please take my words into your bosom and flee. There is a place in the woods to the north. If you leave now, you can make it before dark. The whole town is coming."

"Chanting? The town is chanting?"

"Monk has a book. They are chanting a prayer to weaken you because they say you are a witch."

Pulling back, I peered at him shrewdly. "You're sure?"

He nodded, his eyes pleading with me. "Listen. You can hear them coming."

He spoke the truth. The sounds of a crowd in the distance were already audible and the first pangs of fear rocked through me. "Enrique, we are betrothed, yes?"

"Yes."

"And you intend to give yourself to me, body and soul?"

"Of course."

"Will you pledge your life to me now? Bind your soul to me, whate'er may come, we will be together into eternity?"

With both hands, he cradled my face. "Yes. I love you, Isabella. For eternity."

Locked deep within his gaze, I reached into my pocket. I'd made the ointment for an emergency such as this. Still, I hesitated. I cared for Enrique, and if the spell came to pass, he'd be cursed by my hand. But desperate times called for desperate measures.

Between us, I opened the tiny jar. Under the lid was a razor sharp barb. I captured one of his hands from my cheek, and positioned it palm up, then jabbed the barb into his finger.

He gasped. "What are you doing?"

"Binding us for eternity."

He did not argue, just searched my face with the trust of a child.

I watched his ruby red gift drip into the balm, then plucked my own skin. My darker, older blood oozed over his. Mixing the concoction with my finger, I commanded him. "Unbutton your shirt."

"Isabella, there is no time."

On my tiptoes, I planted a brazen kiss on his lips, snaking my tongue into his mouth, all passion and wet heat. Rick responded with the inexperienced lips of a virgin and another shiver of guilt passed through me.

He unbuttoned his shirt.

I found the place over his heart, yet unscarred, and drew a scythe with the gooey paste. In the old language, I spoke the spell.

"In the name of my mother
Goddess of night
I bind thee, my vessel,
Caretaker of light
Willingly given

Sacrifice thine
Human no longer
Caretaker mine."

The chanting had grown louder, and I could sense the crowd outside the door. Suddenly my skin felt too tight. *Damnation! Where had Monk found that spell?*

The door was kicked in and clawing hands swept me from my home. In a sea of black wool and white collars, I lost sight of Enrique. My body, weakened by their chant, was pinched, yanked, and torn until I was brought to a stake near the church. Once they bound me to it, Monk arrived.

The man of little stature approached with a great book engulfed in his arms. I recognized the tome right away, *The Book of Flesh and Bone.* A sister from Salem had told me about it, but I never thought it would make it this far. The pages were made of flayed human skin, the cover layered with the same. The ink contained human blood, and the inlaid design on the spine was not pearl but human teeth. Legend said it was written by the devil. I wasn't sure I believed in a devil, per se, but if there *was* a source of all evil and darkness, certainly he was the author of this tome.

"Finally, justice."

"Justice? You call this justice? Burning an innocent woman without so much as a trial?"

"Innocent? The fire will prove your innocence."

"If I burn, I'm innocent, and if I don't, I'm a witch? That is my trial?"

Monk turned away, and one of the men approached, torch in hand. My heart pounded. My breath came in pants. Enrique had tried to warn me, but how was I to know Monk had the book?

As the flames caught, and licked up my body, I separated

myself from the excruciating pain, pulling back from the memory, and becoming an observer of my own death.

Isabella's left hand, charred and blackened, rose to waist level, light shooting from her fingers as her final words bubbled from her dying lips. *"Caretaker of the light, always."* Enrique's body seized as the light plowed into him, flopping on the ground and contorting in pain. The crowd turned to watch him fall, but I knew their own fate was moments away. The book would demand its price.

Darkness swallowed the memory, my soul slipping from my charred remains. And that's when *The Book of Light* spit me out into the attic.

14

REVERIE

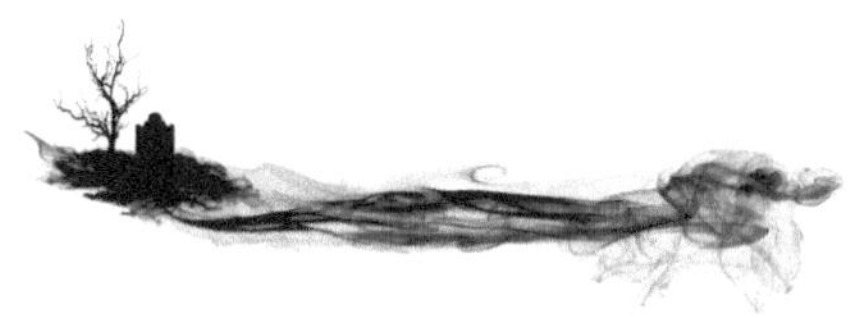

Caw.
    Snap. Snap.
Flap, flap, flap.

I opened my eyes to find Poe dancing on my chest.

"Are you dead?" he asked.

"Do I look dead?"

"Actually, yes. Although more animated than five minutes ago."

Sweeping Poe from my chest, I sat up and straightened my shirt. "How long have I been out?"

"About an hour. I was beginning to worry."

"I saw my own death again. Honestly, I'm not sure how useful the memory was. I barely got a glimpse of *The Book of Flesh and Bone*. Most of the memory was about Rick."

"Maybe that was as close as she could get you. Maybe the book is trying to say that Rick was the last person to see it. If that was your first and last memory, Rick may be the key."

"Fantastic." Sarcasm oozed from the word. "So we are back at square one."

115

"You sound less than enthused about the prospect."

"Poe, I'm not sure I can even trust Rick. After what happened with Gary, how can I know he's being honest with me? And there's something else. Something I never realized before *The Book of Light* showed me."

"What?"

"Isabella, the first…me, she lured Rick into being the caretaker. You should have seen how smitten he was for her. But he never understood who she really was. He gave himself to her without truly knowing the price."

"He must have loved her greatly."

"And resent her presently."

Poe lowered his head. "What are you saying?"

"I'm not sure." I shook my head. "I just feel heavy in the center of my chest, like I've wronged him. Part of me wonders if he's wronged me in return."

The raven flapped to the window where the last light of day was fading quickly behind the glass. "Maybe you should get over it and make up. He's your only hope of finding the book before Julius does."

"Maybe you should mind your own business, Poe," I snapped. I didn't need his commentary. But as I dragged my magic-drained sack of bones from the attic floor and pulled back the plastic flap so that Poe could go hunting in the cold winter's night, for the first time I saw Rick in a new light. Not as a predator trying to capture and dominate me, but as my prey, a prisoner of my past, of my heart. The thought saddened and sobered me.

That night, I flopped on my bed, fully clothed and on top of my covers. Without Rick's blood and sex, my body felt weaker, a racecar running on empty. My mind was filled with sharp thoughts that tumbled painfully. I wondered again where he was and if our last fight was our last encounter. Maybe he'd abandoned me too.

No, I'd pushed him away, and rightly so. Or not. I needed him. Thoughts of my house, the book, my life, flitted through my mind as I drifted, but it was Rick who came back again and again to me, young, innocent, unscarred, and human.

*　*　*

THE BANQUET LAID OUT BEFORE ME WAS SOMETHING OUT OF A dream, all manner of fruit and chocolate surrounding silver candelabras that cast the bounty in a golden glow. Next to the table, spread on a chaise lounge, Rick lay staring out an open window. A warm night breeze ruffled his white shirt, spread open and exposing the scythe-shaped scar I'd given him. In his fingers, he handled a large bunch of red grapes, popping one and then another into his mouth.

On soft silver slippers, I padded toward him but stopped just inside the room. This *was* a dream. The long white night-gown I wore wasn't mine.

"Come to me, *mi cielo*," he said, turning clear gray eyes in my direction. His voice flowed over me like featherlight silk, the flicker of the candles against his smooth golden skin doing the same for me visually. My mouth went dry. My nipples perked to attention under my thin white gown. Step by step, I was pulled forward, the heat in my blood driving me toward the fruit in his hand. One taste would quench this thirst.

When I reached him, I fell to my knees, parting my lips to ask for the sweet, red fruit. No words came out. I tried again. Nothing but a raspy breath of air. I was completely mute.

"Don't speak," he said. "You are weak, *mi cielo*. I will feed you. Close your eyes."

I complied.

Cool flesh brushed my bottom lip and the sweet smell of grape filled my nostrils. I opened my mouth like a bird. The orb traveled the "O" of my lips then landed on my tongue. I bit down. Ambrosia. The fruit tasted of Rick's blood, heady and sweet. It coursed down my throat, flooding my body with a decadent current of energy.

Another grape pressed against my lips. I opened, wrapping my mouth around his fingers and sucking the fruit deep into my throat before sliding my lips and tongue back to extract it. He groaned. When I opened my mouth again, his lips brushed mine, his hands grazing my jaw before digging into my loose waves. Gently, he kissed me. Teasing. Nibbling my bottom lip.

I tried to reach up, to pull him to me, but my hands were dead weights at my side.

His tongue parted my lips, stroking slowly inside my mouth, the taste of his blood filling every corner before he pulled back.

I opened my eyes.

His hands flowed down my neck from my face, sweeping my nightgown off my shoulders. The soft white cotton slipped lower, until it hung precariously from the tips of my breasts. His fingers caressed my collarbones, then drifted lower, teasing the rosy peaks beneath the fabric.

I was still on my knees in front of him, which gave me an unencumbered view of his length, hard and straining against the thin fabric of his linen pants. I wanted desperately to free him from the constraint, but my dream would not comply. So I burned passively, as his fingers massaged my ribs, caressed over my hips, and clutched under my ass.

He lifted me, wrapping my legs around his hips, and pushing my nightgown up to my waist. In this position, his full length rubbed against my core and I tossed my head back from the surge of pleasure the contact elicited. But I couldn't even manage a moan.

"Trust me," he said again into my mouth. "Everything I do, I do for you."

His fingers traced the waist of my panties, then burrowed under the lace. He teased me before dipping one finger inside. Thankfully, my dream paralysis didn't extend to my legs. I rose and fell above him. He plunged a second finger, finding the spot deep inside that he knew lit my fuse and cupping me with his palm. With his opposite hand, he freed my breast, cradling and flicking his thumb over the sensitive tip. The night air caressed me, cold from the sheen of sweat on my skin. I felt a great pressure building and I worked my hips into his hand, frantically searching for release. But he withdrew.

I begged for more with my eyes.

Rolling the side of my panties in his hand, he ripped them off with one swift tug. Then he worked open his fly and lifted me to slide his pants down to where he could kick them off with his feet. He positioned himself. I lowered. Even though I was slick with desire, my body protested at the stretch from his considerable girth. I gasped.

"Trust me," he said again.

As if those words were some kind of medicine, my body finally responded to my commands, my once useless arms wrapping around his neck, my fingers digging into his hair. I worked him deeper inside me. Wildly, I claimed his mouth, my tongue stroking his. I picked up the pace, rising and dropping over his lap. In response, he met me thrust for thrust, the quick drive of his hips causing sharp pants of pleasure to burst from me.

In this position, my nipples brushed his chest with each rise and fall. I arched my back to increase the contact. His hand pressed into my lower back for support, and he bent his neck to take one pert nipple into his mouth. He sucked hard. The tight pinch washed me over the edge. I came apart, my sex gripping him, milking his orgasm as he followed my example. Minutes passed, my core clenching again and again, my breath caught in my throat.

And then his teeth plunged into my carotid. It didn't hurt. I'd heal quickly. But the act was more erotic than what we'd just done. Rick housed a piece of my very soul and our blood connection was an intimacy to rival any.

I returned the favor, clamping down on the web of flesh between his neck and collarbone. Decadent blood flowed over my tongue, and I drank my fill. When I pulled back, Rick's eyes were black disks. The darkness came closer and closer, widening its circumference until it swallowed me.

Trust me was the last thing I heard before my eyes popped open to the sound of Poe thrashing against my bedroom window. The sun was up. I was alone under the covers. As I tossed back my quilt and pushed myself up off my mattress to let my familiar inside, I licked my lips.

I could have sworn I tasted Rick's blood.

15

VALENTINE'S

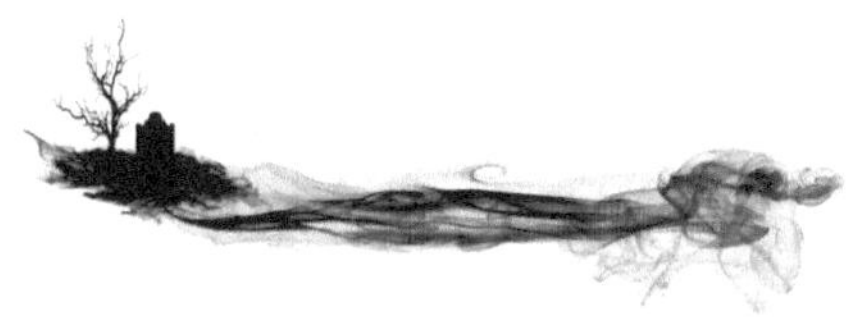

I'd slept until noon but didn't feel rested. All my worries about the increase in supernatural activity in the area, losing my house, trying to find *The Book of Flesh and Bone*, and my dream of Rick drained me to the point of exhaustion. After a quick shower, I pulled on my most comfortable jeans and a warm fleece my dad had brought me from a visit to Canada. I jogged down to Rick's cottage with wild hair and not a stitch of makeup on my face.

Knocking twice, I let myself in again. The Tesla was still gone, my note still on the counter. Where was he?

My phone rang and I pulled it from my pocket. "Rick?"

"Rick? You told me he doesn't even have a phone."

"Michelle! Hi. No, he doesn't have a phone, just wishful thinking."

"Then why did you think he was calling?"

"Rick's been on my mind. We had a fight and then he disappeared. I haven't seen him in more than a week."

"What?"

I exhaled. "I'm sure he'll be back soon. Where could he have gone?" I laughed nervously.

"How bad of a fight did you have?"

"I said I wished I'd never met him."

"Jesus, Grateful, what brought that on?"

"Nothing I feel comfortable telling you over the phone."

"Well, that's okay because you can tell me tonight at Logan's party."

That's right. Tonight was Logan's welcome back party at Valentine's. I'd practically insisted Michelle go, and I'd promised Logan I'd be there. Logan. Fuck. This was going to be our last hoorah. After tonight, I wouldn't see him regularly anymore, now that he was out of my attic for good and done with physical therapy. He'd want to know for sure what we meant to each other, and deep inside I knew he wasn't hoping for "just friends." But I'd committed to Rick, and that was all I had to offer.

"What are you wearing?" I asked.

"Why, are you a creeper?"

"No! Tonight. What are you wearing tonight?"

"Strappy black dress and strappier heels, baby."

I pictured my voluptuous friend in that getup and smiled. She'd be lucky if her husband, Manny, let her out of the house.

"I think I'll wear my green sweater dress."

"The turtleneck?" The scowl was evident in her voice.

"It's classy."

"If you're seventy."

"You just want me to dress sexy for your entertainment."

"Why else would I be going? Gotta live vicariously through my single girlfriend."

Only I wasn't single, *was I?* I left Rick's empty house and started the short walk home. A snowflake landed on my eyelash and was followed by a crowd of fluffy white friends that circled me as I crossed the bridge. "I'll meet you there at seven."

"Are you really wearing the sweater dress?"

"Yes. Non-negotiable."

She sighed. "All right. See you at seven."

* * *

MY PHONE RANG FOR THE TWENTY-FOURTH TIME THAT DAY, and for the twenty-fourth time, I did not answer it. My father's picture displayed on the screen. I wasn't ready to talk to him. I had, however, taken the time to Photoshop a mustache, beard, and horns onto his photo icon. So, for the twenty-fourth time that day, I chuckled at my sophomoric behavior. Hey, whatever worked.

"You look like you're going to a funeral," Poe said from the top of my dresser.

"Actually, I wore this to my great aunt's funeral." The hunter green dress had long sleeves and a turtleneck with buttons that ran from the top of my neck on a diagonal to my armpit. The material was cable-knit wool and the length stretched to my knees.

"What a sensible choice. I'm sure you will be…warm."

I pulled my straightened hair back with both hands, working it into a ponytail, then wrapping the end into a bun. "I don't want to lead anyone on."

"Ohhh," Poe said. "You're afraid if your skirt is short your willpower will be too."

No denying it. I nodded.

"I thought you and Logan were just friends."

"We are."

"Then why the modern chastity belt?"

"It's hard to explain."

"Hmm."

I smoothed the last strands of my hair back and turned toward my familiar. "Can you do me a big favor tonight?"

"That depends. Does it involve watching you awkwardly avoid your 'friend' for fear even the funeral dress won't ward off the hormones?"

I flipped him the finger. "No. I need you to look for Rick while you're out hunting."

"Look where? We've already looked everywhere. We've been looking all week!" Poe protested.

"Come on, Poe! You've got a freakin' bird's-eye view. Look around and try to find him. He's been gone too long. I'm worried. I'm even having dreams about him."

Poe stopped. "What kind of dreams?"

"None of your business."

"Your connection runs deep. Maybe he was sending you a message."

I spread my hands. "He said to trust him."

"Well, there you go."

"You're not getting out of this, Poe. I need to know he's okay."

"All right, all right. I'll search for him."

"Thank you."

I retrieved my black leather bag from beside the dresser and patted the top of my shoulder. "I'll give you a ride to the door." He jumped up to perch over the buttons of my dress.

"Are you sure you want to go to this party?" Poe asked.

"Of course. Why?"

"You only have mascara on one eye."

* * *

THIRTY MINUTES LATER, FULLY MASCARAED YET SUFFICIENTLY frumpy, I arrived at Valentine's. A large sign on the door said the restaurant was closed to the public to accommodate a private party, and judging by the packed parking lot and the thumping bass spilling out into the night, one hell of a party it was. I entered and fought the crowd to the bar. I recognized some of the faces from the hospital and yelled a curt "hello" over the music to be polite. Michelle was right where she said she'd be, getting up close and personal with an appletini.

"Thanks for coming. You look great!" I said, giving her a quick hug.

She returned my embrace. "You're late. You missed the speech by the staff welcoming Logan back. And OMG, you actually wore that dress. You look like a librarian." A slight slur in the middle of "librarian" told me the appletini wasn't Michelle's first drink.

"Thanks."

"Never mind. Pull up a seat and tell me all your troubles. The last time I talked to you, you sounded like hell."

The barstools on either side of her were taken, but that didn't stop Michelle. She jostled the arm of a vertically challenged redhead on her left who was quietly staring into his beer. He seemed shy and somewhat nerdy in green pants and a gold vest.

"Hey, the lady needs your seat," Michelle demanded.

I pulled her arm back gently. "No, Michelle, I'll stand, really."

"Oh, okay, sorry," the man said nervously. When he jumped down, I noticed he was barely taller than the stool. Nice. We'd just ousted a little person minding his own business from his seat at the bar and relegated him to the crowd where he'd likely never be able to get the bartender's attention. When he flipped a tip up to the bartender, my heart sank.

"Wait, sir, you don't have to go." I grabbed his shoulder. A shock wave traveled up my arm, and I released him like a hot rock.

He widened his eyes at me, then disappeared into the crowd. *Shit*. What was that?

"That was *weird*," Michelle said. "Maybe the dress scared him away. Well, never mind, Dustin here will take care of you."

I pursed my lips and plopped down on the empty stool. The bartender came over to request my drink order, and I realized it was Dustin Lynch, Logan's assistant manager. I guess now that Logan was managing Valentine's, Dustin was bartending. "Oh, hey, Dustin. Red wine, *STAT*."

He gave me a nod and a tight smile and reached for the bottle.

"So, why were you all flipped out this morning?" Michelle asked, face weaving toward me.

I suspected she was too far gone to understand, but I told her everything, from Rick's involvement in Gary's turning to Nekomata's purchase of my house. With the music as loud as it was, I doubted anyone could hear as I stage-whispered into her ear, but still, to be safe, I used code words for the supernatural parts, such as saying "Gary's change" rather than the word "vampire." Michelle seemed to get the gist.

"And now Rick's missing?"

"Yeah."

"Crap."

"I know, right?"

"What are you going to do about your house?"

I shrugged. "It's already sold, Michelle. What can I do?"

She lowered her chin and raised an eyebrow. "You can do a lot of things. You wrote the book on magical ways of getting things done."

"Yep. And I'll be consulting that book first thing Monday morning, but first I need to get my head around why all this is happening. This buyer won't be the last if I don't figure out why my house has been targeted."

"You don't think it's the prime location?" Michelle asked, obviously referring to the property's placement next to a hellmouth.

"That would be too easy. I think it's more than that, unfortunately."

A hand clamped down on my shoulder, and I turned my head to see Logan standing close behind me, a wide, tipsy grin coloring his face. "What's unfortunate?"

His green eyes pierced into me, set off by the sharp charcoal shirt he wore. "Someone bought my house," I said.

Logan's face fell, sobering. "What about the attic?"

I searched the crowd of strangers pressing in around us. "What about it?" I laughed.

He slid his hand down my arm and found my fingers. "Can I talk to you in my office for a moment?"

He didn't wait for me to say yes. With a yank, he pulled me from my barstool. I swung an arm out with ninja-like precision and hooked my wineglass with my palm before following him through the crowd. Halfway to his office, a familiar face jutted between us. I put on the brakes, forcing Logan to stop.

"Grateful! Great to see you out and about." Detective Silas Flynn slapped me on the shoulder. "I take it this is a social visit?"

"Uh, yeah. Totally social tonight, Silas."

"Good, because I have the night off." He reached into the crowd and a golden brown hand emerged, followed by the unforgettable presence of a fairy we both knew.

"Soleil." I smiled, and she hugged me hello. "So you two are dating, huh?"

She glanced at the floor and a slight golden glow heated the air around her. "What can I say? He gives me the moon."

Silas turned toward her, and his pupils dilated to the size

of plates. Wow. There were some serious feelings going on there.

"And you give me the sun, darling."

Next to me, Logan cleared his throat.

"Oh, ah, these are my friends, Silas and Soleil," I stated awkwardly. "This is Logan." Logan extended his hand to greet the two.

"The guest of honor! Of course we know Logan," Silas said.

"Good to see you again Detective Flynn," Logan said. "And nice to meet you, Soleil."

"You know each other?" I asked, raising my eyebrows at Silas.

"I covered a break-in at Valentine's a few weeks ago."

"Oh." I nodded a few times, wondering why Silas would have gotten involved, unless they suspected a supernatural. It was the wrong time and place to ask.

Silas fixated on our coupled hands. "How do you know Logan?"

"He's my, er, friend. We're just friends…who need to talk." The awkward aftermath was my cue to move things along. I said my goodbyes and followed Logan into a small room near the back housing a desk laden with stacks of paperwork. He closed the door behind us, and I smoothed my green dress.

"You look beautiful," Logan said, eyeing me from head to toe. "The green brings out your eyes."

"Thank you," I said. Maybe I should have worn pants.

"Now what's this about your house?"

I told him my theory that it had something to do with *The Book of Flesh and Bone*. "Have you seen your mom again?" I asked.

"No, just that one time. But…"

"But what?"

"I've been having these dreams."

"What kind of dreams?" Deja vu. If he said he'd had a sex dream about Rick, I was going to scream.

"There's this woman. I never see her face because she's always in the shadows. She says if I help her find what she's looking for, she'll reward me."

My eyebrows eased down my forehead and squinched over my nose. "What does she want you to find?"

"That's just it. I never find out. The woman motions for me to approach, like she's going to whisper something in my ear, and before I can get close enough to hear her, my mother pops up."

"Your mother? Your dead mother?"

"Yeah. She pops up between me and this woman, just like in my living room, and tells me to find *you*."

"Wait. Your mother is sending you messages in your dreams to find *me*?"

"Apparently."

"So what does she say you're supposed to do when you find me?"

"She doesn't. But I have a theory."

This was too much to take sober. I held up one finger and gulped down my wine. The Cabernet tasted bitter, like maybe the cork went bad before they opened the bottle, but I was so desperate for numbing I finished it anyway. When I lowered my glass, Logan was standing directly in front of me.

He locked eyes with me, lifted the empty glass from my hand, and lowered it to the desk. "I think the hooded woman represents every relationship I've ever had. Sensual but face-less, promising but meaningless, and my mom is telling me to find what's real. She wants me to find *you*."

"I don't think that's what it means, Logan. I can't be with you. I'm, ah, I'm—"

His face was so close, and the wine was rushing to my head. Something else, I was woozy. His eyes seemed to twinkle in a cartoony way, and light played in his hair, tiny dancing bears of white light. *Shit!* I was tripping. There was something more than wine in that drink. What the hell?

"Theresomethinsflibbitygibbit." I was not making any sense. The floor bent up to say hello and I steadied myself on the first thing I could reach, which happened to be his hips. He took that as encouragement and pressed into me, his spicy cologne seeming to waft through me in my altered state.

And then he was kissing me, a human kiss that was nothing at all like the ones we'd shared when he was a ghost. Even in my altered state I couldn't deny the heat. His lips met mine, soft and warm. He pressed me into the wall, his body enveloping me as his tongue invaded my mouth. I didn't so much return the kiss as absorb it.

I felt like I'd gone down the rabbit hole. One moment I was kissing Logan, and the next Rick's face was in front of me. Wait. That was Rick. And he was pissed. He held Logan off me with one hand and held me up with the other. He looked at me with vile contempt.

"Grateful," he said. Wait. What happened to *mi cielo*? "I always knew I loved you more, but I never thought you were cruel. Why did you send Poe to find me? Did you want me to see this?"

"No." I fumbled forward. My hand trailed through the air in front of me. "Mishtake," I slurred.

But he wasn't looking at me. Instead, he was fending off Logan who was getting all "back off, buddy" in Rick's face. I stumbled to the desk, unable to process what he was saying.

"We love each other. We have something," Logan said.

Who was he talking about? I didn't love Logan. Sure, I'd

been attracted to him and we shared a deep friendship, but love? I needed to explain.

I turned toward Rick but he was gone. Logan was on his ass on the floor and the door to the office was hanging off its hinges. I stumbled back out into the crowd, calling for Rick.

"Top of the evening to ya," the shy redheaded guy said to me, blocking my path. "Hope you're enjoying the little something extra in your drink." He grinned wickedly. I noticed he had a number of gold teeth. He leaned in closer. "Nobody steals a leprechaun's seat at the bar. Not even you, Hecate. See you soon." He spit on my shoes, and blended away into the blob of colors I recognized as the crowd.

See you soon? Not if I saw him first. I swam toward the door, hoping I could catch up with Rick. How long did it take me? I have no idea. Time was doing weird things just as the walls were buckling in on me. Somehow, I spilled out into the parking lot, thankful for the deep breath of cold air that filled my lungs.

A broad fist connected with the side of my face. *OW!* I tried to retaliate but my arms wouldn't work. *BAM!* A foot slammed into my ribs. Then the concrete bent up to give me a kiss. Oh, how sweet. Ouch, my head. That's all right, I decided. I could sleep right here on the pavement.

16

RUDE AWAKENING

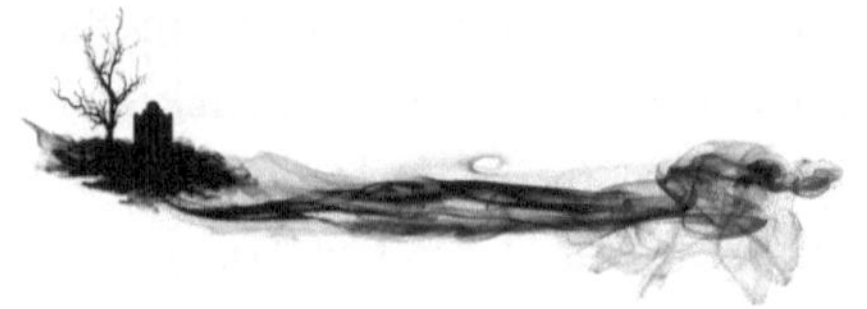

Ch-ch-ch-chatter-chat-chat

Something was clanking together. Oh, my teeth. Maybe that's why my jaw ached. I tried to slide it back and forth and it cracked painfully. I pressed my lips together. *What the hell was going on?* I was shivering too. And one side of my head hurt like a bitch. Actually, my whole body ached, and my wrists were stuck. I fluttered my eyes open. *What the fuck?*

I was not at home, and I was not at Valentine's. The room was dark, but I could make out stone walls supported by thick wooden beams. There were implements on racks mounted to the walls: canes, whips, clamps, and sharp objects that glinted ominously in the light of the single candle that burned on a small table at the center of the room. Either I was in someone's red room of pain, or this was an actual dungeon.

I took a moment to survey myself. The reason my teeth were chattering was I'd been stripped down to the white silk and lace slip I'd been wearing under my dress. Even my shoes were gone, my feet numb from the icy cold stone under them. The ache in my back and wrists was due to the latter being bound above my head to the ceiling. When I tried to tilt my head back to get a better look, I groaned.

"She wakes." The ginger from the bar appeared in front of me, his gold-toothed smile glinting wickedly. An evil leprechaun. Who knew? And to think, I'd felt guilty for stealing his barstool.

"Thank you, Naill," a woman's voice, deep but sensual, crooned to my left. She stepped into my peripheral vision. The way my head hung, I saw her tall-booted leg first, peeking out from the slit in her dress, followed by a long waist. "At last we meet, Hecate, or should I call you Grateful?" Red lips pulled back from pearly white fangs.

"Hecate is fine," I said through the pain in my jaw. "I can think of some things I'd like to call you."

"Anna. Perhaps you've heard of me." She stepped closer, as if she were inspecting my face.

I looked up into her oversized green eyes and searched my memory for the name Anna. My conversation with Gary popped into my head. "Bathory?"

"The one and only." She pushed her bouncy brown curls off her shoulder and turned to pace away from me. Bathory definitely had the Jessica Rabbit thing going on below the neck. Her black dress clung like a second skin, a leather corset boosting her major assets shamelessly.

"What do you want?" I managed.

"I want the book," she snapped. "Tell me where it is, and I will let this incarnation of you live." She closed in. The scent of blood wafted over me. Whether it was my blood or the stench of her breath, I wasn't sure.

"I don't know where it is." At least this I could be honest about. If she had any powers of observation at all, she'd have to believe me.

"Hmm." She paced again, the clack of her heels creating an ominous rhythm on the stone floor.

Or maybe it was the cold that was ominous, or the fact that the warm, wet drip making its way down my cheek seemed to be coming from a painful spot on my head. And one of my eyes was hard to keep open. Yeah, now that the adrenaline was starting to wear off, I was a mess. I dangled from my bindings like a carrion treat for my vampire captor. Where was Poe? Shit, where was Rick? The events of the night came rushing back to me, and instantly the pain of my physical situation was compounded by an emotional pain that weighed down my chest.

Bathory rounded on me with a piranha smile, all teeth and a promise that her bite was worse than her bark. "I was there the day you burned at the stake. Had I known the book in Monk's arms had the power it did, I would have taken it then. As it was, when my next meal collapsed, twitching on the ground, I stepped right over my salvation and moved on to the next town. But you hear a lot as a vampire. Men talk and demons share their secrets in the night. Recently, I've learned what the book can do. I want it. And one of the last people to see it is back from the dead—you."

"I don't know where it is," I mumbled again. My right eye was officially swollen shut.

The cackle that escaped her lips made new goose bumps play leapfrog over my skin. "Perhaps Indiana can make you talk." She lifted a five-foot bullwhip from somewhere I couldn't see and used both hands to make the leather snap in front of my good eye. "Have you met Indiana? I named her after Indiana Jones. Harrison Ford was a master with a whip."

Baring her teeth, she circled the whip above her head and brought the tail down across my chest. I screamed as it bit into my flesh.

"Where is the book?" she growled.

"I don't know!"

The whip sliced across my thighs. "The book?" she demanded.

"I don't know," I whimpered.

Again. This time her anger marred her aim and the tail of the whip bit into my bound hands.

My head listed forward. I heaved but nothing came out. "I don't know," I whimpered. "Why do you want it, anyway?"

"Interesting," she said. "Perhaps, you really don't remember. Allow me to enlighten you. *The Book of Flesh and Bone* gives the spell caster power over life and death. Vampires, as you know, are the living dead, bound supernaturally to a certain set of laws. The book would allow me to change those laws."

"What? Like you'd be able to walk in the sunlight?" I rasped.

"The sunlight, yes. A more natural appearance without the need for illusion. The ability to taste food again. And other things. True immortality. Life in death without limits."

My head listed on my shoulders. Darkness pressed in around me, my vision a constricting tunnel. I was fighting to remain conscious. I couldn't feel my hands or feet anymore, just the ache that racked my torso from shoulders to hips. I felt like I'd been in a car accident. "There has to be limits," I rasped. "Balance."

Her mouth came close to the ear on the swollen side of my face. "I've never been one to follow the rules."

"Mistress!" The leprechaun was back, yelling and flailing his arms from the stone stairs in the back of the dungeon. "I apologize, but you are needed upstairs. It's urgent! There's a fight over a woman and the men have guns."

As if on cue, the sound of breaking glass filtered down

from above. The vampire growled low in her throat, then shot me an evil glare. "I'll be right there, Naill."

The ginger jogged back the way he'd come.

Bathory turned her full attention on me. "You hang around while I take care of a few things," she said with a grin. A sharp fingernail pressed into my chest and I watched a drop of blood trickle between my breasts. "Then we'll see what else we can do to jog your memory." The words held the threat of violence.

I blinked. She was gone. Or maybe I'd passed out for a few minutes. I wasn't sure. Whichever it was, I sensed someone else was in the room. Not Bathory, no. The weight of the supernatural presence was different, lighter. Someone was working at the ropes that bound my arms. Slightly behind me, I couldn't see who it was, and with my face busted up, all I could smell was my own blood.

"Rick?"

"While the pleasure of owning that name isn't mine, the compliment of your confusion doesn't escape me. Perhaps later you can reward me the way you would him." The voice was plush as velvet, sinful, and smarmy.

"Julius." My wrists came loose and my arms fell forward, causing an intense pain to shoot through my shoulders. I screamed.

His hand clamped over my mouth and his face came into focus—dark hair, the color of melted chocolate, and too-large blue eyes. "Shhh. Even with the fight I staged upstairs, Anna is a very old vampire with acute hearing. We have only moments to escape this place before she undoubtedly becomes suspicious."

I nodded. The thought that Julius wasn't rescuing me but rather scavenging me for parts, such as the rest of my blood, crossed my mind. Too bad I had no energy to fight. Remaining conscious was a moment-by-moment battle.

With no effort at all, he tossed me over his shoulder. Pain shot through me once again, ugly, hot pain that made me dry heave. I was pretty sure one of my arms was broken and maybe other bones too. Lucky for me, the added agony pushed me over the edge and blissful unconsciousness took over.

17

OUT OF THE FRYING PAN

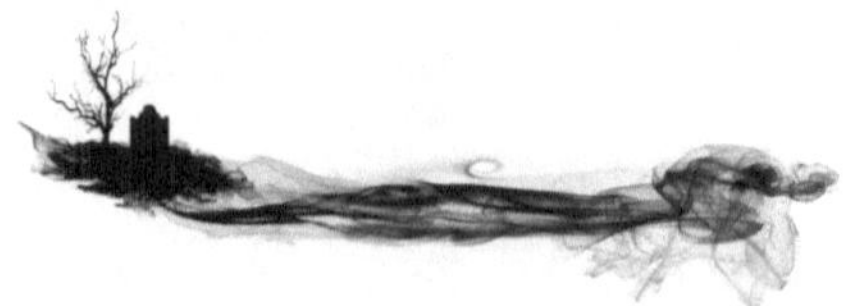

My one good eye cranked open inside a dimly lit room much different from Bathory's dungeon. The other was still swollen shut. Nestled in a plush, white bed with a fluffy down comforter, I ran my hand across the smooth fabric of the sheets and glanced around the room. Clean lines. Dark wood nightstand with stainless steel pull. A rice paper screen. A silver-blue straight back chair. Where was I? Desperately, I tried to sit up to get a better look, but a sharp pain thwarted my efforts.

"I think you have a broken rib," Julius said from behind me.

With some effort, I rolled over to face him. He sat at a larger-than-life desk made of the same almost-black wood of the nightstand. Hunched over a stack of papers, he read by the light of a silver candelabra. That's why the room was so dim. No electric lights. Only candles.

Carefully, I positioned myself to get a better idea of my chances of escape. Comfortable accommodations but not a window in sight. A heavy wooden door was closed up tight, probably locked. Was this a different type of prison? Or maybe Anna and Julius were working together, a good cop-bad cop scenario.

"I'd offer you pain medication, but we have none. Doesn't work on vampires. We have no need for it here. I do, however, have some 1939 Macallan Scotch, if you'd like." His blue eyes didn't lift from the document he was reading.

"No, thanks. I've already been poisoned once tonight. I don't need to make the same mistake twice."

He lifted his head and straightened in his chair. "If I wanted you dead, I would have drained you of every last drop of blood while you were asleep. It's not as if you were putting up much of a fight, and your blood is…" He shook his head and grinned as if even the thought of drinking my blood gave him pleasure. "Besides, if I was going to taint a beverage with poison, it most certainly wouldn't be a ten thousand-dollar bottle of Scotch."

He had a point. "Okay. I'll take a glass."

Julius rose and crossed the room to a credenza bar where he poured two fingers of bronze-colored liquid from a crystal decanter.

"Am I a prisoner?"

He lowered his shoulders in mock frustration. "Does this look like a dungeon?"

"There are no windows, the door is closed, and I'm still in my slip."

Scotch flowed into a second glass. "It's daylight. I didn't have time to find your dress. You are in my bedroom, underground. There are no windows because I would go up in smoke if there were."

"One can only hope."

He handed me one of the glasses and sipped from the other. "Is that any way to treat the vampire who rescued you?"

I looked toward the ceiling. "Are we under TiltWorld?"

The last time I'd seen Julius, his coven had taken up residence in a carnival fun house called the Barn Blast.

"Actually, we've moved to more permanent accommodations. You won't blame me for not divulging the address."

With a wave of my still-bloody hand, I dismissed his comment. "Why *did* you rescue me? It's not like we're besties. How in the world did you even know where I was?" I took a swig of the Scotch. The intense liquor burned its way down my throat and warmed me to my toes. I coughed a few times.

He ran a hand through his hair, loosing a straight lock that fell over his forehead. "I've had you followed for months. Gary volunteered."

A memory from a few months back slipped to the front of my brain. I'd smelled Gary's cologne while climbing into my Jeep after work. At the time, I hadn't known he was a vamp. "Gary? Why?" Julius was evil, but having Gary follow me 24/7 seemed excessive, even for him.

"My coven cannot allow Anna Bathory to gain access to the book."

"What book?"

He laughed until he showed fang.

"Listen, like I told Anna, I don't know where *The Book of Flesh and Bone* is. I'm not sure why she thinks I have it, but I don't."

"Oh, please. Do we have to do this every fucking time?" He slammed the glass down on his desk. "Stop playing coy with me, Hecate. You must know. If the book wasn't somewhere on your property, the nekomata wouldn't be nosing around your house."

I stared at him for a beat. "You know about the nekomata?"

"Every supernatural being this side of the Appalachians knows about the nekomata," he hissed.

I shook my head. "Explain."

He sighed heavily as if trying to decide if he should indulge me. "For many years, rumor among our kind suggested they took the book after your death."

"The nekomata?"

"*Yes.*" Julius shot me an annoyed look. "They are drifters, like your human stereotype of gypsies. They collect things. It is well known that the Pryth Clan frequented New England at the time of your death, scavenging goods from the dead. Thanks to drought, war, and hysteria, there was an abundance of dead."

"Nice."

"But they can't carry everything they steal. Like pirates, they bury their booty to retrieve at a later date. They seal it in vaults under the earth. So, you see, when one comes around after so much time, word gets out."

I lowered my eyebrows, which hurt because of my busted face. "Why now? It's been hundreds of years. Why wouldn't the nekomata come before this?"

Julius downed his drink and returned to the credenza to pour another. Did vampires get drunk? I wasn't sure. "The nekomata seal their treasure inside a vault they create in the earth. Always near a gravesite, since their magic uses the dead. Only during specific celestial events may the vault be opened. As it so happens, the winter solstice is but days away."

"The winter solstice happens every year. Why now? Why this year?"

"Because this is the first year that the hiding place will be accessible to the nekomata, dear witch. This is the first year that your house is not your own." He pointed at me with conviction as if I'd done something wrong.

"So, you're suggesting that the nekomata are buying my house because *The Book of Flesh and Bone* is buried somewhere on my property in a Pryth Clan vault, but they can't get to it without buying my house because of the spell of protection my predecessor put on the place."

He nodded slowly. Julius's mouth spread into a wide, toothy grin. "Your dear old friend died before her time, before she could transfer the title of the house to you."

"Prudence?"

"When she left the house to your father, she meant it for you." He snorted. "Didn't work out. Perfect time for the nekomata to strike."

"So, the nekomata got word the house was for sale. It's been for sale for two years. Why not come earlier?"

He lowered himself back into the leather desk chair and stared at me like I was dense.

"Any protective spell you had on the house would be fully in force until you returned. But a transitioning witch is vulnerable. You should have reinforced the spell when you had the chance. Now, it is already beginning to weaken."

"I thought you were behind the sale, Mr. *Helleborine*."

"Who is Mr. Helleborine? I know the name… Helleborine is an herb you should be quite familiar with, Hecate, but I have never gone by that name."

I looked at him skeptically. "Someone going by that name tried to buy my house earlier this year."

"It was not me, although I wouldn't put it past Anna. She can't be happy about the nekomata getting the book."

"Why? I'm sure she could compel it out of their hands in a heartbeat. She's probably behind the purchase."

"Poor. Dear. Ignorant. Witch." He sighed. "Nekomata and vampires are natural enemies. A nekomata bite is deadly to us, and no, they can't be compelled. They're immune. No nekomata in their right mind would help Anna."

"So, she's trying to get to it before they do."

He shook his head. "Maybe, but I'm not sure why. A Pryth Clan vault can only be opened by nekomata magic. It cannot be forced open by muscle or any other natural means." He sipped his Scotch and stared at a spot on the wall.

"What about magic? She had a leprechaun in her employ. Aren't they, like, super-sorcerers?"

"I'm not sure even a leprechaun could bypass nekomata magic, but I'd rather not find out. You must have wondered why I sent Gary with the money. You are not so naïve to believe it was out of the goodness of my heart." He chuckled.

My lips parted. No, I hadn't trusted Julius's gift, and I still didn't. I turned his words over in my mind, wondering what parts I should believe. I decided, in this case, the shock of honesty might be just what I needed to shake him up. "Nekomata bought my house. It isn't mine anymore. We haven't closed on the sale yet, but unless a miracle happens, it's his."

Julius stood up, knocking his chair back with a clatter. "How? I sent you the money. Why didn't you buy the house?"

"I tried! He bought it first before I could get a loan."

Julius began to pace in front of the door. "This is undesirable."

"You don't say." I pressed a finger into my lips. "There's something I don't understand. You think *The Book of Flesh and Bone* is hidden on my property. If Anna and everybody else knows about the nekomata, why is she coming after me? The city is swarming with supernaturals looking for this thing. If there was any rumor it was in or around my house, why are they in the city and not Red Grove?"

"Anna Bathory has compelled every supernatural creature within a one hundred-mile radius to help her find the book. But make no mistake; she doesn't actually want any of them to find it. Her purpose is to raise an army, so that should the nekomata obtain the grimoire first, they will never be able to leave with it. Believe me, if the book were hidden anywhere but on your property, Anna would already have it. The fact that she doesn't proves it is still protected by your magic. I suspect that's why she might've killed you tonight, to see if your death would break the enchantment."

Shit. So, Bathory wanted me dead. Great. "One more question. Why don't *you* want the book, Julius?"

He stood, leaving his glass at the desk and folding his hands behind his back. With a stony expression, he paced toward me, approaching the bed like a predator. I noticed for the first time that his low-slung jeans and silver waffle-weave shirt concealed an impressive physique. Smarmy, yes, but at one time Julius had been an attractive specimen of a man. I briefly wondered how he'd become a vampire.

He stopped at my side. "I do want the book, Hecate, as much as I want the blood that courses through your veins. You have no reason to trust me. You shouldn't trust me. I was a bad man, and I've become an even worse vampire. Even now I am tempted to drink your blood until I can feel the suction of your veins collapsing and hear the fading rhythm of your heart. Watching you pale would give me great pleasure."

I stiffened in his bed. He was too close. His face lowered toward my broken body.

"But you see, my dear witch, I find myself in the unenviable position of needing to keep you alive. For as much as I want the book, Anna is the older, more powerful vampire. If she gets her hands on it, we will all become her immortal slaves. I'm not willing to bow to her or lose my coven."

The cold curl of his breath forced me back on the mattress. He was in my face now and his fangs had dropped. His blue eyes fixated on my neck.

"Then you'd better keep me alive."

"If the house has already sold, maybe it doesn't matter." A trace of evil permeated his voice, his previously congenial tone swept away by a hungry, lascivious glare.

"Better safe than sorry."

"I best not kill you," he said, more to himself than to me. His icy cold hand swept down my arm to my bloody and bruising wrist. He lifted it above my head, pressing it into the pillow.

I whimpered. The injuries caused by Bathory's ropes throbbed under his touch.

At the sound of my pain, he inhaled deeply. Out of the corner of my eye, I noticed him adjust himself in his jeans. He was hard, and I was in trouble. Flattening my back to his bed, I was too weak to do much else. He collected my other wrist and pinned it above my head.

"They say a witch's blood tastes like silk and gives the energy of ten humans." He parted my knees with his own and stretched out on top of me, propping his weight on his elbows as he restrained my arms. He settled his hips between my legs.

"Please don't." My heart was pounding. My rib ached as his body pressed into mine. With no energy to fight back, a tear rolled down my cheek.

His tongue lapped over my jugular.

"You need me, remember? Don't do it, Julius."

Cool breath chilled the wet spot he'd left on my skin. "Just a taste. I can stop."

I braced myself for the strike but nothing could prepare me for the pain. Unlike with Rick, my flesh didn't part for his teeth; it fought the invasion. I screamed in agony as he ripped into me. I cried in earnest, the sounds of his swallowing bringing back memories of my last death, when Marcus had killed me.

My chest felt heavy, heart struggling against the loss of blood. I was tired. All I had to do was close my eyes and I might never wake up again. "Julius, stop," I rasped.

"Mmm." Julius groaned into my neck. He wasn't going to stop. He was going to kill me.

Rick, help me, I thought one last time. I fought to remain conscious.

Suddenly, a section of the ceiling exploded, wood beams and brick blowing into the room. Light poured through the hole, sending Julius fleeing to the safety of the shadow behind his desk. Sweet sunshine washed over me, around an impressive silhouette. I didn't have to see his face. Deep inside, the most instinctual part of me knew it was Rick. He'd come for me. Even though he hated me, he'd come for me.

To the sound of Poe's caw in the background, Rick hastily swept me up into his arms. What happened next wasn't his fault. He didn't know he shouldn't have moved me. As he folded my body in half, all of the blood rushed from my head and my rib slipped. I couldn't draw a breath. And then I was gone again. I'd lost myself.

Deep, buried under the darkness at the bottom of an ocean, I was drowning. I gulped the salt water, filling my mouth. Too late. It was too late. I'd never reach the surface. Arms flailing, I struggled. It had been forever since my last real breath of air. *Was I already dead?*

"*Mi cielo,* breathe, breathe darling."

Rick. I swallowed what was in my mouth. Not salt water, but blood. His blood. A reflexive gasp broke my lips, and I cranked my good eye open. The sun poured in. I absorbed its energy into my very soul. Pain screamed through my body, Rick's blood working from the inside out. As unpleasant as the hurt was, the ache told me I wasn't dead; I was healing. I was alive. I was alive!

18

MY CARETAKER

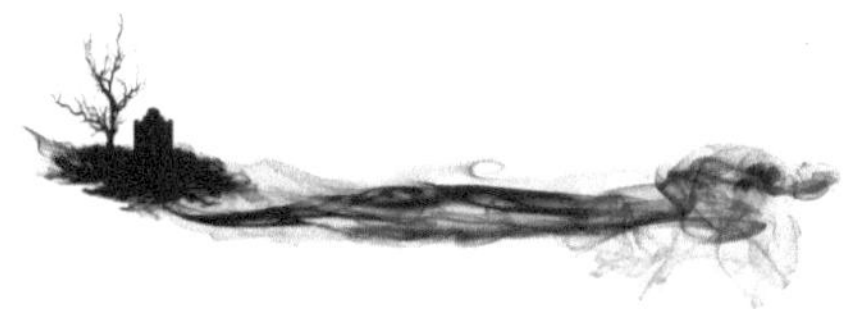

A warm, wet cloth blotted my skin, tugging me awake. My eyes fluttered open. The slosh and dribble of a cloth being rinsed and wrung was enough motivation for me to keep them open. I was in Rick's bedroom, stretched out next to him on his bed, his broad shoulders hunched over a basin of water.

"How are you feeling?" he asked. He ran the cloth back up my arm, rinsing the remainder of dried blood from my skin.

"Heavy all over. Like a truck hit me."

"You're lucky to be alive. Your injuries were extensive, and Julius drained you just short of death. My blood will heal you, but it will take some time for your body to produce what's missing."

I probably needed a transfusion. Not gonna happen. A trip to the hospital would bring questions I wasn't prepared to answer.

"How did you find me?"

"Poe. After I left Valentine's, he tracked me down. It took some time for him to convince me you were in mortal danger."

"And that was the only reason you came? Because I was in *mortal* danger?" I croaked.

He threw the rag into the basin, causing the water to slosh violently. "I came because I am your caretaker. I am bound to you. I have no choice but to come when you call, whether or not I want to."

"I tried to tell you at Valentine's, Rick—"

"That you're in love with Logan? That you want your cake and to eat it too?" he hissed.

"Let me explain about Logan."

He clamped a hand over my mouth. "I don't want to talk about Logan, unless of course you would rather he care for you?"

I shook my head. Hurt darkened his gray eyes. I needed to explain that I hadn't wanted Logan to kiss me. I needed to tell him a leprechaun had drugged me, and it was all a big mistake. But I could see that he wasn't open to more conversation. He was still too raw, and I was so exhausted, I wasn't sure I could find the words.

He released my mouth. "Are you hungry?"

"I should tell you why they tortured me," I rasped.

With thumb and forefinger, he pinched my lips shut. "Not yet. We need you well, and I fear reliving the story will further drain you."

I nodded.

"I will prepare a meal for you."

"Out of what? You don't eat, and you don't have a phone to order food."

A ghost of a smile turned the corner of his lip. "I've been keeping some groceries lately, in hopes that you would stay more often." He spoke the words softly, like an admission.

The surrender in his voice broke my heart. Even though he believed I didn't return his feelings, he'd resolved himself to care for me. Tears pooled in my eyes and I swore that, when I was strong enough, I'd find a way to thank him. Then, I'd explain that I didn't love Logan at all and more, I'd figure out what this feeling was deep inside my chest, and I'd tell him about that too.

* * *

"*MI CIELO*, TIME TO EAT." RICK CRADLED MY UPPER BODY IN one arm while he stacked pillows behind my head.

I tried to sit up on my own and failed. Instead, I managed to wrap an arm around his neck to make it easier for him to reposition me. "Thank you," I whispered in his ear.

He closed his eyes and exhaled a shaky breath, hugging his cheek to mine until it was obvious he'd positioned the pillows as much as needed. Once he'd lowered me carefully into the soft nest he'd made, he lifted a bowl and ladled the soup.

"Open."

I did, and he poured the hot liquid into my mouth. I chewed and swallowed. "What kind of soup is this?" I asked. It tasted like herbal tea with vegetables, not exactly bad but not like my dad used to make...and my dad can't cook.

"I found a spell for a healing infusion of herbs and added some vegetables known to be healthful. The meat I'd purchased was spoiled but I can get some later if you'd like."

I swallowed another bite. It was growing on me. I could definitely feel healing warmth infusing my body from the brew. "It's fine," I said. "I think it's working."

His eyes twinkled with a smile that didn't quite reach his lips but warmed the air between us. Deep inside, that feeling filled me again, the one I'd felt when I'd watched him try to warn me about Monk when I was Isabella. I'd also experienced this when I'd woken up in Maison des Étoiles and when he'd saved me from Julius. I'd been in love before and this wasn't what I remembered; it was stronger. This emotion was a great and powerful mystery I wasn't ready to solve.

"Where did you find me, anyway? Julius said he moved from TiltWorld."

"The coven has purchased the Thames Theatre, now in immediate need of renovation."

"A theatre? Smart. Dark, no windows."

"Yes. Julius is a worthy adversary."

"He's nothing compared to Bathory."

Rick slipped another spoonful into my mouth. "No more talk. You need to rest."

Now that he mentioned it, I was exhausted again. I leaned back into the pillows and held up my hand when he tried to feed me another bite. "Rick, will you do something for me?"

"Of course, *mi cielo*. Would you like something different to eat?"

"No. Tell me about the day we met. The first time. Before you were my caretaker." I dug my fingers out from under the covers and entwined them with his.

Eyebrows rose in surprise. He met my gaze. What I saw in his expression bordered on disturbing: loss, grief, reminiscence, and love. Slowly, he pulled his hand away, but he did not deny me. In a silky-smooth ripple of a voice, he began his story.

"I was only fifteen when we met the first time. You looked the same age but perhaps you were older. Red Grove was a much different place then, with stone cottages like this one distant from each other to allow for the acres of land families must farm to survive. The members of our community lived austere lives of faith. Monk's church was our hub, and his Sunday service, the only time we were all in the same room.

"In some ways it was a simpler time. Expectations were clear and opportunities were few. I was a curious boy with a fascination for the unknown. When I'd finished my chores, I would wander into the woods, sometimes for miles, under the guise of going hunting. In truth, I rarely sought game, but instead visited a freshwater pool at the bottom of a waterfall where I taught myself to swim. My mother would become quite worried at my long absences but would allow it because occasionally I would bring back wild game or fish."

He smiled wistfully. I wondered what his mother was like but didn't want to sidetrack his story, so I nestled into the pillows and listened.

"The day we met, I was swimming, floating on my back in the pool, when I saw you for the first time. I opened my eyes, and there you were, watching me from the shoulder of the waterfall. Of course, I became quite flustered and thrashed to shore."

I giggled. "Why would my fifteen-year-old self fluster you?"

He smiled, and a hint of color warmed his cheeks. "One reason, I was naked, and another, you were a Wampanoag Indian."

"What?" I interrupted. "I was Native American?"

"Yes. Your father was. Your real mother was the goddess Hecate, but I wouldn't find that out until decades later."

I tried to digest that nugget of information while he continued.

"In that time, Native Americans were often dreaded as violent or wild. I feared for my life. Without bothering to dress, I reached for my bow. But when I turned back toward the pool, you were breaking the water's surface. You'd stripped and dove in behind me. You were always like that: brave, strong, unashamed."

"You knew all that from me diving into the water?" I took a deep breath as a wave of pain washed through me.

He brushed my hair back from my face. "You'd never

been there before. Later, you would tell me that your tribe had migrated to the area to escape being sold into the slave trade. You dove into the pool naked, knowing I was watching, with no idea how deep the water was or how safe. Even my fifteen-year-old self knew that made you a force to reckon with."

"Could I speak English?"

"Yes, fortunately for me." He rubbed his forehead, his eyes taking on the sheen of long forgotten memories. "As your head broke the surface of the water, you met my eyes for the first time. I'd never seen anything as beautiful as you. Maybe it was fitting that we should meet completely naked because from that day forward you stripped me of everything. It was like I was born again to a new existence."

"But you didn't know what I was?"

"You didn't know what you were, Grateful. True, you found out before I did, but in the beginning we were both innocent. We met daily after that. You taught me how to hunt and track game the Wampanoag way. I participated in your ceremonies. And we grew together. We became best friends, although my family in Red Grove never knew about you. They only knew that our pot was always full, long after the land gave out and the beginnings of starvation nipped at our community."

I squeezed his hand. "I saw the day Monk came for me in *The Book of Light*. I lived alone, in town. How did that happen?"

He turned away, to face the wall for a moment. "You are getting ahead of me. Wouldn't you like to hear about our first kiss?" When he turned his attention back on me, his face looked wistful, young.

I nestled lower into the pillows, capturing my bottom lip between my teeth and inhaling sharply at the surge of pain the movement cost me. Rick looked at me with concern. I nodded for him to continue.

"We were seventeen. A late kiss by today's standards, but Monk's parish was a conservative congregation. Most men didn't marry until their mid-twenties and physical affection was tightly bound to marriage. Couples had to ask permission of an elder to marry. All very official and reserved. In your tribe, things were different. Any who took a liking to one another could marry; the girl must only demonstrate that she was capable of caring for young, and most women of your tribe could by seventeen. And kissing? Your people loved to kiss."

"You're blushing!" The red tint to his cheeks was endearing. I tried to meet his eyes but he looked away.

"The couples in your tribe were quite affectionate. I was… enthralled. From an early age, you showed an aptitude for healing and knowledge of herbs, so you'd trained with the Wampanoag medicine woman. You took me home one day and introduced me to the leader of your tribe in your native language. I didn't know what you'd said, but he seemed very happy. You turned to me and asked if I would like to marry you, as you had obtained permission from your tribe. Then, in the plaza at the center of your community, you grabbed me by the collar, pulled me forward, and kissed me within an inch of my life." A broad smile spread across his face. "I felt it to my toes."

"Wait, *I* asked *you* to marry *me*? When I was seventeen?"

A low rumble shook his chest and he turned to face me. "You knew exactly what you wanted, Grateful, and after that kiss, if I hadn't before, I knew exactly what I wanted too. Forever."

Our eyes locked, and I tried to picture what it was like for us back then. I had a feeling there was more to the story, and by the way he reacted to my question about moving to town, that it wasn't particularly pleasant. What had we suffered together?

He reached over to tuck a strand of hair behind my ear, then seemed to remember himself and retracted his hand. "I will get you something to drink. It is important for you to stay hydrated." He stood and retreated to the kitchen.

MY FIRST ENGAGEMENT

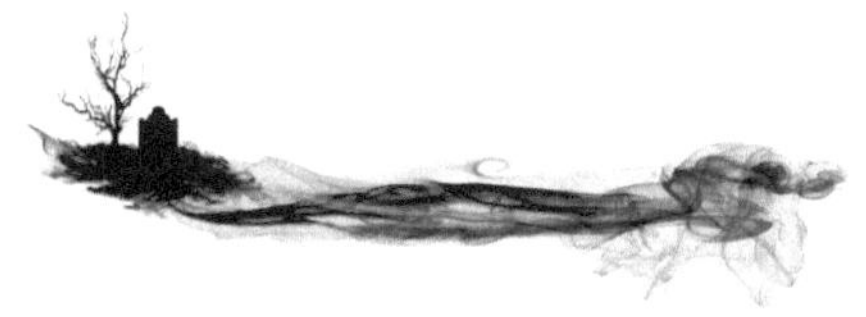

Rick returned with a tall glass of ice water, slices of lime nestled among the ice cubes. Gently, he tipped me up to drink, then placed the glass on the nightstand.

"Refreshing. Thank you."

"You are welcome."

"Why are you Spanish?"

"Excuse me?"

"Puritans were English Protestants. I've never heard of a Spanish Puritan."

"It is true that we were a rarity of our time. My ancestors came over with the conquistadors and migrated north where they joined the Puritan settlers. In truth, my grandfather may have been a criminal, although it wasn't spoken of in my family. I believe he was escaping punishment. The Puritans welcomed my family's practical skills and strength. Survival was priority one for Monk's congregation, although I can't remember any of the English being overly welcoming. Perhaps that is why I spent my time in the woods with you."

I motioned for him to lie down next to me. He hesitated, staring at the empty sliver of bed. Through our connection, his emotions seemed muddled and dark. Being in someone's head isn't like talking to them. Sure, there were times Rick wanted me to know something, and the thoughts came across in complete sentences. But people didn't think that way naturally, and today Rick's head was filled with a mixture of what I would describe as jealousy, possessiveness, hurt, anger, and resentment. I supposed he was still thinking about Logan but suppressing his emotions for my benefit. Grunting, I scooted over to give him more room. That was enough for him to stretch out and get comfortable next to me. Even without touching, the smell of him filled my nostrils—earth, pine, saltwater, and honeysuckle. I breathed him in.

"Did you agree to marry me?" I asked, wanting to get him talking again. Truly, I would have liked the chance to explain about Logan, but Rick wasn't ready to hear it. Not yet.

He laced his fingers over his stomach. "Of course I did. I could no sooner part from you than my own arm. We were to be joined in the official way of the Wampanoag. I was prepared to disappear from my family forever, to live out my life with you and yours."

"But?"

"But, on the morning of our impending marriage, you met me at our pool, hysterical. You told me everyone in your tribe was dead."

"Dead?"

"Drained of their blood. Everyone we knew and loved, dead." His voice cracked.

"Vampires?"

"We didn't know what they were at the time. Vampires are predators and they followed their prey. Just like everyone else that migrated to Red Grove, they came here to feed because so many other places were ravaged by starvation."

"Why didn't the vampires kill me?"

"I can only speculate, but I believe you were protected by your mother."

"My mother…the goddess of the dead, Hecate."

"Yes. I can't be sure, and you never told me, but afterward you…changed, became more powerful. You successfully enchanted Monk's congregation into accepting your presence, no questions asked."

Instinctively, I reached over and placed a hand on his chest as I tilted on my side to see his face. His body stiffened. I removed my fingers and placed them beside me. I cleared my throat. "Nobody asked where I came from?"

"People asked. You told them you'd washed ashore after a shipwreck, having traveled with a band of pilgrims who were killed during your journey. Everyone believed you."

"Sounds plausible."

"Plausible that you would come more than one hundred miles from the nearest port without anything but the clothes on your back?"

I laughed softly. "So, my magic had been awakened."

"Yes. And you'd lost everyone you loved." His fingertips trailed through my hair again. The feeling was comforting, like coming home.

I closed my eyes, slipping into sleep. "Not everyone," I whispered. His story had lulled me into that space between sleep and awake, all my defenses down. "I still had you."

The bed jostled. Through a crack in my eyelids I watched him stand. "Yes, *mi cielo*," he mumbled so quietly I might only have heard it thanks to our connection. "And you still do."

* * *

WHEN I OPENED MY EYES AGAIN, I ROLLED OVER AND LOOKED for Rick. He wasn't in the room; the door was closed, but the curtains were open, revealing a frosty winter's night. I must have slept most of the day. Likely, Rick was out patrolling the graveyard.

Rick. If I'd ever questioned his love for me, I'd been a fool. The story he'd told me was painfully genuine and nagged at a long forgotten memory. Some part of me knew it was truth, as was my past love for him. As confusing as it all was, the warm feeling blooming in my chest was more than heartburn. I was falling in love with him. Not because of my past, although it played a part, but because of the present. He gave of himself selflessly, even when he thought I'd strayed from him. And I was fairly sure, based on everything I'd heard and seen in my grimoire, that I had tricked him into becoming my caretaker, or at a minimum, didn't fully warn him of the consequences. The thought opened up a gaping hole in my chest. Since I'd become the witch, I'd always assumed Rick was the predator, leading me into this life because he had something to gain. Maybe Julius was technically telling the truth about our relationship, but it wasn't the whole truth. I realized, now, Rick had a much greater burden to bear than I originally gave him credit for.

A moment of panic caused my heart to palpitate. Julius wouldn't be happy about Rick's methods of rescuing me, Bathory surely had a price on my head, and Mr. Nekomata could be moving into my house any day now. How long did I have before they came for me? For Rick? I needed to tell Rick what I'd learned and find out what he knew about the possessed woman who died in my ER. We had to be at full capacity, acting as a team, or we wouldn't stand a chance.

I lifted my shaking hands in front of me. The deep, bloody grooves that had etched my skin had filled in, thanks to Rick's blood, but the ache in the joint told me I wasn't completely healed. Another feeding and I'd probably be as good as new. Speaking of blood, I reeked of it. The sponge bath Rick had given me only went so far. I desperately needed a shower, if not to get the stink off me, to wash away the feel of Julius's fangs at my throat or Bathory's bullwhip. With both hands, I pushed myself up and swung my legs over the side.

Near the bed, leaning against the wall, I noticed a long, round purple candle, like the ones you see in church. My intuition hummed. This had not been here before. There was a stamp in the wax, maybe the store logo, in the shape of a scarab beetle. Was this what Rick had obtained during his absence? Immediately, I had to know more. He'd traveled far for this. Why? I reached for the candle.

Apparently, I'd overestimated my degree of healing because my head swam. I tilted forward at the hips and face-planted on the carpet.

* * *

"Mi cielo!" Rick shook my shoulder.

My cheek was pressed into the scratchy area rug next to the bed. I groaned.

"How did you fall out of bed?" He lifted me into his arms.

Morning light shone through the window, warming my face. "I wanted to shower. I feel like I've been rolled in vampire saliva and left to dry."

His shoulders drooped, and he squeezed my waist gently. "I will help you." Gingerly, he undressed me, balling the bloody and torn slip in one hand and tossing it into the garbage can near the bed. As if I weighed nothing, he lifted me and carried me into the bathroom. Holding me up with one arm, he started the shower with the other, testing the temperature of the water with his wrist.

"You must be tired," I said into his neck.

"No, I slept Monday."

"It's Sunday."

"Yes. I am good for a few more days." He tested the water again, then carefully undressed himself while maintaining his hold on me.

I was completely naked but not ashamed. Our connection ran deep, an ancient bond I was still discovering. I tugged at his shoulder. "Bathroom."

It took him a moment to register that I needed to use the toilet, but once he understood, he lowered me to the porcelain.

"Call when you are finished," he said, bracing my arm on the nearby sink. He left me then, closing the door to preserve my privacy.

When I was done, he returned and helped me behind the glass door of the shower. Holding me close, he tipped my head back under the spray. The warm water coursed through my hair, assisted by his fingers, and washed down the length of my body. I watched red-tinged water circle the drain. Rick stepped back, taking me with him, and lifted a bottle of shampoo from the ledge. With his free hand, he squeezed some out into my hair and began massaging my head. I closed my eyes and hummed with pleasure as he worked the suds from the crown of my head to the ends of my long hair. The smell of vanilla and lavender wafted through the steam around us.

I leaned into him, not from fatigue but to indulge the sensory drive of my body. Even through the ache of my muscles and joints, a different kind of discomfort bloomed from my core, an ache for him. My body knew what it wanted, what it needed.

He finished rinsing my hair, and our eyes locked. A torrent of energy and magic spiraled through my body, building as we stood skin to skin. The corners of his eyes wrinkled, but he shook his head, breaking the connection.

Reaching for another bottle, he coated my hair in conditioner that smelled just as good as the shampoo, then grabbed a washcloth from the rack outside the door. He worked the soap inside the cloth, then placed my hands on his shoulders. "Can you hold yourself up?"

I nodded, unable to speak around the lump in my throat.

He kneeled down in front of me, carefully lifting my right foot and lathering it with the rag. He worked his way up my calf, around the back of my knee, and up my leg. As he neared the apex of my thighs, I gripped his shoulders more desperately, not for balance but because my body burned for him. My breath came in shallow pants. He switched to the other foot, the other leg. When he reached my crest, he stood, lathering my abdomen, then my back.

I tried not to register my disappointment as he seemed to skip the parts of me I wanted him to wash the most. My nipples were straining, peaked with anticipation. My core throbbed with desire. And under it all was this hunger, an unnatural, inhuman craving for his blood.

Supporting the base of my neck, he tilted my head back, rinsing the conditioner from my hair, then positioned me, a rag doll in his arms, under the spray to wash the lather away. I slipped my arms around his neck and pressed myself against him until no space was left between our wet bodies. He wanted me too. I could feel the hard length of him against my belly. Why was he hesitating?

"Please," I whispered into his ear. I followed up my plea by wrapping my lips around his earlobe and sucking gently.

He moaned. "Are you strong enough? I don't want to hurt you."

"I will be. I need this…to heal."

"My blood first."

Unlike my skin that moved aside easily for Rick's teeth, I had to cut or bite him for access to his blood. I didn't have my blade, and I was too weak to bite through his skin, so he did the honors. With a partially shifted hand, he dragged his talon across the space where his neck met his chest. As his flesh opened for me, I latched on, suckling the sweet ambrosia that was his blood. Warmth and strength spread outward from my stomach. My hand trailed down his abdomen to his thick shaft, partially sheathing him with my palm. He gasped. I stroked as I drank until his hips began to thrust into the ring of my grip.

Feeling stronger, I pulled back and licked the opening in his flesh. It knit together, healing itself. He didn't wait a moment to replace flesh with flesh. His mouth came down on mine, his velvet tongue stroking inside until I thought I might explode from need. He bit my lower lip gently, then worked his way along the bone of my jaw and up to my ear.

"I haven't finished washing you," he whispered. I heard the soap jostle in the dish and then felt him back away. He built up a lather between his palms, replaced the bar. Those soapy fingers gripped my waist and twirled me around. Sandwiched between his large hands, one on my belly and one on my lower back, he slid both down, cupped my sex, worked his soapy fingers along my most sensitive area. I hinged forward, catching myself on the shower door, my chest pressing into the cool glass. His other hand rounded over my ass, washing me in the spray. Back and forth, around and around. I arched my back to give him easier access.

Every time we'd had sex before felt like a feeding—pleasurable, erotic, his excitement pulsing through our connection and mingling with mine. I could tell he was holding back, keeping me from seeing all his emotions. But oddly, his guarded soul didn't put a damper on my attraction. After the last twenty-four hours, I felt exposed and vulnerable. I wanted him to own me, to control me. I wanted to be his in every way possible.

I pressed into his massaging hand, needing more. The

spray rinsed over me, his palm smoothing the soap away. I inhaled sharply as he pressed against my backside while his hands swept up my sides to knead my breasts.

"Please," I begged. "Take me."

He pinched my nipples hard, making me moan with ecstasy. The head of him pressed at my opening and I eased back until he was completely inside me. His hand swept down my side, to the back of my leg and hitched one knee up, setting my foot on the ledge of the tub. I answered by raising my hips to get a deeper angle. That was all it took. Gripping my shoulders for leverage, his hips unhinged. The glass door rattled with his advance and retreat. At the same time, he reached between my legs, massaging and stroking until the pressure grew to the point of no return. I exploded around him, my sex constricting as I called out his name again and again. I held nothing back. If our connection was open at all, he must've felt the change, that he owned me in that moment. But I felt nothing in return. He was closed off to me.

Patiently, he slowed while my body calmed, then pulled out just long enough to spin me around. He was back under me in a heartbeat, bending his knees to thrust inside of me from tip to base in one lithe move. He gripped me under the ass, and I wrapped my legs around his hips, my back crashing against the opposite shower wall. Joined, he stopped, ran his nose up the side of my face, and looked at me with hooded black eyes.

"I am yours, *mi cielo*. You own me."

"I don't—"

"You hold my chain as surely as if I were your dog." The words were matter of fact. No hint of resentment.

"You're not—" Didn't he know he had it backward? I was his.

He pressed a finger over my lips and tilted his hips so he

was deep inside. "You own me, but I am a jealous slave, and if you cannot be mine in return, I can only assume you are better off without me." In and out, slowly he stroked. "Are you better off without me?"

"No," I moaned.

"Can you be mine?"

"Yes!"

Holding on tight to his neck, I braced myself as he began to slam into me in earnest, his entire body fully engaged in the act. And wasn't that a turn-on? Watching him lose himself pushed me over the edge again, my orgasm milking his until the spray of the water ran cold and my fingers turned pruney.

Rick reached back and shut the water off, then kissed me at the base of my neck.

"Do you need to feed?" I asked him.

"Not yet. You're not strong enough."

"I am. I feel good." It wasn't a lie. The sex and the blood had chased away the remaining ache. I grabbed the nape of his neck and pulled while tipping my head to give him access.

He pressed his lips to my throat but didn't bite.

"Please, Rick. I don't want the last set of teeth in my neck to be Julius's."

For a moment, he hesitated. Then, with a possessive growl, he struck. My flesh moved aside, accommodating his teeth. I stroked the back of his head as he drank from me.

20

THE BOOK OF FLESH AND BONE

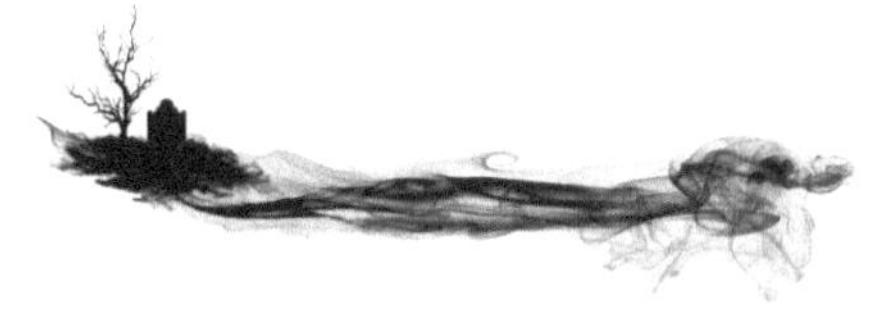

Several hours later, I changed into a heavy pair of Rick's sweats and allowed him to drive me home. Once he established the house was safe, he left, and I climbed the stairs to the attic to find Nightshade. I was done going out without her. Not with my face on Bathory's supernatural wanted posters.

As I turned the key in the lock and entered my most sacred abode, Poe dive-bombed me at the door, flapping black wings and squawking like a chicken. "Poe! What the hell?"

"Where have you been?" Poe demanded. "Your phone has been ringing off the hook. I can't answer it, you know." He waved a wing in the air. "No opposable thumbs. And some of the messages sounded quite urgent."

"I've been recovering at Rick's."

"Recovering? Is that what they call it these days? You do look better than the last time I saw you outside the Thames Theater. You were the color of death. I thought we might be worm fodder."

"We?"

"If you die, I die, remember?"

"Death sounds so permanent. Wouldn't it be more accurate to say we'd be recycled?"

He bobbed his black beak introspectively. "I'm not ready to be recycled, Miss Witch."

"Me neither. So, who left messages?"

"Your father, every day times three. Logan, my God that man needs a hobby, and your friend Michelle."

"I think the leprechaun who poisoned me stole my handbag. I'm sure they're just freaking out because I'm not answering my cell phone."

Poe flapped his wings and took off for the corner of the attic where I kept my trunk full of witchy paraphernalia. He grasped something in his talons and flew it over to me, dropping it in my hands.

"My purse!"

"I had to claw the little shit's face for it, but he was more interested in delivering you to the vampiress Bathory than keeping your bag."

I grabbed Poe by the shoulders and planted a huge kiss on the end of his beak. "Thank you, thank you, thank you!"

He chuckled, then cast me off with a ruffle of his feathers. "You realize you weren't this excited when I saved your life from the mountain troll? My God, what's in the bag? Rare, uncut diamonds?"

I reached in and retrieved my smartphone. The screen was cracked but still useable. "Better. My life, in digital form." The voicemail icon displayed a red number in the double digits. I jabbed it with my finger.

Damn! Logan sounded beside himself with worry, and Michelle was pissed. She'd covered a shift for me at the hospital. My father's real estate agent voice devolved into his father's voice and then to something I wasn't proud to be related to.

He'd tried pleading with me to call him again and again and bribing me with various apartments in the city (one of which was in Logan's building), until finally he left a message that the nekomata sale would close on Friday, December twentieth at ten in the morning. I'd have to be moved out by then.

"Shit, Poe. Julius told me the nekomata are waiting for the winter solstice. They need the energy of a celestial event to open the vault that the book is stored in, the one Julius thinks is under *this* house."

"The winter solstice happens December twenty-first."

"Exactly. What the fuck are we going to do?"

Poe didn't have the answers, but he did demonstrate a very un-birdlike behavior. He began to pace. "Can you ask your father to push back the closing?"

"We're not exactly on speaking terms." I tapped my foot nervously.

An exaggerated sigh told me what Poe thought of my excuse. "Might you consider a reunion, considering it is the fate of humanity at stake?"

"Of course, I'll ask him, Poe. I'm not stupid. I'm just saying that he might not be receptive. Especially not with Seraphina around."

"Who's Seraphina?"

"Dad's new girlfriend."

Poe fluttered over to the desk and rested his chin on the tips of his wings. "Do tell. Is she a bimbo?"

"I wish. No, she's gorgeous and intelligent, and as condescending as they come."

"Ahh."

"Anyway, she's got my dad on this kick that I should move closer to them. It's going to be a hard sell pushing back the date."

"Then we have to move the book," Poe said.

I spread my hands in frustration. "I told you, I don't know where the book is!"

"Not that book. *The Book of Light!* God help us if they obtain both of them. They'd be unstoppable."

"You're right. I'll ask Rick to guard it for me."

The raven groaned. "Bad idea."

"Why?"

"Rick's cottage is one story, right?"

"Yeah. You've been there before."

"Here's the rub, Spam-witch, if I'm not mistaken, your elemental power source is air. His is earth."

"Yeah, Rick may have mentioned that to me once before."

"You store *The Book of Light* in his stone cottage and you will literally be hiding your light under a bushel. It will render you powerless. Not advisable if Nekomata does get his hands on *The Book of Flesh and Bone*."

"Fuck. Where, then? Maybe I should have my father buy me that apartment in town."

Poe opened his beak to answer me when the doorbell rang. "Who might that be?"

It rang again. I blinked slowly and crossed my fingers. "Let's hope it's not Mr. Nekomata. I'm not sure I could spare the opportunity to kill him." Just in case, I grabbed Night-shade from her space near the wall before jogging down the stairs. I checked the side window first and breathed a sigh of relief before opening the door.

"Logan—"

"Jesus H. Christ, Grateful. How could you do this to me?" His face was red.

"Hello, Logan. Nice to see you again. Please, come in."

He was not amused. He paced into the house, fuming. "You storm out of my office, disappear before I can catch up to you, and then don't answer your phone for two days? I thought you were dead in a ditch somewhere!"

I stared at him, mouth agape, never having seen him so angry.

"Well? What happened?" He spread his hands expectantly.

"I was poisoned by a leprechaun and taken prisoner by a crazy-ass vampire named Anna. She's looking for *The Book of Flesh and Bone*. Seems your mother's ghost was right about that one. Then Julius abducted me from the dungeon where Anna tortured me. When I didn't give him what he wanted, he drained me of most of my blood. Rick and Poe saved me just in time. I've been recovering at Rick's the last two days."

Logan's forehead wrinkled. "My God, that was way worse than the ditch."

Dropping my chin, I stared at the one piece of good news I'd gotten today. "Poe was able to rescue my phone." I held up the electronic device. "Screen's cracked but I can get it fixed at the kiosk in the mall."

He bobbed his head. "So, it wasn't a complete loss."

A slaphappy chuckle machine-gunned out of my mouth, fueled by a combination of nervous energy and relief. "I know this must sound incredibly ridiculous, but it's my life and the honest truth."

"Oh, I know. I was part of it once, remember?" He took a step closer to me, reached for my elbow.

As his hand approached, I jerked back. I didn't mean to, at least not in such an obvious way, but something had happened to me the night before. I'd given myself to Rick in a deeper way and made promises I had no intention of breaking. "Logan, we need to talk."

"That's readily apparent." His hand hung awkwardly in the air between us, and he grimaced at the arm I'd jerked away.

I sighed. "I'm with Rick."

With a roll of his eyes, he slid his hands into his jeans

pockets. "I know. He's your caretaker and you're his witch. You need each other to do what you have to do—"

"No." I shook my head. "It's more than that. I didn't understand at first. This isn't obligation or a shared history. It's more." I wasn't sure how much more, only that I wanted to find out. I owed it to Rick to give this a chance. I owed it to myself.

"I know you have feelings for me, Grateful. I didn't imagine the connection we shared."

"When you were a ghost? That was the soul sorter in me. We were naturally attracted to each other because I was supposed to help you move on."

"And now?"

"Friendship."

A low grunt punched from his chest. "You didn't kiss me like a friend."

I huffed defensively, hands moving to my hips. "I was high on leprechaun roofies! Believe me, I didn't know what I was doing."

"Bullshit."

"Excuse me?" Now I was pissed. Who was he to say what I was feeling?

He pointed a finger at the end of my nose. "The first hint of a fight with Rick and you came running to my apartment. Why did you do that, Grateful? Unless some part of you still feels something for me?"

"I do feel something for you. Friendship."

"Fuck!" All the color drained from his face, and his eyes fixated on the cabinets over my shoulder.

The disappointment must be eating the guy up. "It's gonna be okay, Logan. You'll meet someone else."

He glanced back at me, annoyed, and gestured over my shoulder with an open palm. "My mom is in your kitchen."

"She is?"

"She wants us to follow her."

I glanced over my shoulder but couldn't see anyone. Frustrating. "Lead the way."

With a curt nod, he followed the spirit to the door to my cellar. Why did everything creepy happen in the basement? I hated the basement.

He stopped at the bottom of the stairs. Between the wine cellar and us was an ancient looking pool table with a marble top. Logan paused for a moment, then turned back to me. "She says we need to move it."

"What? The pool table? That thing must weigh a ton."

"Come on, Hecate, put those magic muscles to work." He placed both hands on the corner of the table and lowered his shoulder.

"I guess when the ghost of your mom tells you to do something, you do it." I widened my eyes and dropped down into pushing position.

"On three. One…two…three."

Logan grunted, and I pushed with everything I had. The table moved about two inches. On his count, we pushed again and again. Finally, what Logan's mom had wanted us to see was right under our feet.

I didn't understand the ancient carvings that decorated the rectangle of stone we were standing on, but my whole body detected the magic. Dark magic. Demonic magic.

Freeing Nightshade from her sheath, I tried to wedge the blade in the seam and pry the vault open. *Crack!* A bolt of electricity blew me backward. I landed on my ass, sword in hand. "Ow!" I said, rubbing my tailbone. "It's testy."

"The Book of Flesh and Bone is there," Logan said. "And Mom's warning me, we are in grave danger."

21

GRAVE DANGER

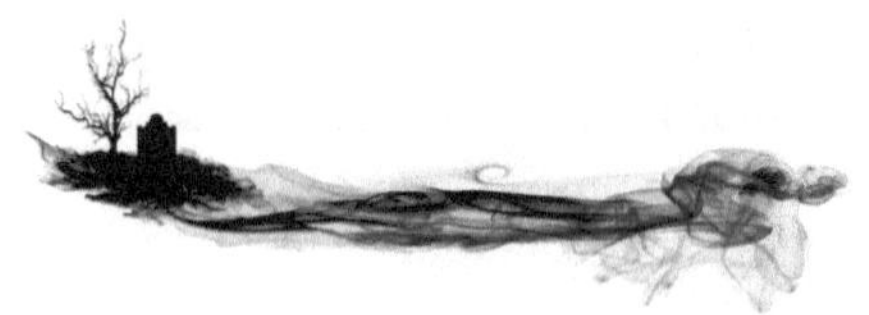

"Grave danger?" I raised eyebrows at Logan and broke into the type of laugh that starts out loud and then peters out when you run out of breath. I had to hug my knees to my chest. Tears formed in the corners of my eyes.

"What's so funny?"

I inhaled loudly. "Oh, come on! We are standing on top of *The Book of Flesh and Bone*. Satan's own wicked grimoire." I grabbed my shaking stomach. "And we're in a house next to a graveyard. *Grave* danger. Of course we're in *grave* danger. When am I ever not in *grave* danger!" The fit of laughter overcame me again. Could. Not. Breathe.

Logan's hands wrapped around my shoulders and shook. "Snap out of it. I don't think my mother meant it as a joke. What should we do?"

I got control of myself and pushed up from the floor, eyeing the symbols on the vault and trying to call on my emerging witchy instincts for direction. "Poe! Get down here," I yelled toward the stairs.

Flapping. The muffled thump of wings against wood. I was sure we'd left the door partially open but it sounded like he was struggling to fit through. A black streak passed by my face and landed on the leather pocket of the pool table. "Eww. The vibe down here is making me molt." He ruffled himself and a few stray black feathers cascaded to the floor. "What's under the stone, Witcherella?"

"Rumor has it, *The Book of Flesh and Bone*."

"Rumor has it from whom?" Poe fixed Logan with a beady black stare.

Logan stepped back. "The bird talks?"

"This is my familiar. His name is Poe."

"Yes. I am Poe, keeper of this witch, and I say, sir, that it seems a bit coincidental that you should know exactly where the book is."

"I—"

"Poe, he used to live in the attic as a ghost. Besides, he didn't actually know. It was his dead mother. He's a medium."

Poe flapped and plumped his breast skeptically. "Likely story. Can you see this so-called dead mother, Miss Witch? How do we know he's not possessed? Or a nekomata in disguise?"

"I'm not a demon!" Logan said, extending his hands to the sides. "Or a shapeshifter."

I scratched my jaw. "He came through the front door, Poe. He's not supernatural."

"Did you invite him in?"

Oh crap. I had invited him in. And come to think of it, I couldn't see the ghost of his dead mother, and it *did* seem rather coincidental that he knew just where to look. "Oh my God, Logan, are you a demon or a shifter?"

"No," he insisted as if the mere idea was ridiculous. "No!" he repeated more emphatically.

Poe hopped to my shoulder. "Prove it."

"How exactly am I supposed to prove it?" Logan's

outstretched hands balled into fists and came to rest on his hips.

I pulled out my phone and searched my database for a spell to detect supernatural beings. "Stay right there." I ducked into the downstairs bathroom and filled the empty soap dish with some water. When I returned, Logan looked more than a little put out. I held the dish toward him.

"Tip forward so that I can see your reflection in the water."

He hesitated for a second but indulged me. I placed my free hand on his head and repeated the phrase I'd learned from my spell database. "Ostendil mihil teipsme."

The water glowed cerulean blue then rippled from the inside out as if a teardrop had fallen from his face and landed at the center. When the rings settled, I could see his reflection clearly. It looked just like Logan, with the addition of a blue star glowing in the center of his forehead.

"See! He's one of them," Poe accused, pointing a talon toward Logan.

"Wait up, Poe. The spell said the supernatural would appear as shadows in the water. Logan's reflection is clear, aside from the star.

"What does that mean?"

"I think it's because he's a medium. He can channel and talk to the dead. That's all."

"You think? You're not sure." Poe narrowed his eyes.

"I'm sure he's not anything maleficent."

Logan stood straight, rubbing his head. "Can we move on, please? Honestly, if I was a demon, I'd have plowed over the flying rat and gotten the hell out of here while you were in the bathroom."

Poe's beak dropped open at the flying rat comment. He squinted his eyes at Logan. "I don't like you."

"Feeling's mutual."

In answer, I turned my back to them and stared at the symbols in the concrete. "Now that that's settled, how do we open this?"

Poe hopped down the table's edge to get a better view. "You can't. These symbols are ancient nekomata runes. It says it can't be opened until equinox on the winter solstice."

"Not even with magic?" I asked.

"No. It says when the sunlight hits the stone at midday of the solstice, the treasure will be revealed."

"We're inside. How does the nekomata expect sunlight to hit the stone?"

Logan looked over his shoulder at the sliding glass door to the backyard. "I saw a *Scooby-Doo* episode where the bad guy used a series of mirrors to reflect the light."

Poe stared at him incredulously. "Were you eating Fruity Pebbles at the time?"

"Hey, it's a viable alternative."

Poe squawked, "Perhaps we should entertain ideas from more reliable sources than Saturday morning cartoons?"

"It could happen, Poe." I shot the bird a warning glare. Why was he being such an asshole to Logan? "I wonder if this was why Mr. Nekomata said he wanted to bulldoze the house. Maybe he plans for the sun to reach this directly."

"Could he do that?" Poe asked, fluttering to my shoulder. "You said the sale closes on Friday, the day before the solstice. Could he bulldoze this place in a day?"

"It's hard for me to believe he could get a crew out here in the middle of winter on a Saturday. But I'm not ruling anything out."

Logan blew out an exaggerated breath. "Not to be an ass, but shouldn't we be trying to stop the closing? Best-case scenario, Nekomata never has the opportunity to shed light on the vault."

"I'll call my father back and beg. I'll come up with an

excuse. We should all be prepared though. I'm not the seller; my father is. Technically, he could sell it right out from under me."

Poe yanked my hair with his beak. "What father could deny his own little girl? A few tears and I'm sure he will accommodate you."

"I'll bawl my eyes out if it will keep Nekomata out of here until after the solstice."

"Good plan, my dear spell caster," Poe said. "However, as I mentioned before, it would be prudent of you to move *The Book of Light*. If all else fails, we will need it to manage the consequences."

That's right. I needed a place to hide the book, a place with enough air to enhance its magical properties and where it could be safe and protected in my absence. I couldn't keep it at Rick's and after what happened with Marcus the vampire a few weeks ago, I didn't want to involve Michelle. Which left only one person who could help me.

"Logan, I need to ask a favor of you."

"My mother is smiling and nodding her head. Whatever you are going to ask me, looks like I'm supposed to say yes."

AFTER LOGAN AGREED TO BABYSIT *THE BOOK OF LIGHT*, WE moved it to his condo, feeling like I was leaving my first-born baby in his home office. He wasn't completely keen on the idea. Fortunately, his mother's ghost persuaded him to go along with it. I spent the better part of the day laying protective spells around his place, something I'd wanted to do anyway. Nothing could come in without his invitation, aside from me. By the time I'd finished, the place was a magical Fort Knox.

"The front desk already has instructions to let you up, day or night, but here's a key."

I looked at the silver specimen he dangled in front of me. For some reason, the thought of having a key to his place made me uncomfortable. "I don't think I'll need my own key," I said. "This is only temporary."

"Are you kidding me? I'm gone most nights at the restaurant. If you need to get to the book, this is your only way in."

Reluctantly, I accepted the key, noticing the Valentine's emblem on the stainless steel keychain. The engraving was of an artistically designed heart pierced by Cupid's arrow, only the point was actually a spoon and the feathers, a fork pointing in the opposite direction. *Valentine's* was scrawled across the artwork.

I turned the key over in my palm. "I know this might be awkward for you."

"You mean because I basically threw myself at you and you turned me down." He rubbed the back of his neck.

I locked my eyes on the toes of my boots. "Uh, yeah. Listen, I'm sorry about that, Logan. I never meant to lead you on or to hurt you."

He took a deep breath. "You didn't. Not really. What happened between us, when I was corporeally challenged, caught us both off guard. I guess it just meant more to me."

"What happened between us, when you were a ghost, was an accident. I didn't understand the source of our attraction, and I let things get out of hand."

The dejected look on his face had me walking for the door.

"This won't be for long." I held up the key. "I'll be out of your hair in no time."

"I like you in my hair."

I stopped at his front door and turned to face him, squirming under the pressure of the moment. "It's not that the night we shared didn't mean anything to me, Logan. It did and you do. We shared a connection when you lived in my house, and I'll always cherish those days. But while I like and respect you, even love you in some ways—"

"In some ways?"

"It's as a friend. You are a dear, dear friend. And it would kill me to lose you from my life. But I'm...I..." God, I wasn't sure I could say it.

"You love him," he offered.

I cleared my throat. Logan was the wrong person for me to say this to, especially the first time. "My affections are spoken for...and happily so."

He nodded. Met my eyes. I said my goodbyes and headed for home.

THE DOGHOUSE

On my way back to Red Grove, I tried to call my father to begin the supplicatory process for a later closing date. He didn't answer his phone, an oddity for my super real estate agent dad. Usually, he could sign papers, show a house, and answer his phone simultaneously. Hell, I had suspicions that he answered his cell on the toilet.

And that's when my anxiety really took off. What if Anna Bathory had gotten her hands on him to get to me? Julius said the nekomata and the vampires were sworn enemies. The nekomata were close to obtaining the book, which would mean Anna was desperate. My dad might be strung up in her dungeon at that very moment. Or drained by Julius! Worse, what if either one of them compelled him to do something really drastic, like jump off a bridge or be used at the Mill Wheel by any female vamp who wanted him? I started to sweat thinking he might be dead or permanently missing. Why hadn't I thought to give him some sort of protective charm while I could?

When the phone did ring, I snatched it up so fast I swerved into the opposite lane. "Dad?"

"Um, excuse me. I'm trying to reach Grateful Knight?"

"This is," I said. I recognized the voice but couldn't place it.

"It's Silas, Detective Silas Flynn."

"Oh, Silas. What's up?"

"Unfortunately, I'm calling on official business related to the crime scene at Maison des Étoiles." I pictured the were-wolf in my mind. I'd seen him at Valentine's but voices always sounded different to me over the phone. I'd completely forgotten I'd given him my number, and that he'd promised to call with information on the finfolk and mountain troll attack.

"I traced the finfolk back to a community living in Red Grove Lake. The finfolk king claims he knew nothing of the perpetrators' plans. I expected as much. No supernatural in their right mind would admit a connection."

"Uh-huh."

"But here's the interesting thing, Grateful. He claims there've been nightmares in the area. Became a little flustered just talking about it. A few of his people have gone missing and he blames them. He believes our perpetrator was possessed by one and didn't know what he was doing."

"I had a woman come into my ER possessed by one. She was infected at Red Grove Lake. Sounds like we have an epidemic on our hands."

"Do you know much about them? We've never encountered this problem before on the force. Normally, nightmares are a mild annoyance to humans, not a threat," Silas said.

"You know about as much as I do. A magical entity has to be facilitating the possessions. Nightmares can't do that on their own. Any idea who might be helping them?"

"None."

"Did you find out about the troll? Was he a victim as well?"

"We can only assume. The trolls were…uncooperative. I couldn't get any information out of the community and narrowly avoided becoming a lot thinner under one of their clubs."

"Ah. But given the trolls' natural tendency to avoid humans, it would fit the profile."

"I was thinking the same thing."

"What can I do to help, Silas? What are your next steps?"

"Since you live in the area, would you mind investigating again at Red Grove Lake, maybe seeing if you can find where the nightmares are organizing?"

"They're incorporeal. My understanding is they have to go back to the netherworld during the day unless they've possessed someone."

"Exactly. With this type of activity, I wouldn't be surprised to learn they're congregating in that region, a mass possession. You mentioned the human was possessed at the lake. Did you ever find out why she was there?"

"No. It's not a popular tourist attraction, especially in winter."

"Can you investigate? See if you can find out why she was there and when she became possessed. Maybe look for signs of a nightmare settlement."

"Of course."

"Good. I'd do it myself but I'm going to be indisposed for a few days. Full moon."

"Oh. I thought when you were dating Soleil—"

"That I didn't have to change unless I wanted to? That's true. Her sunlight can keep the moon away. A fortunate advantage of our mating."

"Then why—"

"She hasn't returned my calls. When I call the Maison, the girls tell me she's busy and can't be disturbed. I guess you could say I'm in the doghouse." He chuckled, but I could tell it wasn't remotely funny to him.

"I'm sorry. I thought you two made a cute couple."

"Yeah, me too. Such is love." He cleared a lump from his throat, and we said our goodbyes.

I tossed my phone into the cupholder, thinking about how I'd never gotten the chance to ask Rick how he'd found the woman. But I didn't stop when I reached his stone cottage. I was too worried about my dad. As I crossed over the stone bridge, I considered calling his office line and asking his secretary where he was. I'd never had to do that before and would have to look up the number.

Thankfully, when my house came into view, I could put aside my fears. My father was in my driveway, leaning against his car in the cold winter sunshine. Thank goodness. He was safe, and by the looks of it, extremely pissed.

* * *

"You are acting like a two-year-old," my father said, helping himself to the bottle of Scotch I kept in the little cabinet over the refrigerator for him.

"How could you say that? You sold my home right from under me. Take some accountability. I told you I wanted to buy it from you and you sold me out to the highest bidder. What kind of father does that?"

He poured the Scotch over ice from the freezer and sat down on a stool at my kitchen island, pulling off his gloves and hat. He was still wearing his coat. Lifting his glass, he said, "The kind of father who needs the money."

I narrowed my eyes at him. "Since when? You're one of the top real estate agents in the Carlton City area."

"You might have noticed the real estate market has been

in the toilet lately, Grateful. It's not just this property that isn't selling. Very few of my listings have sold in the last two years, especially the big-ticket properties in the city." He sipped his drink.

Arms crossed, I leaned against the sink and pouted in his direction. "Gary paid me back. I can give you sixty thousand in cash today, if you'll sell the house to me."

"Gary? Your ex-boyfriend? I thought he was dead or missing or something."

"You and me both. He showed up on my doorstep and paid me back everything he owed me, plus interest. So, I have the money."

His head swam back and forth on his shoulders. One well-manicured hand lifted to scratch his five o'clock shadow. "I'm sorry, Grateful. Contracts have been signed. Deposits made. I can't just undo it."

A dull ache was beginning at the base of my neck, a tension headache threatening to take over. I rubbed the spot with both hands. "I can't tell you why, Dad, but staying here is very important to me. I love this house. I love Red Grove. I have a new boyfriend who lives just up the street."

"Ah, so that's the real story. Why is it always about the boyfriend with you?"

Grrr. "It's not about the boyfriend. It's about me. I've built a life here."

The ice in his glass clinked together as he drained the last drops. He poured himself another. Geesh, at this rate I'd have to drive him home. He dug his fingers into his hair as if I was literally driving him insane.

"Is this house not positioned over a sinkhole?" he snapped.

I frowned. "Actually? No. I staged the rumble to scare your buyer away."

His mouth dropped open at my admission. "How did you do that?" He held up a hand. "Never mind. I don't want to know. What about the rat?"

"Same."

"Grateful!"

"I was desperate." I placed my hands on the counter and leaned forward. "Is there any way for me to buy it, Dad?"

"No."

Tears pricked at the corners of my eyes. "Can I ask you for one tiny concession, then?"

He propped his face against his palm and gave me an exasperated sigh. "Okay. What is it? I'll do my best."

"There is no way I can be packed and moved out of here by next Friday. Can you push back the closing?"

He pulled out his phone, looked at the screen as if he'd gotten an email, then started keying in something. I waited patiently. It was only my life in the balance. Couldn't he see how important this was to me?

"Done," he said.

"What?"

"I texted the buyer and said I had a personal emergency, could not make the closing on Friday, and we'd have to push it back. So, there you go."

I walked to his side of the counter and hugged him around the neck. "I'm sorry I acted the way I did. I should have called you back earlier."

"Darling, you have your father's temper. I should have spoken to you before I sold the house. But, in my defense, the last house I sold was also in Red Grove and over market value. This town is booming."

"You sold another house out here?"

"Yep." He pointed his thumb over his shoulder. "On the other side of the lake. Little cabin-in-the-woods style place off Route 3. Used to belong to Elmer…"

"Bishop?"

"Yeah."

"I bought my desk at his estate sale."

"You bought a desk? I thought you were broke?"

"I'm recovering. I really could have bought this house."

"Huh."

"Who bought Elmer's place?"

"Some woman, all by herself."

A tingle traveled from my toes to my scalp. "A woman by herself?"

"Yeah. She said she was into nature. Loved the lake. A writer I think, an introvert. Wanted time alone."

I swallowed hard and tried to find my voice. It took me a few tries to get out a suitable question. "You know, I think I heard about someone from work who was looking for a house. What did she look like?"

"Big woman. Not fat but like a shot-putter, you know, big boned. Brown, wavy hair. Not into makeup. Attractive in a natural way."

For a moment, I was sidetracked by the thought that my dad had found a shot-putter attractive. But then when I had seen her last, she'd been half-drowned and fully possessed.

I cleared my throat. "I know her from work. I think I'll stop by and bring her a house warming present. Do you remember her name? I keep forgetting it."

"Sure, honey. That would be kind of you. It's Avery Bane."

Dad was acting a little tipsy and a lot compliant. I was fairly sure he shouldn't have given me the name of his client. Probably a breach of privacy laws or something. His secret was safe with me.

What was Avery hiding in that house? Was she possessed before or after the sale? I didn't know, but I intended to find out. I needed to talk to Rick. Avery did have a reason to be at the lake after all; she lived behind it. So, who had tried to drown her?

"I should probably get a move on," my dad slurred. His head had drooped toward the counter and his eyes were rimmed red.

"Why? Is Seraphina keeping you on a short leash?"

He took a deep breath and exhaled through his nose. "I don't think it's going to work out between Seraphina and me."

I molded my face into the most surprised expression I could muster, fighting down the pure joy that threatened to expose itself. "Why?"

"She's just too young. Works all day and stays out half the night. It was fun while it lasted, but now she seems, I don't know, distracted. Not to mention, she's obsessed with knowing where I am at all times. Probably wigging out right now."

"She doesn't know you're here?"

"Hell no. I'm just waiting for the right time to let her down easy."

"So then, you can stay a little longer to…" I was going to say "sober up" but the face he gave me clearly indicated he would not be receptive to his daughter taking away his keys. I needed to be smart about this. "I have a movie I was going to watch, and I don't want to watch it alone." I put the bottle of Scotch away in the cabinet and retrieved a Coke from the fridge to replace it. "Would you mind hanging out for a couple of hours? It would mean a lot to me."

He fixated on the Coke, then lifted his eyes to mine. "What movie?"

"*Young Frankenstein.*"

"You've had that movie for years."

"Never a bad time to watch a classic. It's your favorite, right?"

He nodded slowly. I led him and his Coke into the family room and started the movie. He was asleep on my sofa before Igor retrieved the abnormal brain from the brain repository.

23

AVERY'S SECRET

As it so happened, Dad spent the night on my sofa. It was okay with me. I'd rather have him sleeping on my couch than dead on the side of the road. My dad drank but rarely to the point of being drunk. This slip was a sign that he was truly uncomfortable with what had transpired in his life recently. I could blame Seraphina for some of that, but I supposed I was also at fault. After just twenty minutes of him not answering his phone, I was ready to call in the brigade to find him. I'd gone a week without returning his calls. He'd acted angry when he walked in my door, but as I watched him sleeping on my couch, I wondered if worry was what tipped his glass one too many times.

We ate a quiet breakfast together, not talking about my soon-to-be homelessness or his overindulgence. With a big hug, I sent him back out into the world, forgiven, and drove myself to work. I was lucky to have my job after dropping off the face of the earth while I was recovering. I owed Michelle, big time.

After a long morning in the ER treating the latest flu epidemic, I texted her to see if I could take her to lunch as a thank you. She agreed and met me in the back parking lot, outside the hospital.

"Valentine's?" she asked.

I shook my head. "I think I'm off Valentine's for a while."

"No. No! Come on, Grateful, the only other place within lunch radius of the hospital is Aunt Bee's and we'll be bumping into the octogenarian dinner crowd. Are things between you and Logan so bad?"

"No…yes… Just awkward right now. But Logan's not who I'm worried about."

Michelle stopped our journey to my Jeep and made a gimme motion with her hand.

"Remember that short redheaded nerd you told to move?"

"Yeah."

"Leprechaun. Drugged me, then kicked my ass."

She inhaled sharply. "What? Oh my God, did he go postal over the barstool thing? I'm so sorry, Grateful. I wouldn't have been so rude if I'd known he was a super or if I'd been less drunk."

"No. Nothing to do with you, actually. The little shit had my number. Get in the car. I'll tell you the story on the way to Aunt Bee's."

Ten minutes later we were nestled in a brass-accented booth with toile fabric seats, having ordered French toast and crepes because the lunch options waxed geriatric. As predicted, we were the youngest people in the place. I eyed the curly white head of the woman at the table across the aisle. She raised her floral teacup in greeting. When she smiled, I noticed she was only wearing her top teeth.

"The special today is stewed prunes," Michelle said flatly.

"Okay. I'll try to get over my fear of Valentine's. But you do know my bloodstain is still visible in the parking lot."

"Maybe you can make the restaurant safer with a spell."

"Good idea. I'll run it past Logan."

"So, what are going to do about your house?"

"Dad says I have to move out next Wednesday. I haven't found a new place yet. I don't suppose you would have an extra room or attic…"

Her cheeks contorted back toward her ears, showing teeth but not in a smile. What was that expression? Somewhere between surprise and getting a whiff of a really bad smell. "I'm so sorry, Grateful, but Manny's mother is staying with us right now."

"What? I hadn't heard."

"Just moved in last night. She's divorcing Manny's dad."

"Haven't they been married for like fifty years?"

"Yes. The whole thing is kind of silly. She says the romance is dead. She's seventy-six years old. How alive is the romance supposed to be?"

The waitress plopped my French toast in front of me and topped off my coffee. I cast an irritated glare toward the cup and tried not to direct my ire at the unwitting waitress. How could she know she'd touched on a hot button, a major pet peeve. She'd completely upset my coffee-sweetener-cream ratio. Now there was too much coffee, but I had no way of knowing what percentage of sugar and cream to add to even it out because I hadn't looked to see how much was left in the cup.

"What is wrong with your face? You look like you're having a stroke," Michelle said.

"She totally changed my coffee chemistry. Now I won't get it right again until I start over."

Michelle swallowed a bite of strawberry crepe while I fussed over my cup. After a few experimental additions, the color was right and the taste was close. I moved the cup to the other side of the table so the waitress couldn't top it off without reaching over me.

"When did you become so anal about your coffee?"

"Always. I actually prefer it with cinnamon. Rick always makes mine with cinnamon."

Her eyebrows shot up. "Your relationship has evolved to morning-after breakfast preparation?"

I played with the paper wrapper of my sweetener packet. "Actually, yes, but he's always known how I liked my coffee. He knows stuff about me I am just figuring out about myself. And he's so selfless about our relationship. I haven't given him enough credit."

For a moment, I entered a trancelike state thinking about my encounter with Rick in the shower. The next time I came into the present moment, half my French toast was gone.

"Huh." Michelle had finished her crepes and leaned back against her seat, arms crossed. "I didn't see this coming."

"See what coming?"

"You're in love with him."

I tried not to react to the word but jerked a little anyway. My mind had been dancing around the "L" label for a few days, but I wasn't ready to say it and even if I was, some part of me knew that Michelle was not the right person to say it to, not the first time. I shrugged impassively.

"Hmm. I see."

"What do you see?" I finished my coffee and stared at the swirly stain the brew left at the bottom of the mug. An uninvited thought stormed into my brain; my soul was the cup and Rick was the stain. Had he marked me before or after my cup was filled with this life? Funny, I always thought my soul was inside my body, but suddenly, like the illumination of a freshly flipped light switch, I could see that my soul was the greater part of myself, the cup, and this life was the coffee. Rick had kept the cup safe to fill again and again and again, his presence leaving an indelible mark on every cup, changing the chemistry.

"Grateful!"

"Uh, what?"

"Where are you going to live?"

"I'm not sure."

"Hmm. Based on the empirical evidence, I'd say you should ask Rick. I'm pretty sure he'd house more than your disembodied soul."

Warmth flooded my chest at her suggestion. Yes, that was exactly what I would do.

* * *

THE ER WAS OVERSTAFFED THAT AFTERNOON AND I WAS LET off early. I wanted to stop and talk to Rick, to ask him if I could stay with him until I had a chance to find my own place and to tell him about Avery and my house. But I reached Red Grove as the sun began its descent. I had maybe an hour of daylight left and I wanted to investigate Avery's house before dark. I giggled a little thinking I was going in search of nightmares. There was something irrational about that statement, like running into a burning building.

Then again, in Red Grove irrational was the new black.

Nightshade hummed in her sheath on my back as I rounded the lake on Route 3 and came upon the cottage that used to be Elmer Bishop's. A car was in the unshoveled driveway, snow heaped around and on top of it. I parked in the street and walked toward the house through the knee-deep snow, unmarked by any other set of footprints. I presumed Avery had set off on foot to the lake behind the house, which was why the car was left. No one knew she was dead. She'd come into the ER without any identification. I was hoping her residence would be exactly as she left it and give me some clue to understanding her predicament.

I decided to start by walking around the periphery of the house to get a good understanding of what I was dealing with, in case the house was still occupied by humans or something else. A light shone from the kitchen window, illuminating a half circle of snow in the twilight. I edged along the woods, taking coverage in the trees while positioning myself to best see behind the glass.

Inside, a small pine table was topped with a vase of dried flowers. A painting of a basket of vegetables nailed to the pale yellow wall above the table was emblazoned with the phrase *Give Peas a Chance* in old-fashioned letters. I could see the faucet of a white porcelain sink and the back of a hand-worn wooden chair. After several minutes of watching the kitchen through the window, I took a step forward, only to retreat when a shadow cut through my line of sight.

I ducked behind a leafless maple and watched a man walk to the sink and wash his hands. His deep-set eyes flicked up. I tucked myself more completely behind the trunk. He wasn't a vampire, that was for sure; he didn't have the nocturnal features and there was a blush of windburn on his cheeks, a condition the undead didn't suffer. But he wasn't exactly human. As he lathered his hands, his muscles rolled beneath his skin as if he had extra joints at the wrist, elbow, and shoulder. Almost catlike.

The man disappeared. I picked my way carefully from tree to tree until I could see inside the main area of the house. Mr. Nekomata! The man who was buying my house was sitting in the brown recliner, the light from the TV giving his parchment yellow skin a blue glow. Of course his name wasn't really Mr. Nekomata. Nekomata was the type of creature he was, and I realized the rest of them were too. This was a nekomata clan. I could make out a female, the male from the kitchen, and the older male who had toured my house.

Now I was confused. I pressed a finger to my lips and flipped the happenings of the last weeks over in my brain.

The woman who'd lived here had definitely been human, possessed by a nightmare. I'd seen the black vapor pour out of her body firsthand. The creatures inside Avery's house? Not human. What was the relationship? Was Avery possessed before or after the nekomata moved in? If before, did that mean the nekomata and the nightmares were working together? There were no tracks coming or going from the house. With the recent snow, all that meant was they'd been in the house a couple of days.

I allowed the forest to swallow me, backing into the protection of the trees as I tried to put the puzzle pieces together. The sun had completely set, opening the door to the chill of night, and I hugged my parka around me. On instinct, I moved toward the lake, retracing the steps the woman must have taken through the trees. Maybe the finfolk would give me, or Nightshade, answers they wouldn't give Silas.

Odd. When I arrived at the shore, the lake was frozen over. I stared at the white sheet of ice in confusion. How had Silas interviewed finfolk? Were they living under the ice? Did they come through it? I shuffled to the edge. The snow was deep here, past my knees, making it hard to move. By the light of the full moon, I tried to discern any movement. Legend said finfolk lured their victims into the water. I was prepared to be lured, but nothing caught my eye.

Nightshade was quiet in her sheath on my back, but I drew her anyway to see if she could sense anything supernatural. I passed the blade over the ice. Nothing. Had they all left? Had the nekomata driven them off?

Snap. I twisted toward the woods. I was in the middle of nowhere, the skeleton-bare deciduous trees of Red Grove forest hugging tightly to the evergreens and blocking out the moonlight. I couldn't see two feet into the trees. A rustle came from a distance to my left. I turned. Nightshade flickered to life, her pale blue glow intensely beautiful against the snow.

The wind picked up. I shivered. I wasn't scared; I was cold. I'd been outside much too long, and the temperature was dropping fast. I had to get out of here or I'd be risking frostbite. Hoping to flush whatever it was out, I took a few steps in the direction I'd come. I lost my balance in a particularly deep drift and tripped forward, Nightshade plunging into the bank in front of me. I did not immediately rise but waited, listened.

My ploy worked. A black beast tore from the trees with an impressive growl. I didn't waste time analyzing if the flash of fang, fur, and claw was bear, wolf, or demon. My hand gripped Nightshade's hilt. With a wail I cut through the snow, exploding forward just as the beast's claws swiped for my head. Nightshade arced into the beast's side, my hand following through to strike the creature off its trajectory. At the same time, I ducked, sparing my head for another day.

The thing yelped and curled into a furry heap near the ice. I approached with caution, Nightshade glowing brighter as I neared so I could see clearly. A wolf. A great, black wolf constructed of long sinewy muscle that couldn't be mistaken for a common dog. I'd sliced it from belly to shoulder, but the wound itself wasn't what had incapacitated the creature. Nightshade's enchantment had a greater effect than her slash.

The beast twitched. I lowered the point toward the ribs, prepared to run it through. Black smoke oozed out the wound and curled around my blade, a wicked screech echoing through the night. It twisted vigorously, caught in Nightshade's enchantment. A nightmare! The wolf was possessed!

"I sentence you to eternity in Monk's Hill Cemetery," I proclaimed.

With one last shriek, the thing twisted into itself and blinked to the hellmouth prison I'd condemned it to. As soon as it was gone, the wolf seized, foaming at the mouth and bending into an unnatural and painful-looking arch. I thought about putting it out of its misery. But before I could think too hard about what was happening, the muscles twisted and the bones broke.

By the light of my blade, Silas Flynn took shape at my feet.

24

AWAKENING

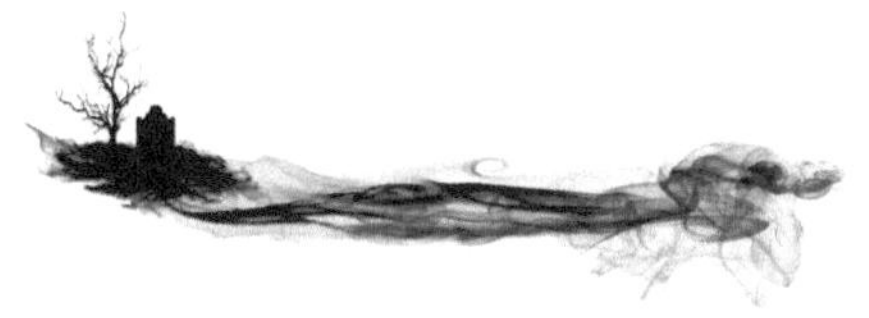

"Silas?" I dropped to my knees in the snow and pressed both hands over the wound, trying to stop the blood flow. "Shit."

Flapping wings turned my attention skyward. Rick. His beast landed on the bank behind me, his gossamer wings blowing up powder. The only gentle feature on the beast was his face. Doglike with large black eyes and a leather-like snout, he lowered his head next to me.

"Don't change back, Rick. I need your help getting Silas to your place. He was possessed. If we can heal him, he might be able to give us more information about how this happened."

The beast snorted his acquiescence.

I sheathed Nightshade and gathered the werewolf into my arms. Lifting that kind of weight would have been impossible before I was the witch, but super-strength came with the job. I still had physical limitations, but my abilities hovered around Olympic athlete rather than couch potato nurse.

With some effort, I climbed onto Rick's back, cradling Silas in one arm and gripping a tuft of hair with the other.

Three running steps and he was airborne, flying low over the treetops until his stone cottage came into view. Conscious of my tentative grasp, the beast landed in the front yard. I dismounted and carried Silas inside, laying him gently on the sofa.

A moment later, a naked Rick followed through the open door and came to my side. "How did this happen, *mi cielo*? What were you doing in the woods without me?"

"I was investigating that woman's house, the drowning victim I thought you left for me last week. Her cottage is teeming with nekomata, including the one who bought my house from my father."

"Bought your house? You cannot sell your house. There could be horrific consequences."

I widened my eyes sarcastically. "No kidding." I should have told him what was going on before, but he was MIA and then I was injured. "Get me a balm for this wound and I'll explain."

He left for the kitchen and came back a moment later with a gooey concoction of herbs and a roll of gauze. As I ladled the stuff on Silas, I explained about the detective calling me to check out Avery's house and how that had turned out.

"Who is this Avery person?" Rick asked.

"The woman who died in the ER last week. She coughed up a nightmare when she died. I thought you sent her."

"I did no such thing, *mi cielo*. I left town after our argument about Gary's turning to obtain a magical object that I thought could help our situation. I did not return until Poe came to get me."

"But your kitchen floor was wet when Poe and I came by."

Rick thought for a moment. "The snow. The night I left, I'd tracked it in with me. I left quickly and didn't clean up after myself."

"Oh. But if you didn't find her, who did? No one has access to the lake except you and… Oh, the nekomata! You didn't leave the woman for me to find, they did. They were sending me a calling card."

Rick rested his hands on his hips, calling attention to his naked flesh in a way that caused my blood to heat even though my arousal was completely inappropriate to the situation. I closed my eyes, took a deep breath, and turned my attention back to Silas's wounds.

"Why? If the nekomata want to obtain the book, they should be avoiding your wrath until the solstice."

"I don't know." I felt for Silas's pulse. He was breathing but his heartbeat was weak. "It's clear the nightmares want me dead. They used Silas to lure me to Red Grove Lake and tried to kill me. I don't think there were ever finfolk in those waters. It was a trap."

"Finfolk?" Rick shook his head. "Not in these waters. You are lucky to be alive. Werewolves are deadly."

"I had Nightshade drawn, trying to find the finfolk. Otherwise, it might be me on the couch."

Back and forth, I paced in front of the television I'd never seen Rick use even once, rubbing the palms of my hands together. "Let's say the nekomata and nightmares are working together. They must be since the nekomata have overtaken Avery's home. The nekomata wanted a place close to the book to case the area, so they made a pact with the nightmares to possess Avery and cause her death, thus leaving the house for their purposes."

"Sounds plausible."

"Part of me thinks they tried to kill me because my father pushed back the closing, but Silas requested that I investigate Avery's house before I talked to my father."

"Which means they wanted you dead regardless of the sale."

"Exactly. When I was his prisoner, Julius said Anna would have killed me, thinking my death would break the enchantment around the house. It could be the nekomata are making the same presumption. If I'm dead, they don't have to worry about the technicalities around the sale."

"Agreed."

I faced him and swallowed hard. "But beyond that, my death would make things…easier. Closing or no closing, you and I are the thorn in their sides. We are not going to allow them anywhere near that book, no matter what. They tried to take me out of the equation."

Silas moaned. We both rushed to his side. After shaking him gently and calling his name, it was clear he wasn't waking up, although his pulse beat steadily against my fingers.

"He seems stronger. Maybe when he's conscious he'll tell us what we're missing." I stared at Silas, willing his eyes to open.

Rick's fingers stroked my hair, and I turned my cheek into his palm. Our eyes met. I came unglued. The stress of the day poured out of me in the form of tears I'd been hoarding for days, and I threw my arms around him, hiding my face in the crook of his neck.

"I will protect you, *mi cielo*." The thick muscles of his arms wrapped around me and his lips pressed into my forehead.

I pulled away. "Fuck, my car! I left it on the road near the cabin. Will you fly over to get it for me? I don't want the nekomata to know I'm on to them."

He nodded, eyes lowering to his naked body as he spread his hands. "Still dressed for work."

With a reassuring smile, he disappeared out the door, and I took a seat on the floor near the sofa, watching the rhythmic rise and fall of Silas's chest.

* * *

I came awake to Rick shaking my shoulder. "Your car is here. You should go home and sleep."

In a half-awake fog, I reached for him, noticing he was fully dressed but his eyes were still black, a sign he'd recently shifted. I ran my hand down the vee of his button-down, hooked my fingers over the first button, and pulled him toward me. Instead of accepting my kiss, he stood up.

"What's wrong?" I asked.

"I am afraid recent events have left me drained."

"I can help you with that," I purred, standing in such a way that I was flush against his chest.

"This time I need sleep, and so do you. Tomorrow is the solstice. It's important I am rested." His voice was firm and cold as ice. "I will call you if Silas wakes."

"You don't have a phone."

"I'll use our connection. You will be home?"

"Yes."

Skeptically, I stared at him. Rick wasn't himself. He'd never turned down an invitation for sex. I'd thought we were growing closer but he seemed distant and aloof. "Okay," I whispered. "I'll see you tomorrow then. We should be vigilant, just in case."

He nodded.

I turned and began a slow, even walk toward the door but stopped short of opening it.

"Rick, are you sure there's nothing wrong? You don't seem yourself."

"Maybe I am more myself than ever. I want to give you what you need, Grateful. I want to give you choices."

"What's that supposed to mean?"

He scrubbed his face with his hands, suddenly looking

weary. "I need my rest. You need yours. When the book is safe, we will talk."

Why did this feel like a brush-off? I twisted the knob and let myself out, my chest heavy with longing, not just for sex but for the closeness we'd shared when he was caring for me. What had happened over the last, I looked at my watch, *two hours*? Why had it taken Rick two hours to get a car parked less than a twenty-minute walk away? And he could fly.

I climbed in behind the wheel of my Jeep, keys dangling from the ignition, and spaced out at the wheel for a minute. Was it possible that Rick was possessed? Had a nightmare caught up to him in the woods and taken control? He called me *Grateful*; he only did that when he was angry. If he wasn't angry, maybe he was possessed. *Shit!* If they could possess Silas, they could possess Rick. Could I trust him tomorrow?

Nightshade poked into my back as I straightened in my seat. She would know. I climbed back out, prepared to storm into Rick's house and shove my blade into his face. I had to know he was the only soul in his body. I paused when the glint of metal on the passenger's side floor caught my eye. I rounded the car, opened the door, and reached for the crushed metal object. It took me a minute to figure out what it was, but the key hanging off the little chain was a major clue. The crushed Valentine's logo now looked like a piece of gum, chewed up and spit out.

Ugh, Rick was jealous! He'd seen the Valentine's logo and based on the story about losing my house, he probably assumed I was planning to live with Logan. I had to set him straight. All along, I'd been planning to live with Rick. I just hadn't had the chance to ask him.

I rushed toward the door, knocked lightly. There was no answer. I tried the knob. Locked. He never locked his door. I knocked again. "Rick?"

Nothing.

With a deep breath, I took a step back, and then another, until I was back at my Jeep. After seeing what he'd done to the keychain, maybe he legitimately needed his space. Besides, before I broached this subject with Rick again, I had to be sure exactly what I wanted to say. After years of failed relationships and suffering from the blonde paradox, I'd sworn the next time I said *I love you* it would mean forever.

And a night like tonight was not the right time to start forever.

25

KNIGHT AND DAY

I went to bed with the curtains open, my eyes fixed on the silver white circle of the moon through the naked branches of the tree outside my window. I did not sleep. My mind played an endless loop of warnings. Protect the book. Move. Tell Rick you love him. Stop the nekomata and the nightmares. Kill Bathory. Beware Julius. Rinse and repeat.

Poe landed on the branch nearest my window, tossing a mouse into the air before swallowing it whole. He tapped his beak against the glass, and I reached over to open the window and let him in, shutting out the blast of icy air that followed him into the room.

"Must be hard to sleep with your eyes open," he said. "Something keeping you up?"

I told him about Silas and what I saw at Avery's house. "Where were you?" I asked him. "As my familiar, aren't you supposed to sense when I'm in distress and come to my aid?"

"Sure, if I know you're on witchy business, but you hadn't come home from work. I thought some human was giving up their ghost in the ER, so I didn't respond."

"Nice, Poe."

"Hey, you wouldn't want me flying into the hospital windows every time your heart raced during the day. If you want me on the job, give me a heads-up."

Harrumph. I crossed my arms over my chest and stared at the ceiling. Why in the world did the woman in the garden give me a raven as a familiar?

"Do I need to remind you that I saved you from the troll and delivered Rick to rescue you from Julius? It's not as if I haven't earned my keep."

"Sorry, Poe. You're right. I should have stopped home and got you before I went to Avery's."

He waved his wing. "Exactly my point."

"Can I ask you something?"

"Sure." He hopped from the windowsill to my nightstand.

"Who was the woman who gave you to me? The one in the garden?"

Poe cracked his beak in a movement I'd come to interpret as a smile. "Hecate, goddess of the dead, otherwise known as Santa Muerte depending on where you are in the world, and a host of other names. She's your first mother and the source of your power."

I closed my gaping mouth and raised my eyebrows. "Truly? That was her?"

"Yes."

"And you, like, hang out with her when I'm dead?"

"Something like that. She remakes me each time for you, but a part of me is always with her." He nested down next to my lamp.

"Why a raven? Why did she think I needed you, Poe?"

He twitched, blinking his eyes.

"Sorry. No offense. I like you a lot; I'm just wondering why you weren't a cat or an owl."

"I don't know for sure, but I can tell you my honest opinion."

"I want to know."

"Cats are for manifestations who need independence. A cat won't come when you call it. It will help you only when it comes to respect you." He paused, taking me in. "You didn't need independence."

"No?"

"No. An owl is for manifestations who need wisdom or common sense. An owl familiar is perfect for an uneducated lass trying to make it in the world. You are not uneducated, nor lacking in wisdom."

I smiled. "I'd like to think I'm smarter than the average witch."

He nodded. "Ravens, on the other hand, are given to those who lack self-worth. A raven will intervene only when a witch can't do something herself, and then only when she decides what to do. I will tease you within an inch of your life, and I will expect you to take care of yourself. I will also make you brave and strong, trusting in your intuition. I'll challenge you to know what you want and to take it. A raven as a familiar will make you a *warrior*."

"Are you saying I have low self-worth?"

"I'm not saying anything. Don't shoot the messenger, m'kay? But since we've met, have you done more on your own?"

I thought about that. "I guess I have."

"And do you know what you want?"

My head immediately filled with images of Rick. "I think I do."

Poe shook his head and coughed. "Don't think, know!"

"Okay, I do! I know what I want."

He met my eyes. "And do you feel you are worthy of what you want?"

I searched Poe's face and my innermost thoughts. "Yes. I'm worth it. I deserve Rick. I deserve this house. Gary wasn't my fault and neither was the financial situation he put me in. I'm a great witch, Poe."

"Very good." He hopped back to the windowsill. "Then I was the right familiar for you, after all. Big day tomorrow. I recommend you get some sleep." He tapped on the glass.

I obliged by partially opening the window again. "Thanks, Poe."

"Don't mention it."

* * *

Bono's croon of "Mysterious Ways" popped my eyes open. My ringtone. I pried the phone from my bedside charger; the screen read eleven a.m. My heart started to palpitate. How had I slept so late? One hour until the winter solstice and I still had sheet marks on my cheek!

My dad's face filled the screen, his real estate agent smile promising unicorns and rainbows. I punched the screen and brought the phone to my ear. "Dad?"

"Grateful, I'm glad I caught you."

"What's up?"

"I just wanted to give you a heads-up. Mr. Nekomata is going to stop by the house this afternoon. He was completely fine with you living there another week, but he wants to survey the property."

"Wait. What? Today is not a good time, Dad."

"He said it would only take a few minutes."

"Call him back and tell him he needs to come a different day. Today is bad for me. Very, very bad." My heart was threatening to jump out of my mouth. Down deep, my intuition was playing a dirge, throwing up caution flags like confetti.

"Nekomata is a very busy man, Grateful, and it is his house now."

207

Across the inside of my arms and down my sides, a prickling sensation scampered like an army of tiny bugs had invaded my skin. I forced myself to swallow before confirming what I knew to be true. "You sold the house."

"Don't worry, honey, I got it in writing that you have permission to stay there a few more weeks."

"But you sold it. The house is no longer legally yours."

"Correct. We closed this morning. The paperwork is still being processed, but he effectively owns the house."

"Oh, Dad. Why? Why!" I screamed into the phone, but I knew, the nekomata would make it impossible for him to deny them. If they couldn't convince him the human way, they would simply have a nightmare possess him, like Avery. Nothing was going to stop these guys from reaching the book, especially not a human man.

Silence. Our call was still connected, but Dad didn't respond to my screaming. After a few awkward moments, he finally said, "I'm sorry. If it makes you feel more comfortable, Seraphina is with him. You won't be alone with a strange man in the house."

"Seraphina? Why would Seraphina be with him?" I thought my Dad was breaking up with her, not sending her out with clients.

"She's his niece, Grateful. That's how we met."

A series of images seized me, causing my fist to clench around the phone. Her superhuman beauty and grace, the way she made my chest tighten. How could I have missed it? Seraphina was a nekomata. The whole time, she wasn't interested in my father, she was interested in making sure he sold my house.

"I've got to go, Dad," I mumbled.

"Call me when you're ready to look at apartments." He hung up on me without saying goodbye.

Okay, I probably deserved that. After all, Dad didn't

understand that he might have signed my death certificate. He was just doing his job.

I needed a plan. Every cell in my body pinged against my skin in warning. My heart raced. My palms broke out in a cold sweat. Coping skills first, plan second. I took a deep breath in and let it out slowly to the count of three. And again, slow breath. I wiped my mind of every thought and simply listened to my breath. Once I was in control, I focused on the task at hand.

Priority one, determine if the protective enchantment around the house was still in place. I tapped my *The Book of Light* app and searched for a spell to detect enchantments. Thankfully, the magic was there; Michelle and I had made it past "E."

With one last deep breath to steel my nerves, I stripped out of my pajamas, fetched Nightshade from the corner, and strapped her to my back. Then I dressed like a ninja, black stretchy pants, military boots, long-sleeved black shirt with a large neck to give me access to my blade.

I rushed from the room, stopping in the attic for some things from my chest. Salt, silver bowl, a sprig of St. John's wort. Down to the kitchen. One part salt, one part lemon juice, a drop of my blood, a cracked egg with the yolk broken by my blade. I placed the bowl next to the front door. When nothing happened, I opened the door and placed it on the threshold. The yolk of the egg swam a little in the concoction, reaching for my drop of blood. It didn't mix with the spot of red, but surrounded it. I checked my app, then gawked at the bowl like a pregnancy test with an unwanted result. The enchantment was fading. Fully in place, the yolk would not be able to touch my blood. I'd know when it fell completely because the yellow would blend with the red. Already the yolk pressed against the outside of the bubble of blood.

"It's only a matter of time," a deep voice said, snapping my head up from the threshold. Mr. Nekomata stood at the base of my porch stairs, and what do you know, Seraphina smirked at his side. "Give yourself over to us and we will let you live. We only come for what is rightfully ours. Invite us in, give us the book, and we will consider you a friend of our clan."

I stood up and faced him from inside my doorway. Salt and pepper hair, distinctively Japanese features, exceptional height. His camel hair coat caught a spray of powder from the snow and flapped in the breeze that chilled me to the bone.

"I've recently learned Seraphina is your niece," I said, lowering my chin and narrowing my eyes.

His thin lips pulled back. "Yes. I believe you've already met."

Seraphina wiggled her leather-gloved fingers, her fitted wool coat undulating against her legs in the winter chill. "Nice to see you again, Grateful, especially considering I don't have to eat your cooking."

I squared my shoulders and drew Nightshade from her sheath. The blade glowed blue, although I could barely tell in the daylight. "May I presume you are Uncle Kai?" I was pleased with myself for remembering what Seraphina had said about her family.

Mr. Nekomata nodded. "I am Kai."

"Good. I always like to know someone's name before I kill them. Any next of kin I should notify after I slay both of you?"

He cracked his neck, then turned his chin slowly toward the woods across the street from the house. Monstrous creatures stepped out from between the trees. Even from a distance I could make out sharp teeth and claws on hairy cat-shaped bodies the size of saber-toothed tigers, all with forked tails—the nekomata in their shifted forms. Kai had brought an army. "These are my kin."

I muttered a curse my brain tossed out for me like a life vest. Kai bent slightly at the waist, as if a minor discomfort had washed through him. Any sign of distress was gone in an instant. He loosed a patronizing laugh. Why couldn't the solstice happen at midnight? I was my weakest during daylight hours.

"Looks like there will be a meal today, after all," Seraphina said. "And you're the main course."

The nekomata closed in. I could see them clearly now—long tawny fur, black stripes, and spots over their flanks, and a long, cougar-style snout that would undoubtedly lock on to you and never let go.

"Join us, witch, or die," Seraphina demanded.

"You say 'die' like it's a big deal or something. I've died lots of times, bitch, and you're not worthy of a repeat." With a sneer, I kicked the silver bowl inside and slammed the door, locking it behind me. I looked down at the contents of the bowl. Orange. The yolk had permeated my blood; the expiration date on my enchantment had officially come to pass.

SOLSTICE

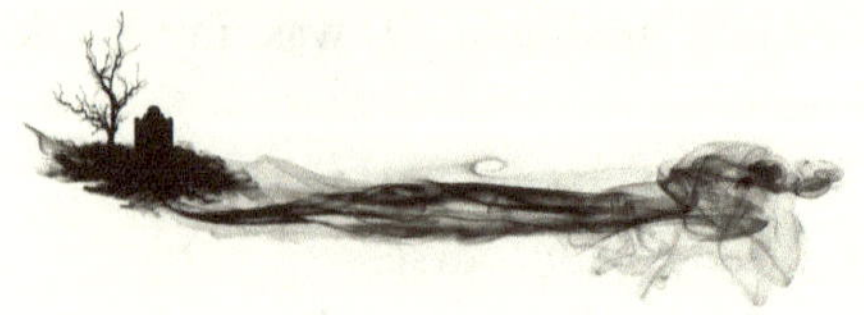

Nightshade in hand, I bolted up the stairs. My kindergarten teacher, Mrs. Chloe, would have been very disappointed as the razor-sharp length of bone in my hand was much worse than running with scissors. Behind me, the nekomata pounded on the door, hurrying my feet. I ducked into my room sending out mental vibes with everything I had, calling Rick and Poe to me for help.

The raven flew full speed toward the glass and I popped open the window just in time to let the streak of feathers inside.

"They've surrounded the house!" Poe squawked.

"No shit. Where's Rick? Did you see him coming?"

Poe shook his head. "He wasn't anywhere. Maybe inside the house?"

"You tried the door?"

"Briefly. I knocked. He didn't answer."

"Crap. I knew he was angry, but I didn't think he'd completely give up on me."

"What's he angry about?"

"No time, Poe. We've got to stop Kai and Seraphina."

"How do you plan to do that?"

I poked my tongue into my cheek and fiddled with Nightshade's hilt. "I'm going to run Kai through with my blade and send him to hell."

"And the rest of the nekomata?"

With a huff that lowered my shoulders and blew back his feathers, I said, "I'm going to kill as many as I can before I die."

We stared at each other until the pounding on the door was joined with an ominous crack. I suspected it was the wood beginning to split. I repositioned Nightshade and moved for the door.

"May I make a suggestion?" Poe interrupted. "A self-protection spell might keep you alive a few minutes longer. Some magical armor or accelerated healing might be in order."

Two bounding steps and the kiss I planted on the raven's head made him cringe away from my grip.

"Control yourself, woman!"

"You're the best, Poe."

"Make haste, dear witch, or we are nekomata fodder."

I tore my phone from my pocket, trying to ignore the time (eleven thirty-eight—shit!) and started searching my *The Book of Light* app. No healing spells. I hadn't made it to "H" yet. But there was one for *armor* under "A," and best of all it was a simple incantation using Nightshade as a magical amplifier.

Extending the blade in front of me, I spoke the incantation, but the power flaked impotently around me. "This daylight is killing me!"

"Would you like me to help? Familiars are known to amplify magic."

"Um, no, I'd rather be torn apart. Get over here!"

Poe circled the room and landed on my head, digging his talons into my scalp.

"Ow."

"Trust me, it will sharpen your focus. Say the incantation."

"Alligo corpus meum impenitribility meorum mucro." I pronounced each word distinctly. The magic obeyed. A swirl of darkness came from the corner of the room, circled my feet, then bit into my skin. "Oh!" It slithered up my calves to my knees and continued north until I could feel the spell heavy in my eyelids. Poe jumped down to my shoulder and for the first time, his claws didn't hurt.

"Gives new meaning to growing a thick skin," Poe quipped.

"Let's do this thing."

Below us, the heavy sound of something barreling through the front door spurred me into action. I raced for the stairs. Poe took flight, leading the way. The beast who'd broken down the door shook off the remnants of wood, glass, and hinges and headed for me with a growl. Thickly muscled shoulders narrowed to sinewy haunches, but I focused on the teeth and the clack of the monster's claws with each step on the wooden stairs.

"Big mistake," I said to the beast, narrowing my eyes and opening my arms to welcome his attack. "Haven't you ever seen a horror movie? Never be the first to enter a haunted house."

The thing leaped for me and I flattened to the stairs, stabbing rather than swinging my blade. I sliced into its neck. Paws the size of my head swiped at my shoulders and chest, while deep red blood, almost purple, gushed over me. Without the enchantment, I would have been shredded.

Ach-ach-achhh. The nekomata choked above me, drool dripping from its fangs and running down my cheek. Out of the corner of my eye I saw a second one enter the house. My only blessing was the shifted nekomata were so large they could only fit through the door one at a time. I placed both boots on Number One's stomach and heaved. It toppled off me, somersaulting down the stairs into the entering pack.

Poe was circling the head of Number Two, trying to distract the beast and slow the entrance of Three while I got to my feet. With one swipe of its paw, Two sent Poe flying into the dining room. I heard his body thump against the far wall. My hand found purchase behind my head, and I pushed, flipping up onto the middle stair and immediately flinging myself over the banister. I landed squarely on my feet in front of the advancing pack. Nightshade sang through the air, decapitating Two.

"Poe, are you okay?" I yelled as Three clamored over the mountain of Two's body to get to me. No answer. The beast charged. I waited until the last second, then executed a sideways aerial cartwheel, landing on my feet behind the kitchen island. The nekomata were big and brutal but not agile. In a wasted moment, while Three scrambled to change its trajectory, I buried Nightshade in its skull. There was no time to celebrate the kill.

Four thrashed at me over the top of the counter, crashing through the pots and pans hanging from the pot rack, like a freight train pulling into the station. A paw rebounded off my neck. *Holy crow!* My armor had protected me from a certain torn jugular. The creature's surprise at my durability bought me a precious second of time. I extracted my blade from Three and swiped it through the center of my attacker's jaw. The nekomata stopped abruptly as if it had run out of batteries. I exhaled and the top of its head slid off onto the floor. The beast crumpled.

Poe chose that moment to swoop through the family room and onto the counter behind me. "I'm good!" he announced, stretching a wing that hung awkwardly from his body.

No time for a reunion. Five advanced through the door more cautiously, eyeing the bodies littering the foyer, the hallway, the living room, the kitchen. Lowering its head, it stalked me, weaving right, then left, deciding how to best get around the island to reach me. It chose left. I leaped straight up in a leap that would have been impossible for a human, landing with a thump on top of the island. The beast pounced. I aimed for its heart but missed and sliced into its abdomen.

"Ahhh," I yelled with the effort of rolling the creature through the air. Nightshade slipped from its flesh. The body landed with a bone-cracking thump on its back on the wood floor. I hopped down from the island and positioned my blade over its heart. I paused as the body shivered, twisted, bones snapping and muscles stretching. When the nekomata had shifted, Seraphina stared up at me, hand gripping the wound in her side.

"You can't kill me, Grateful," she whined. "You'll break your daddy's heart." Her strange green eyes locked onto mine.

"Didn't he tell you? You're not his type." I leaped into the air, landing one boot on her chest the other on the floor, and sank my blade straight through her ribs, directly into her heart. She writhed beneath my boot for a moment, half shifting before the light in her eyes dulled. Her body went limp. I kicked it off my blade.

I turned to face the door but no more entered. "There were more than five, Poe. Where are the rest?" The sound of shattering glass below us answered my question. I bolted for the door to the basement, throwing it open with enough force for it to bounce off the far wall. I could hear a struggle and the sound of crunching glass under scampering feet.

"Do it!" Kai ordered.

When I reached the bottom, I came up short at what I saw. Soleil! Kai stood next to the pushed aside pool table at the base of the vault, one hand around the fairy's long, graceful neck, the other gripping her hands behind her back. Her eyes flicked to mine for a split second before a lightning-fast blast of energy threw me against the wall, knocking Nightshade from my hand. Before I'd known what hit me, Naill, Anna Bathory's pet leprechaun, had straddled my chest, knees over my arms and dagger pressed to my throat. "Don't move a muscle, Hecate, or I will cut your throat out."

"How are you here?" I blurted, eyes flashing to Kai and Soleil. "I thought nekomata hated vampires and you, Naill, are definitely aligned with the vampires." I made the revelation for Kai's benefit, but he didn't even flinch.

"You *are* blond, aren't you?" Naill said. "Why do you think Anna and I helped the nightmares escape the graveyard? The nekomata have to open the vault, and you are right, they hate vampires. Fortunately, the clan is known to blindly follow their leader. A little leprechaun magic and our vaporous friend ensured Kai would be sympathetic to our cause."

"Kai's possessed by a nightmare?"

"A nightmare that owes Anna a favor."

"And expects a reward," possessed Kai said, pushing Soleil by the neck toward the vault.

Naill nodded at Kai. "You must do it now. The solstice is upon us. Her Majesty will have your head should you fail."

Trapped under Naill's knife, I searched the room for Poe.

"Looking for this?" Naill pointed at a sack to my right containing the thrashing form of a raven-sized object. *Fuck*, I hated that ginger. How did his tiny legs move so fast? "Don't get any ideas. He can't break through the bag. It's soaked in helleborine."

"Mr. Helleborine! You!"

Naill laughed wickedly.

"Don't do it," I begged Soleil and was rewarded with a stubby hand over my mouth.

Kai thrust her forward, and I watched his grip tighten around her neck, reddening the skin there. Soleil's eye's filled with tears. She was holding back, I could tell, but it was painful.

"Now, Kai!" Naill demanded.

The nekomata dug in harder, until Soleil's neck began to bleed, but the blood was not red like human blood. Soleil's blood was liquid sunshine, so bright I had to partially close my eyes as it dripped onto the stone vault and sizzled like acid.

Kai's voice filled the space as he spoke the incantation, and Soleil glowed ever brighter under his assault. I closed my eyes fully and sent out my strongest plea yet for Rick's help, but nothing came down our connection. Either he couldn't hear me, or he wasn't answering.

A mighty crack echoed through the room.

I opened my eyes to see the dusty, cobweb-covered interior of a crypt exposed to Soleil's light. Before I could react, Naill pounded the hilt of his dagger into my temple, so hard my teeth clanked together and my skull bounced against the tile floor with a resounding crack. I fought against the temptation to pass out, sure that the last of my armor enchantment had dissipated with the force of surviving the onslaught.

Unable to move, I watched Naill push Kai and Soleil aside and hop into the crypt, emerging a moment later with a book powerful enough to fill the space between us with a heavy, palpable dread. This wasn't just a grimoire. The darkness leaching from it pushed Soleil's light back inside her skin. The fairy moaned and listed to the side in Kai's grip.

In an army crawl, I pulled myself forward for a better

view. I recognized the corner of the tome as a shoulder blade. A human spine bound the pages. Slivers of bone framed the cover made from leathered human skin. I'd heard the pages were also made of skin, and the writing, not ink but blood. The book appeared to have a clasp or lock of some kind constructed of a human jaw and other smaller bones.

Naill chuckled wickedly and held *The Book of Flesh and Bone* above his head like a prize.

"Let me see it," Kai demanded, casting Soleil to the floor and reaching for what he wanted. "Give it to me."

"Patience. The mistress will be here to open it at dusk."

"Bathory had better remember our deal. The first spell must be used for me, then the book is yours." A flash of black fog passed behind Kai's irises.

"Of course, that is the deal. Soon you will have your own flesh, and the mistress will have true immortality."

Silently, I crawled forward, reaching for Nightshade. I pulled myself up on the pool table and Naill made a face like a cockroach just poked its head out of his macaroni salad.

"You're Mr. Helleborine. You helped kill the last Hecate," I stated dumbly, possessed by some unexplainable need for closure. "You and Anna were the ones helping Marcus from the outside. And now you're trying to kill me again."

Kai tilted his head and his eyes flicked to something behind me. I followed his gaze to see Naill grinning, his hand charged with green energy. Holy crow that little guy was fast!

"Fuck," I mumbled before he zapped me with his magic and a bag slipped over my head, plunging me into darkness. Yeah, that protection enchantment was definitely done for, and probably, so was I.

CEREMONY

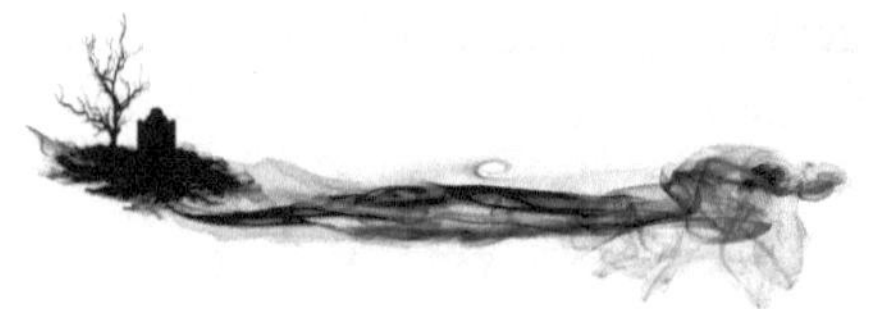

I came around but didn't open my eyes. Better possessed-Kai didn't know I was conscious. Cold, so cold. As I shivered, my back bounced against a rock-hard surface. I was bound—hands, waist, and ankles. Damn, I was getting sick of waking up bound. Listening carefully, all I could make out was wind across my ear, the crackle of burning wood, and icy wet hitting my skin. I was outside, maybe freezing to death.

"Are you alive?" Soleil's voice whispered.

I cracked my eyes open. The dim winter sky above me dribbled tiny snowflakes that stung my eyes and cheeks. I blinked them away and turned my head to the left. Soleil was tied to a tree a few feet away from me, and she looked like hell, as if someone had beaten her within an inch of her life, then smothered her in mud.

"Deep water mud dulls my power. I'd warm you, but I can't even muster a faint glow," she said sadly.

With a ridiculous amount of effort, I strained my neck to look down my body. I was tied to a stone slab, about three feet off the ground. I couldn't see much else except that we were in the woods somewhere. A small fire to my right barely nudged back the frosty weather, but because of my restraints, I couldn't see beyond the topmost flicker of the flames.

I whispered to Soleil, "Can you see what I'm tied to? Is there any way for me to free myself?"

She shook her head. "You are bound to a stone altar. She plans to cut out your heart." Her voice sounded hopeless, and a shiny gold tear cut through the mud on her cheek.

"My heart? Wha—" I struggled against my restraints. "Can you see Nightshade?"

"Shhh." Soleil warned me to calm down with stern eyes. "Your blade is resting on top of the tied bag that holds your bird, about fifteen feet to your left, guarded by a sleeping leprechaun."

Shit. Think. Think. Think. Think. "Is there anyone else here at the moment?" I asked, trying to picture our surroundings.

Soleil swallowed and another star-bright tear carved down her face. "Your caretaker."

"Rick? Where?" My head flip-flopped on the stone, the back of my skull aching from the effort.

"Shhh," Soleil chastised again. "Above and behind you."

I arched against the unforgiving ropes and tilted my head back as far is it would go. What I saw broke my heart. Rick was unconscious, imprisoned in a medieval metal cage that dangled from a tree branch at least twenty feet above the ground. Dried blood was caked on the bars, and even with my impaired vision, I could see long wounds striping his skin. What happened? Why hadn't he shifted?

Rick? Rick? I tried to use our connection to wake him but got no response.

"Why doesn't he shift?" I whispered, although I didn't expect Soleil to answer me.

"He is very weak. Perhaps Naill has done something to him. Leprechaun magic is extremely powerful. "

"Is he alive?"

Her eyes narrowed. "You would know better than I."

I should know better. Normally our connection was so tight I could sense his thoughts if I wanted. But now, looking up at him dangling there, he seemed so human. So disconnected. I tried again. Digging deep, I felt for the thread that tied us together, the trail of metaphysical breadcrumbs that always led me back to him. I thought of the day we met, the first time, how the water had felt coursing over my brown skin and the look of him exposed, shocked, staring at me with his full lips parted from the shore. A boy on the verge of becoming a man. My man. He had always been mine, from the very beginning. And I had always been his. I understood this now in a way I hadn't before. It was like being eight years old and thinking a trip out of the state was seeing the world. The older I'd gotten, the larger the world became. This love was the same. When I'd met him, everything was flat, simple, odd but explainable. Now, I realized it was ageless, endless; a love that transcended lifetimes.

Julius and Gary had posed the question, if I had the power to do so, why hadn't I made myself immortal? Why had I given Rick that particular gift? They tried to convince me I could have had the power all along, that Rick had somehow tricked me into binding himself to me. But now I understood. I had made Rick my caretaker so that we could be together for eternity. If anything, I'd ensnared *him* in my trap of immortality, bound us together because I couldn't bear the thought of living without him. And he had endured this curse lifetime after lifetime while I had the luxury of death, of a relatively normal childhood. Rick was not the monster. I was the monster.

As tears flooded down my cheeks, freezing near my

jawline, I found the thing that bound us to each other. Flimsy, like a spider's web, our connection was the weakest I'd ever remembered it being. Consciously, I fought my way along it, psychically transcending the space between us until the magic inside of me was in his head and I was shaking him by the shoulders. How could I touch him when I was tied to an altar and he was in a cage dangling above me? I can't explain the how, only that I held him in my arms in the white, empty space of our consciousness. We'd left the world behind, temporarily.

"*Mi cielo?*" He woke in my arms. *Damn*, holding this state was almost painful.

"Rick, you've got to wake up. You've got to shift and get us out of here!"

"I can't. It's too late for that."

"What are you talking about?"

He met my eyes. "You told me you didn't want me anymore, that you couldn't forgive me after Gary. You told me you wished you had a *choice*."

"We had a fight. I'm doing my best to—"

"No. You were right. I could have stopped Bathory from taking Gary, but I didn't. Too many lifetimes." He shook his head. "I became impatient to love you again."

"Rick, I understand, okay? Can we talk about it later? We need to find a way out of this."

His face fell. "I lit the candle," he muttered.

"What? What candle?"

"After our argument, I left on a journey to obtain a magical object to help our situation."

"You said something about that. What was it?"

"I visited another Hecate. Tabetha, Salem's witch. She gave me a candle to break our connection. All I had to do was light the candle, and when it burned all the way down, I would be human again. I could die."

I froze. My hand gripped his face, forcing him to maintain eye contact. "Why? Why would you do that? We'd reconciled. I told you I'd stay true to you."

"I know what you said, but I did it to free you. You don't want me. I saw Logan's keys in your car. You love him. When the candle burns down, you can make him your caretaker, or grant yourself the immortality you've given to me. You will be free of me." His eyes drifted from one of my eyes to the other and the pain in his expression broke my heart. "And when I die, I will finally be free of loving you."

"Is it such a burden, Rick?" I asked without thinking.

"Would it be a burden to you to love someone with everything inside you, only to know they would never love you back, that they thought of you as an affliction, a beast to be tolerated for the good of humanity? Yes, it is a burden, one I can bear no longer."

Tears dripped from my face, and the entire space we were in turned grey from the pain that echoed through me. "But I do love you." On my knees, I tried to plead with him. "The only reason I had those keys was because I stored *The Book of Light* in his condo. I don't love Logan, Rick. I love you. I know you saw us kissing. I know it was painful for you. But I'd been drugged by Naill, and Logan initiated it. I didn't want him to kiss me. I wanted you. I only want you."

"You think of me as your dog," he spat. "You don't want me as an equal, you want me as a tool."

"No," I choked. I lowered my forehead toward his, sobs racking my chest. "Please, Rick, I want you. Only you. Don't do this. Can't you see I'm yours? I've always been yours."

He reached up and tangled his fingers in my hair. "It is too late, Grateful. Already, my power fades. My only regret is I thought it would take longer. I thought I could save you first. But the moment I lit the wick, it began. And now it's too late. The candle burns inside my cottage, and in a few more hours, I will be completely human. And then I will die." He lifted his hand from a particularly nasty wound in his chest.

Grateful. He called me Grateful, not *mi cielo*. Not his sky. He'd already let me go. He'd resigned himself to his humanity. I sobbed until my shoulders shook violently.

He stroked my hair back from my face. "I suspect this emotion has more to do with your survival than your true feelings. Don't you see that what is inside of you is more powerful than anything inside of me? All you have to do is access it. An entire universe of magic and power is at your fingertips. Call the power to you. I can't help you anymore. Not this time."

As if I'd bungee jumped into his brain, the cord of our connection snapped me back into my body abruptly and with enough pain to make me scream. Or was the scream from the torture happening behind my breastbone? Rick had left me. My own caretaker had given up on me.

"She wakes," Naill said, walking his stubby legs over to my side. "Relax. Queen Bathory is preparing for the ceremony."

"What does she want with me? She already has the book."

He ran a thick finger down the length of my arm and flashed a smile wide enough to show all his gold teeth. "I'm so glad you asked. Legend has it that there is a spell in *The Book of Flesh and Bone* that will render a vampire truly immortal. Impervious to daylight, strong without the need for blood. After sunset, the queen will open the book and know the exact preparation for the spell, but one ingredient is a certainty, passed down to her from generations of vampires."

"My heart."

"Any supernatural heart will do. We'd planned to use one of the lesser vamps. We thought you'd be dead by now, after all. As it turned out, you and the book are a convenient two-for-one deal. Frankly, I was surprised you survived the army of nekomata who attacked you, but then we hadn't counted on lover boy joining the fray." Naill glanced toward the cage.

"Rick?"

"He killed most of the clan outside your house before we took him down. Lucky for us about the candle. And to think we had nothing to do with that. He did it to himself." His wicked laugh drilled into me like machine gun fire.

But he came. The thought gripped me, sending a bolt of electricity down my spine. Rick had already made the decision to become human when he joined the fight. He was willing to die for me—a real, eternal death. That must mean something.

I leaned my head back against the stone as Naill wandered off toward the fire.

"Soleil?"

"Yes."

"Any chance you could grant me that favor you promised?"

"Unfortunately, the mud has rendered that impossible. I am sorry."

The sky was darkening. Sunset. Soon, Bathory would come for my heart. But she couldn't have it. My heart wasn't mine to give; it already belonged to someone else. And whether or not he liked it, I was going to get us out of this and end that candle before it was too late. Because at that moment I realized Rick still loved me. He had to. Not only was he offering to give up his immortality for me, he'd risked his humanity too.

He loved me, and I loved him. I knew it in my bones—whether or not Rick chose to admit it. Bathory was about to find out just how powerful those feelings could be.

SUNSET

As the sun set and darkness swallowed the clearing where I was held prisoner, Vampiress Anna Bathory emerged from the night as if she were part of it, cut from the shadows and stitched into a bloodthirsty seductress with more body than dress. She cradled *The Book of Flesh and Bone* in her arms, closing her eyes and inhaling the scent of the tome as she approached me. I winced at the thought of the smell of dried flesh, bone, and blood. *Sicko.*

She rested the massive book on a tall stump that Naill provided for her and unhinged the jaw clasp, flipping the pages. "Ah, here it is. True immortality." She looked at me and smiled her piranha smile with no attempt to hide any portion of her massive teeth. "The spell calls for your heart and lots and lots of blood. Shall I use yours? Or your care-taker's?"

I tried to fix my expression. I didn't want to give her the benefit of knowing she'd got under my skin. But I felt my eyes widen slightly when she mentioned Rick, and I could tell she noticed.

"Yes. I think we will use his blood. Much more entertaining. Plus, a more powerful combination, I think. Two deaths are better than one."

Damn, I hated this chick. "Why not two hundred deaths like Monk?" I said. "Worked out well for him. Oh wait, no it didn't. The book drives a hard bargain, Bathory. It will take you down with it, just like Monk."

She stroked her hand down her shiny black tresses, nudging the ends back over her shoulder. "I don't think so. The problem with Monk was he didn't know how to wield the book. In his heart, he had good intentions. Only true evil can control evil. The price is you, your blood. I will be immortal."

"Have you forgotten our deal?" Kai's deep rumble of a voice came from outside my field of vision, somewhere near my feet. He sounded pissed and I had every intention to use that to my advantage.

I addressed the nightmare within Kai's body. "She won't do it. If she wastes her first spell on you, the book will extract a price on her that could make it impossible for her to perform her own spell. It could strike her dead like it did Monk or take her voice so she couldn't say the incantation. She would never risk her precious flesh to give you what you want."

"Shut her up!" Bathory growled. Naill was beside me in a split second, shoving a nasty stretch of rag into my mouth. Hmm. Maybe speaking up wasn't such a good idea.

Kai stepped into view, hooded eyes digging into Bathory. He did not look happy. The vampiress took a step back.

"Allow me to perform the immortality spell first. Once it is done, I can create a body for you without fear of provoking the book's wrath."

"Don't bullshit me, Anna," Kai said through clenched teeth. "Once you get what you want, you will never pay me my due. You must perform the embodiment spell first, as we agreed."

"Or what?" She laughed, low and breathy, in his face. "What are you going to do to me? Need I remind you that Naill's magic restricts who you can possess? No undead. My body is off limits. You knew when you agreed to our arrangement that you were at my mercy. Now be a good little wisp and wait for your queen to finish her business and maybe I'll throw you a bone."

The flush of red that washed over Kai's face made it clear he wasn't down with that plan. I could be mistaken, but I think it was the "good little wisp" comment. Even I thought that was offensive.

"Without me possessing the nekomata clan leader, you'd never have gained the book. You owe me."

Bathory shrugged.

The nightmare snapped. I saw him go over the edge in Kai's body. The possessed nekomata hurled himself at Bathory who rolled backward, ass over teacup, as Kai pummeled her with everything he had.

Upon seeing this, Naill got his miniature, probably golden, undies in a bunch. "My lady? My lady?" he blubbered, dancing around the skirmish.

"Call the others!" she demanded between clawing Kai's face and rolling on top of him. Big mistake. Kai shifted. With a series of blood-curdling pops, his bottom jaw elongated into a long, toothy snout, and razor-sharp claws extended from his knuckles. One swipe sent Bathory flying, blood pouring from her neck and chest. Kai's nekomata exploded out of the camel hair coat, a tawny-haired whirling devil.

But Bathory wasn't born yesterday. Hell, she wasn't born last century. Her wounds healed themselves in seconds and she readied for his attack. Taking advantage of the same weakness I'd detected in the shifters, she waited until he was in a full-out run, then leaped sideways, hitching onto the creature's mane and tossing a leg over its back. As her arms clamped around Kai's throat, he bucked wildly. Naill bounced and clapped near the fray like some prepubescent cheerleader.

I took the distraction as an opportunity to work on my bindings. By bending my knees, a feat only possible by pressing them together to the point of pain, I was able to slide my back down the rough stone and loosen the ropes. If I strained my neck, the tips of my fingers could reach the gag. I yanked it out of my mouth and cast it aside. With a little more contortion, I was able to move one wrist to my mouth. The rope dug into my bloodied skin, but I set my teeth to work.

As I maneuvered the binding, it occurred to me that my years as a bar rat in college actually might pay off. I'd tongue-tied plenty of cherry stems into knots in my day. This was just the opposite, right? Only I wasn't as drunk or as distracted with whatever fraternity cohort was on the barstool next to me. Still, I had skills. The knot loosened slightly between my incisors.

A growling mass of supernatural rage rolled between the fire and me. I paused momentarily, but there was no way Bathory or Kai was paying any attention. Both were bloody to the point of serious injury, even for the undead. She was ghostly white from loss of blood, and he gushed red where she had torn into his front leg.

Victory! The rope loosened enough that I knew I could pull my hand out. Only, now wasn't the time. An army of undead emerged from the woods, at least thirty vampires, some of whom I recognized from the Mill Wheel. Bathory's reinforcements swooped down on Kai, ripping him apart, limb from limb. I watched in horror as the nightmare inside emerged from the beast's body, a smoky black cloud of menace, and pinged around the incompatible undead before racing toward me. The cloud paused as if considering my body, but then plowed into Soleil.

"Get out of her," I seethed.

"Not a chance," Soleil said in a tenor version of her voice. "This is the safest place to be. The fae is the only one on this merry-go-round Bathory can't kill without harming herself.

Soleil was made of sunlight. I guessed ripping her open would be dangerous for a vamp.

Everyone stopped. I flattened on the altar, effectively playing dead.

Bathory glared at Soleil over my stomach. "Smart. Only once I am immortal, Soleil's talents won't be able to hurt me." Bathory staggered back toward the book, weak from the loss of blood.

"My queen," Naill called, wrestling a bound man forward. "I had them bring this for you from the bar."

The human looked around forty with a balding head and beer belly. I had a flash of sympathy, then remembered that if he was hanging out at the Mill Wheel, he was likely paying vamps to compel young girls to have sex with him. My sympathy faded.

Bathory gave Naill a small nod, then sank teeth into the man. There was a moan, gurgles, loud swallowing, and then a thump as his drained body hit the dirt.

Slowly, painstakingly, I worked my hand free from its binding, hooking my fingers in it to keep it from falling. I did not want to draw attention. Timing was everything.

"Now," Bathory said, "the cauldron."

Naill dragged a pot almost as large as he was to her side. "Yes, my lady."

Oh dear Lord. If that nugget got his nose any farther up her ass, he'd become a permanent part of her backside.

He handed her a silver-hilted dagger. She lifted it in her

still bloody hand and strode to my side. Her perfectly arched brow lifted. "Nice knowing you, witch. Too bad about your caretaker. Looks like you won't be coming back from this one." With both hands gripping the hilt, she raised the dagger above her head until her upper arms covered her ears, then with one final gaze at my chest, plunged the steel toward my breastbone.

The movement was lightning quick, but so was I. Some part of me—the goddess of the dead part, I suppose—knew what she would do before she did it. Rick had said that everything I needed was inside of me and surely he was right, because at that moment, I knew every undead cell in the super standing next to me. I owned what she was. I had knit her out of the ether in some former life.

Releasing the binding, I rolled out from under her falling dagger. She howled an obscenity as the blade hit the stone and not me. I rolled back, flattening the knife under me while bringing my elbow to the side of her head. Three of my limbs were still bound to the table but I used what leverage I could get to throw my entire bodyweight into it, aiming not for her head but through it. She hissed and fell to the ground.

Quickly, I began working the knot on my other wrist. I wasn't fast enough. I'd barely loosened it when she popped up next to me. One hand gripped my throat while the other clawed my shirt open.

"There are two ways for me to cut out your heart. Since you've taken my knife, we'll do this the old-fashioned way."

I punched into the side of her head as her nails dug in over my heart. Her grip on my neck was brutal, and the lack of oxygen made my vision swim. I thought I was dead, until a black wind blew over me, knocking Bathory's hand away. From my supine position, I watched the darkness collect into a familiar vampire.

"Julius!" Bathory growled. "Back off. The book is mine."

"Over my undead body," Julius crooned. He brushed a stray tress out of his face and lowered himself, ready to brawl.

I turned my head to see the Mill Wheel vamps close in around the two, but Julius hadn't come alone. A small army emerged from the darkness. I recognized Gary right away. His nocturnal eyes passed over me but didn't linger.

"Leave now, Julius, or I will be forced to end you," Anna said.

Julius laughed. "Give it your best shot."

They collided in fast-forward, teeth and claws, a tangle of black fog. The other vamps rushed in to help, only to be thwarted by the other side. A battle raged around the book and the fire. I watched Naill slowly back away, disappearing into the woods to save his lucky ass.

I began working on my other wrist in earnest. Yes! I'd moved to my ankle when a beast I recognized crept out of the forest. I supposed it could be any werewolf, but the wound in its side and the way it limped toward me told me it was Silas. I jerked back as his weighty paw lifted and swiped for me. Only his aim was purposefully off. The rope binding my ankles split in two. Silas meant to free me.

"Thank you, Silas," I whispered quickly, then bound off the table and raced for Nightshade.

THE SUN ALSO RISES

My limbs tingled from the cold and numbness of immobility, but I forced them to obey my command. I leaped over the fire and reached for my blade. Nightshade's hilt slid into my hand with urgency, as if she'd been straining to help me. Underneath her blade, the burlap sack rustled. I untied it and freed Poe. "Help Rick down," I ordered. He nodded once and took to the sky.

A hand landed on my shoulder. I whirled around to face a Mill Wheel vamp. He yanked me into a bear hug. Poor sucker must have been young or stupid. My blade sank into his gut and he exploded into a shower of ash. The other vamps were distracted with the fight, although that wouldn't last forever. Some were already down for the count, the winners joining in the tussle between Julius and Bathory. It didn't matter who won that fight. If either was left standing, I'd lose.

What I needed was to get out of there, but I couldn't leave Rick, Soleil, or the book. *Think!* I noticed Silas then, sniffing Soleil like a dog whose master comes home smelling of another pooch. The nightmare was still inside her, throwing off her scent. "Smart doggy." I smiled and sprang into action.

Rounding the skirmish, I shuffled to her side. I pressed Nightshade into Soleil's chest. At the site of the knife, Silas growled at me menacingly. I wondered how much of himself Silas had left when he shifted. "Don't worry. I won't hurt her."

"What are you doing?" the tenor voice asked through Soleil's mouth.

"Banishing you." Nightshade glowed ever brighter.

The nightmare growled and squirmed against Soleil's bindings.

"I sentence you to an eternity in hell." I felt rather than saw the immediate results of my sentence. My blade suctioned to her chest and then slowly, like a worm being drawn from the dirt, the nightmare wrapped around the blade, inch by inch from her chest. Tighter it squeezed until it poofed into nothingness. Soleil took charge of herself.

"Ew. I need a shower," she said, shivering.

"Just what I had in mind." I cut her free and pushed her down in the snow.

"Hey!"

"The mud, Soleil! Get it off." I turned my back to her and faced the brawling vampires. One by one, they noticed me, turning fanged faces in my direction. Even Bathory and Julius recognized the threat, pausing their war and fixing deadly eyes on me. I raised Nightshade. "Any time, Soleil. Could really use some help here."

"Almost there." I glanced back to see her rubbing herself with snow, steam filling the space around her.

Glancing back was a big mistake. Bathory barreled into me, thrusting Nightshade above my head. In no time, I was at the bottom of a very large heap of vampires. Fangs ripped into my flesh. I heard Soleil scream and knew she was in the same predicament.

I was battered and bleeding. And then, like a far off

memory, Rick's words came back to me, "An entire universe of magic is at your fingertips." He was wrong. It wasn't at my fingertips. It was in the air I was breathing, the night air that surrounded us. Night air that was the source of my power.

The magic slammed into me like a tidal wave when I called, the air thickening to the density of pea soup. The power yanked me from under those vamps with windy tendrils that circled the camp, casting the undead aside in a wintry hurricane. The vamps covered their eyes against the blowing snow.

I used muscle and the mounting storm to reach Soleil. "Come on. You've got to flame out now!" I yelled. My power was already draining. The vamps were pushing through the wind to get to us. I couldn't hold them back forever.

"I can't," she yelled. "I tried. The mud's effect lingers."

Bathory and Julius reached for me, leaning into the wind and snow. "Sorry, Soleil, but desperate times call for desperate measures."

"What?"

I yanked her into my arms. Holding her, screaming, in front of the vamps. I used Nightshade to slice a shallow cut across her chest, shoulder to shoulder. She screamed, but the cut paid off. Sunlight bled from the wound, and then the sun rose. Far from the dingy gray of a winter's morning, a blazing hot ball of orange swept through the clearing. Vampires burst into flame. Bathory wrapped one dying vamp around her like a coat and fled into the darkness of the woods, Julius right behind her. All of the vamps scattered or burned in the sunlight. When all were gone, I released Soleil, spinning her around to check her wound.

"I am fine!" she said, clutching the cut. "The vampires are gone. We are saved!"

"Sorry I had to do that."

Gradually, she began to pull her light back inside and heal

herself. "It is nothing. I should have thought of it sooner." Her rose-colored lips pressed together.

I nodded, turning in a circle to assess our surroundings in Soleil's fading light. A few vamps lay burning near the fire. All the others had made for the shelter of darkness. My eyes swept across the trees, looking for any stragglers that thought they might try to return for *The Book of Flesh and Bone*. I raised Nightshade when I saw a man stagger from the woods. Only, it was Silas, human again, naked and shivering. Soleil's light had broken the moon's hold on him. She opened her arms and he ran into them. The embrace was desperate, therapeutic. How long had Silas been possessed? Soleil captured? Seeing them together was a beautiful thing.

The romantic scene in front of me brought my eyes up to the cage where Poe was nudging Rick with his head and beak. "He will not wake," Poe said worriedly. "I cannot cut him down like this. I might kill him."

I nodded, sheathing Nightshade and rushing to the place the rope was tied to on a nearby tree. I worked the knot free, then carefully lowered the cage. When Rick was at my level, I could see how bad he'd been hurt. His fight with the neko-mata had left him with an arm bent at an awkward angle, probably broken, and long shredded wounds still oozing blood. I swung open the door and he collapsed into my arms. With two fingers I felt for his pulse. Weak. He was barely alive. I positioned myself to feed him my blood, then stopped. Was he human? Did the candle burn all the way down? If it had, my blood could make him sick. I had to find out.

"I need to get him home." I looked from Soleil to Silas to Poe.

It was Poe that came to my aid. "I cannot deny a witch who knows what she wants." He rolled into a ball, stretched, and gathered himself, morphing into a beautiful black stallion.

"I love you, Poe," I said.

"I know," he answered.

Calling on my witchy strength, I slid Rick's body over Poe's shoulders and pulled myself up behind him.

"Can I trust you two to protect the book?" I looked at Silas and Soleil.

Soleil spread her arms to display the gash across her collarbone. "There is no place safer than with me. I will keep it for you. Save your caretaker."

I nodded. "Silas, which way to Rick's cottage?"

The detective looked at me with pity. "About a mile that way." He pointed into the trees.

Just as I thought. We were near Avery's cottage in the woods behind Rick's place. Using every ounce of strength I had left, I gripped Rick against my chest and prodded Poe forward, praying for the first time to my goddess mother for help.

* * *

BY THE TIME I REACHED RICK'S HOUSE, MY ARMS AND LEGS burned. I was exhausted—mentally, physically, emotionally. But I refused to give up. This man in my arms who had always seemed larger than life—now so human, so fragile— was suddenly more important to me than anything—even *The Book of Flesh and Bone*. I still couldn't believe I'd left the tome under Soleil's watch. If you added up all the minutes I'd been in the same room as the fae, it wouldn't equal a day. Maybe not the smartest thing I'd ever done, but necessary.

The door to Rick's cottage was hanging open. But then Silas's werewolf probably didn't have good door-closing skills. I thanked Poe, and half carried, half dragged Rick inside. A ring of skulls glowed from behind the couch. At the center, the three-inch thick purple candle I'd seen before with the scarab beetle imprint had burned down to its last inch of wax. A tiny blue flame struggled at the top of a pool of wax.

"Rick? How do I stop this?" I jostled him carefully in my arms.

His eyelids fluttered. "Out the flame."

"Put out the flame before it burns down? And you'll get your power back?"

His head listed to the side in what I interpreted as a nod.

Carefully lowering him to the floor beside me, I licked my fingers and shot my hand out to snuff the candle. Bad idea. My fist bounced off the barrier of the skulls and a magic zap landed me on my ass.

"Rick?" I shook his shoulder. "How do I get to the candle?"

He opened his eyes and looked up at me, the ghost of a smile crossing his lips, a deep breath of air escaping through his nose. "You don't." His gray eyes were wet.

"Bullshit. There has to be a way."

"Only I can do it."

"Then do it! You'll die if you don't."

He shook his head. "I do not want to live this way. I've loved you too long to spend a lifetime watching you love someone else."

I lowered my head until my mouth was almost touching his bloodied face. "You won't have to. I promise you, I am yours. Only yours."

"You are saying this to save me. I don't want your pity. I want your heart."

I lifted his hand and placed it on my chest, my eyes searched each of his as tears welled and spilled from my face. "You have it. How can I prove it to you, Rick? I am yours." It wasn't enough. If I was going to give myself to him, I had to give it all. "I…love you. I love you. Not the memory of you, not what you do for me, but *you*. I think I always have. I was just confused because everything happened so fast. I didn't want to get hurt again. Everyone I've ever thought I've loved, I've lost. My mother, Gary, a dozen boyfriends, even my father has pulled away from me. I just couldn't open myself up to it. You suffer enough pain and the walls come up. It's a protective instinct. But I'm opening up now. Fuck, I am wide open. I've painted a bull's-eye on my chest, okay? I love you. I do. Please don't hurt me again." The last part came out on a whisper that cracked in the middle like a brittle bone. With my whole self, I begged him to stay with me, tears falling, lips hovering over his, and my body tensed as if one heavy word from him would break me. My muscles shivered with the strain of waiting for his answer.

He swallowed hard, closed his eyes, then opened them again. "On one condition."

"Anything."

"Marry me."

I froze. Warring empires collided within me; fear of commitment battled a love that was ancient, although new to me. Out of the corner of my eye, I saw the candle flicker. There wasn't time for logic, only feeling, only intuition.

"Yes," I said, breathless. "Yes, I will marry you."

Our eyes locked and a current of magic traveled through me. I wasn't sure what it meant, but I suspected my promise was binding. His fingers reached out, knocking one of the skulls aside, breaking the protective ring. I did not hesitate. I threw myself into the candle, snuffing it out and knocking it to the floor. The hot wax splashed over my fingers, burning me, but the candle was out.

I turned back toward Rick, but he looked the same—weak, in pain. "Did it work?"

"Yes, *mi cielo*, it did. But it will take me some time to recover." He held up a hand. "For now, I am…human."

I knew what he meant. The way he stretched on the floor and even his hair were as mundane as could be. While the candle burned down over the last day, he had transformed into a normal man, and although I'd stopped the magic in time, it would take just as long for him to transform back. Unless I helped him recover.

Glancing down at myself, I noticed I was covered in blood, mud, and other unidentifiable but grotesque things. I stood, then helped him to his feet, half dragging him into the bathroom, where I situated him on the floor.

"Rest here for a minute."

Eyes already closed, he dipped his chin in response.

"I'm going to give you a bath."

Rick's eyes popped open, and he raised an eyebrow, a smile breaking through the exhausted expression on his face.

I winked at him and started the water to warm it up. While I was waiting, I started peeling off bloody clothes, leaving them in a pile next to the toilet. Thankfully, most of the blood wasn't mine. The last thing I removed was Nightshade. I leaned her against the wall near the cabinets.

"We got our caretaker back," I whispered to her, glancing at Rick, who'd fallen asleep against the wall. The hum that came from her thin bone edge seemed to say she understood.

HEALING

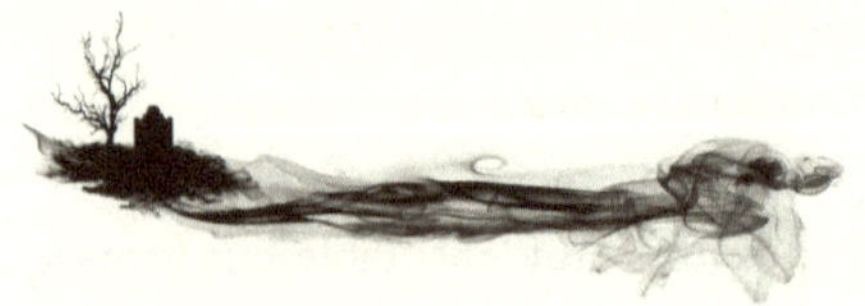

Rick had fallen asleep against the wall. I sensed he needed the rest and took the opportunity to shower. Blood washed off me in maroon waves, and the deep grooves the ropes had left in my wrists filled in minute by minute. The bumps and bruises, as well as the sore muscles, were well on their way to recovery. Part of the healing was due to my advanced regenerative abilities as a Hecate, but the speed of my cell repair was also thanks to Rick. He'd given me so much blood after my last run in with Bathory, it was still in my system. Now it was time for me to return the favor.

After drying off and brushing out my hair, I dug in his drawer for a candle, a fat red one I'd seen in there before. I placed it on the side of the sink. Although I couldn't find any matches, I'd learned I didn't need any. Placing my hand behind the candle, I blew across the wick, picturing a flame in my mind. The air curved against my palm, circled the candle top, then ignited, blazing a good three inches before settling into a more even burn.

"You are learning, *mi cielo*." Rick's eyes were open again.

I straddled his body and lowered myself to a squat over him, not even worrying that I was naked and exposed. I wanted to be at his level to talk to him, and there was nothing he hadn't seen before. "I'm not so much learning as remembering. Some things I know from copying into my database. Others just pop into my head when I least expect them."

"You were amazing tonight. Strong. Intelligent."

"I thought you were unconscious."

"I was in and out, but I saw enough."

I sighed. "I got lucky. If Julius hadn't shown up to challenge Bathory, I'd probably be a heart lighter." I rubbed the spot on my chest where the vampire had dug in her nails.

"Judging by the storm you called, I'm not sure you needed Julius at all."

"I couldn't hold it for long."

"Not everyone would have thought to use Soleil as you did, especially after she'd been compromised by the nightmare. How did you know the mud's effect wasn't more than skin deep?"

"I didn't. I just knew I couldn't take them all out on my own and hoped for the best."

He nodded, eyes traveling down the length of my arm as if he'd just noticed I was naked.

"I left *The Book of Flesh and Bone* with Soleil and Silas. Do you think that was a mistake?"

"No. I've known Soleil for more than one hundred years. She'll guard it with her life. And I believe Silas is as trustworthy."

"Me too."

In the silence that followed, the fluorescent bathroom light suddenly became annoying, competing with the gentle glow of the candle. On a whim, I raised a hand and blew a strong breath, willing the lights off. I meant to throw the switch. Instead, the bulb exploded in a shower of sparks. "Whoops."

"I never liked that bulb anyway."

I watched him for a second, his gray eyes twinkling crisp and clear in the candlelight, more human than usual. His lips twitched, and I broke into laughter.

"I'm going to clean you up." I nodded toward the full tub and tugged at the bottom edge of his shredded sweater. "This needs to come off."

He obliged, sitting up a little so that I could peel it over his head. The shirt snagged on his wounds, dried to the skin with so much blood, and he cried out as I pulled it off.

"I'm sorry," I said. "I'll be more careful."

I removed his shoes and socks, then helped him stand and stripped off his jeans. Slowly, I helped him lower himself into the warm water. He winced as the liquid hit the lacerations. I climbed in behind him so that he was leaning against my chest, his waist between my thighs. The tub was large, but still he had to bend his knees to fit.

With a washcloth, I started with his face, removing the layers of blood, sweat, and what I thought might be tears. He allowed me to do it, didn't even try to pry the cloth from my hands. I was thankful for that. I wanted to do it.

I soaped up the cloth and moved to his right hand, scrubbed each finger, circled his palm, up the inside of his wrist to the elbow and back down his forearm before lowering the trail of lather into the water to rinse away. I started on his other hand.

"There's something I want to say to you," I began. I needed to get this off my chest, to begin with a clean slate.

"I am listening."

"*The Book of Light* showed me some things about our first lifetime together, the day you became my caretaker. When I go back into my memories, I don't just see what happened, I *feel* as I did that day. I don't just remember events, I experience them."

He nodded.

"Rick, I think I pressured you into becoming my caretaker. Clearly you didn't know exactly what I was or what committing yourself to me entailed. I trapped you."

At my coaxing, he leaned forward so I could wash his back. While I did, I waited for his response. One breath, two breaths, the guilt weighed my chest.

"I knew enough," he finally said. He flopped back down against me as if the effort of sitting up was too much for him.

To give us both a moment, I resumed washing his chest, careful around his wounds, and tried to reposition to reach his legs. He felt what I was trying to do and pivoted, settling across the tub from me, so that we were face to face.

"You couldn't have known I would make you my caretaker or how painful it would be," I said.

He swallowed, closed his eyes. "There was not a day in my life with you that I thought you were normal. I call you *my sky* because I've always considered you above me, something beyond my understanding."

"Hmm. Strange, considering you seem to understand me better than I understand myself most of the time." I started washing his foot, rubbing my thumb over the arch, moving the soapy rag up his ankle and calf.

"After your father and your people were killed, you moved to the colony. One afternoon, I met you behind my parents' barn. You told me your mother had visited you, your real mother, and you tried to explain to me who she was. I didn't believe you. I hushed your words, fearful you would be charged with blasphemy. You showed me. You picked up a stone from the ground and set it on fire in your palm, then in the blink of an eye made that flame fly away, a bright red butterfly."

"I could do that?"

"You did. I knew you were a witch, *mi cielo*, even if I didn't understand who Hecate was. While I didn't know you were binding me all those times we were together, and *caretaker* wasn't a word in my vocabulary, I knew you were different and if anyone in Monk's parish found out, both of us would hang or burn. I accepted that most certain fate because the idea of living without you was…unbearable."

"Do you regret it? Do you wish I would have allowed the candle to burn down?"

"Are you sure about marrying me?"

I locked eyes with him. "As sure as a person can be about a thing."

"I don't regret it."

I washed up his inner thigh. A hiss escaped his lips as I reached the length between his legs. Wounded or not, this part of him was responding normally, and a warm current rushed through me at the feel of him through the washcloth. I made sure he was clean, stroking his length, around his base, between his legs, until I was so worked up I could hardly think. I tossed the cloth into the corner of the tub. He groaned at the absence of my hand.

"I need to heal you first. I don't want to hurt you," I said. Gingerly, I shifted in the warm water until my knees landed on either side of his hips. I leaned forward, exposing the length of my neck. "Bite."

I heard his lips part, felt his breath on my skin, but he didn't strike. "I can't shift yet. I only have my human teeth."

Lowering my lips to his ear, I pressed my pulse point to his mouth. "Bite harder." To demonstrate, I sucked his earlobe between my teeth and bit gently.

He struck, and it was not gentle. Flashbacks of Julius's painful bite messed with my head. But this was not Julius, and Rick desperately needed what my body had to offer. He drank greedily. Swallow after swallow created a rhythm I heard and felt against my naked chest, and then the ultimate reward. The wounds between us began to heal, knitting themselves together from the inside out until nothing was left but stripes of pink flesh.

One last swallow and he lapped over the bite, sealing the wound. My head swam a little from the loss of blood, but no part of me wanted to give any less than the last drop he needed to take. I knew he'd had enough when he grabbed my backside and lifted me from the tub, wrapping my legs around his hips.

His eyes were still gray, not black like they usually were when we made love. The beast within was distant, at least for now. It didn't matter. This man, supernatural or not, wanted me. It wasn't magic; it was emotion.

He carried me to the bed and lowered me to my back. His hands caressed from my hips to my bottom rib, thumbs teasing along that erogenous length of bone. I placed a palm on his cheek, guiding his face to mine. Mouths melded, tongues stroked. His capable hand made its way to my breast —stroking, kneading, teasing my nipple until it reached for him.

Ever so slowly, he lowered his body to mine, never breaking eye contact as he positioned himself. Somehow, even after all of the times we'd made love, this felt like the first. Maybe because I was emotionally bared. I loved him. He knew it. And he loved me in return. Or maybe it was because we were equals. Both human now, but not quite.

Whatever it was, as his hands stroked up my arms over my wrists, and meshed with my fingers on either side of my head, and he sank into me, the length of him owning me inch by inch, I gave myself to him fully. In the dim wash of light from the candle in the bathroom, he began to move above me. Gently, ever so gently. This human sex was quiet and soft.

He trailed kisses down my jaw, over my neck, behind my ear. I melted beneath his touch. As his pace quickened, so did mine. A rush of pleasure played out like a storm through my limbs, winds building and lightning striking from that source of heat at my core. I reached up to snare his lips, kissing him deeper as the tension grew. It wasn't enough for me.

I flipped him over on his back, rising above him, allowing the goddess within me to take over. Meeting him thrust for thrust, I lost myself, untamed and reaching to catch the building swell. I came apart, felt him arch and call out as his own pleasure gripped him. Riding out the storm, I eventually found myself again. Shockwaves tipped me forward. I rested my cheek on his chest. After some time, I slipped off him and onto my side. He curled his entire body around mine. Tucking his face into the crook of my neck, he whispered, "I love you."

"I love you, too," I said, and I meant it.

His breath evened out, and I drifted into a much-needed sleep.

THE FAVOR

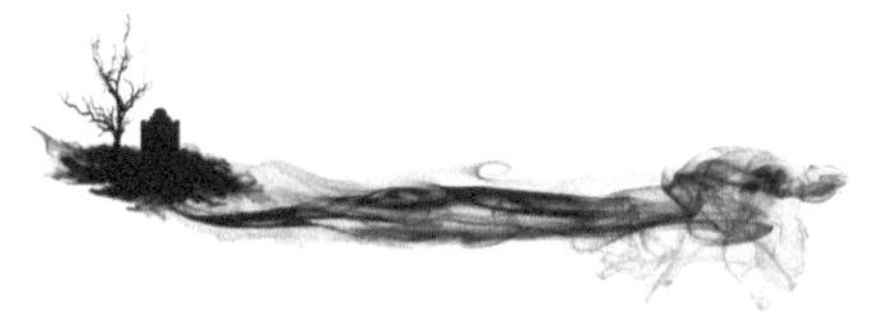

I woke in the circle of Rick's arms to a loud buzz that I assumed was his alarm. It wasn't. He was snoring. Snoring! I decided to enjoy it while it lasted. It might be the last time I ever got to see him sleep. With a contortion of my body that would put a ninja to shame, I disentangled myself from his limbs and climbed out of bed. I dressed quietly, retrieving Nightshade from the bathroom. I was surprised to find him asleep when I returned. He didn't even flinch when I kissed him goodbye on the cheek.

I left a note on the counter and left for home. *Shit.* Could I still call it my home? As I walked up my driveway, dead nekomata stained the snow to my left and right, signs of Rick's bloody battle apparent all around me. A gaping hole had replaced my front door. What did I expect? Kai, or the nightmare controlling his body, and Naill were certainly not going to close up shop before they kidnapped me. I trudged over the mound of snow that had collected on my threshold and had a second to consider what the wet stuff was doing to my hardwood floors. My phone, still parked in its charger next to the stove, began to ring. U2's "Mysterious Ways" and

Dad's picture blasted at me from the screen. I stepped over the bodies piled at the bottom of the stairs, grimaced at Seraphina's half-shifted form at the base of my kitchen island, and answered it.

"Hello?"

"Grateful! Finally. Are you still avoiding my calls? I know you're angry, but—" Dad's voice sounded raw and gritty, like maybe he was getting sick.

"No. Just needed a good night's sleep and turned the ringer off. Listen, Dad, I'm sorry I was so hard on you before. I was just disappointed about losing the house."

"Grateful, something terrible has happened."

The sound of a footstep in my foyer brought my attention to the hole in my wall. Silas Flynn, dressed in a brown suit and tie, stepped over one of the bodies and met my eyes.

I nodded my hello.

He gestured toward my driveway and two monstrous men came inside. They had broad foreheads and biceps the size of tree trunks. Although they looked human, something inside me was hiccupping "ogre." One smiled a mouthful of razor-sharp teeth in my direction. Yep, ogres.

"A Detective Silas Flynn called me this morning," my father said, voice breaking. I placed a hand over my mouth. Dad was crying. "Seraphina and her uncle Kai were killed in a car accident last night. She had my information in her purse…" His voice trailed off.

"I'm so sorry," I said. For more than I could safely say.

"How could this happen, Grateful? One day here, the next day gone. Life is…fleeting. She was… I didn't love her, but I could have. We had something."

"Aww, Dad." My eyes misted over, even as the two men loaded Seraphina's stiffening body onto a stretcher and carried her toward the door.

"The guilt… Before she'd left for the night, we'd talked

about her moving out. What if something I did, our fight, somehow distracted her?"

I walked to the window and watched the men load the body into a large box truck. "That can't be true. You said she was with her uncle Kai. Who was driving? He wouldn't have allowed her to drive if she was upset."

He sobbed.

Hell, this was killing me. "I'm so sorry, Dad. Do you need me to come down there?"

"No. I've just got to pull myself together. Detective Flynn said he'd be notifying the rest of the family. I just hope they include me in the service. Besides Kai, I never met any of them."

"Mmhmm." What could I say? I was pretty sure the entire family was being piled in the back of the truck.

"Dad, I don't know how to bring this up, but what will happen with the house?"

He gave a deep sigh. "Kai's lawyers included a clause in the contract that in case of death on or before the closing date, the property would revert to the seller. Some folks do that to avoid adding debt to the estate. The house is mine. I know how much you wanted it. If you still want to buy it, it's for sale again."

I frowned, my heart breaking at the sadness coming over the airwaves. "Thank you, Dad. I'm truly sorry for your loss. I still want the house. Give me a week to get my finances in order. I'll pay full market price."

"I still don't know why you want it so badly, but after almost losing you over this sale, I'm not going to fight you anymore. You're all the family I have, sweetheart. Please tell me all is forgiven."

"All is forgiven," I said, and I meant it. I missed him, and I needed him.

"I'll see you at Christmas," Dad said.

"Wait, Dad, is it okay if I bring a guest?"

He coughed. There was a long pause. "I thought it would be just the two of us."

"It could be, if that's important to you. But there's someone special in my life. I'd like you to meet him."

"Who?"

"Er, Rick. The caretaker of the cemetery. We've been dating."

Another long pause. "Sure. Why not? Bring him." That was the real estate agent voice, held together by a plastered-on smile. The timing wasn't great with his girlfriend freshly dead, and based on my trail of failed relationships, he probably thought this one was doomed as well. But I was sure he'd come around once he knew how serious Rick and I were.

We said our goodbyes and I tapped the screen just as Poe flew in through my front hole and landed on the banister. The ogres carried out the last body, and Detective Silas Flynn approached me, handing me a piece of paper.

"A bill?" I asked defensively.

"The Malmot brothers don't work for free. That price includes disposal *and* cover-up." Silas raised his bushy eyebrows and shrugged.

"Twenty-two hundred dollars!"

He slapped me on the shoulder. "You have thirty days to pay. And just so we're clear, you don't want to stiff the Malmot brothers." The corner of Silas's mouth tugged downward. "Good to see you again, Grateful."

I nodded dumbly, staring at the bill as he slipped back out the door. I watched him climb into the box truck with the Malmot brothers and back down the drive.

"Not that I don't love the open-air feel of the place, but maybe we should call someone to fix this," Poe said.

Yes. The door. My door. To my house. Needed to be fixed.

I stared at the mountain of melting snow in my foyer for a minute, then at the shards of wood and metal scattered across the house. I let out a deep breath. "Let me try a trick I learned." I raised a hand under my chin, and picturing my foyer as it once was, I called all of the magic I could muster from the house and my night with Rick. I blew. Air left my lungs and tornadoed toward the foyer, picking up snowflakes and ushering them out the door. Slivers of wood lifted from the floor and implanted themselves back into my walls. The door stood up and walked itself back into place, followed by the etched glass oval that melded and became whole again.

Again and again, I huffed and puffed, until the last gust of air seeped from my lungs and my foyer was restored.

"Wow," Poe said. "Practically a miracle."

"No. Just practical magic."

I made for the stairs. "Take the day off, Poe. I'm going Christmas shopping."

"If you insist." He didn't sound disappointed. "I'd love to try guinea pig if you're asking."

I stuck my tongue out at him and turned the corner for my room.

* * *

SEVERAL HOURS LATER, I ARRIVED AT MAISON DES ÉTOILES, arms laden with gifts. My feet ached like my boots had a vendetta against me, and the handles of the shopping bags cut into my skin, even through my thick wool coat. I would have loved to go straight home, maybe with a side trip to Rick's, but I needed to check on the book first.

This was the first time I'd come through the front door. I supposed I wasn't Soleil's regular clientele, but I could appreciate the allure of the place. A stone walkway lined with ornate lampposts traversed a wrought iron fenced lawn. A blanket of pristine snow glistened, reflecting the bright colors of the leaded glass in the lampposts. When I reached the oversized red door, there wasn't a traditional doorbell. After searching for an alternative, I yanked a chain dangling to my left. An old-fashioned doorbell rang inside.

With slight complaint from its hinges, the door opened and a petite blonde with unnaturally green eyes welcomed me. The silver swath of fabric wrapped around her petite body seemed to defy gravity. I stepped into the foyer.

"Soleil is waiting for you in her room. That way," the fae said, pointing.

I followed her directions, down a hallway lined with judges paneling, sophisticated oil paintings, and red damask-curtained doorways that led to the clean lines of well-appointed parlors. The place was Wild West meets East Coast chic. Sophisticated, but clandestine.

The light filtering from under the door at the end of the hall told me I was in the right place. I knocked as a courtesy and let myself in. Gold heat washed over me. Soleil's room was white on white with the only color coming from the hundreds of plants and flowers growing from pots lining the walls. The place reminded me of a Greek garden of the gods. Fitting, I thought, considering Soleil could rival Apollo. A sculpture of a brass sun spit water into a pool to my left. Soleil herself stood in front of a window overlooking the backyard, shining so brightly in her gold and white dress I could hardly bear to look directly at her.

"Good afternoon, Grateful. Thank you for coming."

I set my bags down and gave her a quick hug hello. "No problem, Soleil. I was in town, anyway. Good to see you looking like your old self again."

She blinked slowly. "Yes. I am thankful for your help once again."

"So, where is it?"

"I've sealed it here." She pointed to a slab of marble that looked no different than the rest of the floor and passed her hand over it. "Only sunlight can open it." The square levitated and I squatted to get a clear view of *The Book of Flesh and Bone* inside the vault underneath.

"Good."

"You may take it now," she said. "I will hold it open for you."

I stood, shaking my head and stepped back. "It needs to stay here."

Her eyes flared and the marble tile dropped noisily back into position. "No, no, no. You can not leave this here!"

"It's the safest place, Soleil. The vampires wouldn't dare search here for this, and my home isn't safe, not when Naill, Bathory, and Julius are still walking the streets of Carlton City. Not to mention there could be relatives of the Nekomata clan out there who still know its original burial place.

"But Bathory and Julius will suspect I have it."

I stepped forward and took her hands. "You promised me a favor."

Calm washed over her, and she searched my eyes. "Are you sure? The wish could be used for your own personal gain—material things, relationships...children."

The last hit me hard. I couldn't have children with Rick. For a moment I was tempted to save the wish for myself. Then I thought about Bathory getting her hands on the book.

I squared my shoulders. "I have everything I want or need, except for this."

She nodded.

"I ask that *The Book of Flesh and Bone* be bound here forever, unable to be reached by anyone who might use it for evil."

Soleil nodded her head and then clapped her hands in front of her chest. A ripple coursed out from those joined palms, passing through me and echoing off the walls before plowing back into her like a strong wind.

"It is done. Be forewarned, the results will only last for my lifetime."

"Would it be rude for me to ask how long your kind typically live?"

"A few thousand years."

"And you are…"

"A few months from my nine hundredth birthday."

I smiled. "Good enough."

Digging through my bags, I pulled out a small package I'd wrapped for the occasion and presented it to her. "It's a few days early, but Merry Christmas."

"You shouldn't have." Her actions didn't match her words as she ripped into the plaid paper.

She laughed when she saw what was inside. "Sunglasses?"

"I thought they might be a cool accessory for you to wear when you're a bridesmaid at my wedding?" I raised an eyebrow in question.

She gasped, then reached forward and drew me into a hug. "You do have everything you want."

I nodded.

"And yes, I would be happy to be your attendant. Rick must be so happy."

Lifting my packages, I smiled and moved for the door. "You know, I think he is."

EPILOGUE

I should have known something was up when Rick said he would meet me at my father's on Christmas morning. We'd spent every minute possible together since our engagement, unless I was working at the hospital. It seemed odd to arrive at Dad's brownstone alone.

Rick met me at the door wearing dark washed jeans and a holiday sweater with a reindeer on the front.

"Nice. Where'd you get that one?"

"The salesperson at Macy's said they were, and I quote, 'all the rage.'"

"I can honestly say that sweater has never been sexier." He kissed me and ushered me inside, his hand finding the small of my back.

After a meal of roast lamb and red potatoes (my favorite) we gathered around a professionally decorated artificial tree in my father's living room. The place still looked like a museum, not so much as a grain of dust to disrupt the sterile ambiance. Thank goodness the cabinet was open. The Christmas parade was playing on mute in the background.

Something was missing though. Dad was distracted. As

expected, no one had called him about a service for Seraphina. My guess was all her clothes were still hanging in his closet. My heart drooped into my stomach. I'd never seen him this down.

"Here, Dad. Open mine first." I handed him the gold wrapped box I'd brought, hoping to cheer him up. He tore off the paper and smiled. "Scotch! The good stuff. Jeez, Grateful, thank you."

I smiled. I'd splurged a little to buy a high-end label. After the taste Julius had given me of the good stuff, it felt wrong to get stingy on Dad. It wasn't as pricey as the vampire's, but the purveyor had sworn my father would enjoy it. I figured the extra money Julius had sent my way should be put to good use since I couldn't get a loan with it to buy my house. A problem I swore I'd solve after Christmas. In the meantime, I'd left *The Book of Light* at Logan's, not knowing whether I'd be evicted again anytime soon. He'd agreed to keep it there, even after he'd learned of my engagement to Rick.

"And now you." I handed a smaller box to my caretaker.

After an elaborate spectacle of opening it, he dangled my gift between his thumb and forefinger as if it smelled. "A cell phone?"

I nodded. "It's time."

Rick grimaced and looked inside the box as if the phone might be a joke and the real gift was still inside. I'd suspected he wouldn't love it; a more than hundred year habit was hard to break. Still, he *needed* it.

"He doesn't have a cell phone?" Dad asked incredulously.

I glanced at Rick, who quickly masked his disappointment. "Long story," we said at the same time.

There was only one gift left under the tree, the size of a thick manila envelope. My father presented it to me ceremoniously. "From Rick and me."

"Both of you?" I asked. Odd, considering I wasn't aware they'd ever spoken before today.

I tore into it, curiosity making short work of the wrappings. Inside was a thick stack of documents.

"I have to be honest, Grateful, this isn't just a Christmas present," Dad said.

I looked at him and then at Rick, who pulled a small silver box from his pocket. He flipped open the lid and I saw the blue shine of the antique oval diamond ring that had once been mine.

"I asked your father's permission." Rick smiled nervously. "Will you marry me?"

I wasn't sure why he was so nervous, or why he felt the need to ask me again. I'd already said yes. But then, it was like Rick to want to do things the old-fashioned way. He'd want to make it official.

"Yes. Of course." I gave a breathy laugh and held out my hand so he could slip the ring on my finger. It fit perfectly. Glancing up at my dad, I saw a happy tear slide halfway down his face before he wiped it away. "So, the paperwork?" My heart beat harder as I finished pulling it from the envelope.

"The deed to the house," Dad said, beaming. "An engagement present from Rick and me. To be fair, he was going to buy it for you himself, but when I learned why, I gave him a very good deal."

My hand went to my heart. "It's mine? The house is mine?" The two most important men in my life nodded their heads.

When you are the Monk's Hill Witch, there's a lot of uncertainty in life. I wasn't sure who might try to kill me next. Bathory and Naill were still out there. I owed them justice and they'd be difficult opponents. So much about my existence was dangerous, even brutal.

But as I held out my hand, watching the blue diamonds reflect the Christmas lights glowing red, green, and gold from the tree, I had my house, I had my family, and I had my man. I hadn't cast a spell or made a wish, but somehow after everything, tonight was *magic*.

* * *

THANK YOU FOR READING KICK THE CANDLE.

After saving her caretaker, Rick, from certain death, Grateful Knight is ready for their happily ever after. The date is set and wedding plans are in the works. But when the witch responsible for the candle that almost ended Rick's life shows up in Red Grove expecting payment, the price is more than Grateful can bear. She's about to meet the greatest challenge of her life. The only thing she knows for sure? Rick is worth it.

Find out if Grateful can rise to the challenge of her magical life and navigate her supernatural romance in **QUEEN OF THE HILL**, Knight Games Book 3, available now.

Turn the page to enjoy a free excerpt of QUEEN OF THE HILL , available now!

EXCERPT: QUEEN OF THE HILL

KNIGHT GAMES BOOK 3

1

WAKE-UP CALL

Sex is different with someone you love. New sex extinguishes a fire; old love stokes the embers. In a way, sex is a lot like wine—drinkable as soon as it ferments. But if you allow it to age, the result is a visceral experience—a nirvana of the senses.

When it came to Rick and me, we'd aged together for multiple lifetimes. Every touch elicited an irresistible array of memories. Each caress ignited a new flavor on the emotional spectrum. Sweet and aromatic. Complex. Layered. Having a long finish. An enticing intoxication of hormonal chemistry and raw heat.

I loved Rick.

In bed beneath me, he dug his fingers into the hair at the nape of my neck and tugged. I lifted my cheek from his chest to meet his gaze. His hooded stare held nothing short of reverence, his pupils almost black with need. "You must know you bewitch me in a way that has nothing to do with magic. I have crossed oceans of time to be with you. Lifetimes. I would do it again, but I hope I never have to."

"You won't," I promised. "We're together now, and I plan to be careful with myself."

I trailed my fingertips up the side of his chest and over the length of his arm. Iridescent purple magic followed my touch, markedly beautiful beside his dark hair and the silky red pillowcase under his head. The streak wasn't something I was consciously producing. Power poured out of me with so much love. At journey's end, my left hand linked with his, my engagement ring squeezed inside the web of his long fingers.

The blue and silver cushion of gems that marked our coming nuptials was both old and new. The ring itself was antique, commissioned in the 1700s, but its place on my finger was a novelty. Rick had asked me to marry him only a few short weeks ago, and I had said yes. I was engaged. To be married. To Enrique Ordenez—Rick. My caretaker.

I pressed my lips against the side of his neck. The heat of my breath brought his blood to the surface. Liquid ambrosia. My personal recipe for the elixir of life. During my first lifetime as a witch, I'd made the decision to store an immortal part of my soul inside Rick when Reverend Monk burned me at the stake in 1698. Of course, I don't remember all the details, having died and been reborn several times since. But I had pieced together this much: I didn't have to give Rick my immortality. I chose to. By using magic to create a symbiotic relationship between the two of us, I'd ensured we would be together forever. A lovely side effect was his blood healed me, and my blood strengthened him.

"I need to be inside you," he whispered into my ear. His hand found purchase between the dimples of my lower back. I obliged, shifting my hips to join with him. He groaned and rolled me over.

Nestled under his rock-hard body, his lips brushed my ear as he whispered a mellifluous string of Spanish syllables. The exotic adoration lulled me into a blissful state with each magnificent thrust. I had no idea what he said, but I knew exactly what he meant.

"Look down," Rick whispered.

"Down?" I tipped my face to the side. My hair swung below me in my line of sight. We were levitating above the mattress, suspended in midair.

"Me?" I asked.

"You," he whispered.

I sighed. The power from our connection flowed through me as Rick gently guided my chin back to center and his mouth crashed down on mine. His lovemaking became more fervent, and I was quick to respond in kind.

Knock-knock-knock.

We both ignored the sound at the door and came together in a mind-blurring crescendo. I clung to him fervently through airborne aftershocks. The internal fireworks were still going off when the interruption came again.

Knock-knock-knock. "I have returned twice. I shall not return again," came Soleil's shrill voice.

We dropped like a two-ton weight. The bed groaned in protest.

"She sounds pissed," I said.

Rick rolled off me, pulling the sheet over our spent bodies. "Enter," he called.

The door swung open to reveal Soleil's tight expression and ballerina-like physique. I was sure the lock had been engaged from the inside, but then, as the madam of Maison des Étoiles, Soleil had ultimate control. Each room was enchanted to bring to life the desires of the patrons. Soleil was celestial fae. In fact, her sunny disposition had saved my ass from death by vampire in the past—the winter solstice, to be exact. Fae magic played a big part in the lure of her bordello, too, and was why Rick and I were there. I'd had my first threesome in this room with Rick and… Rick.

"Grateful, may I remind you that you have a dress fitting today at noon?" Soleil asked. She tucked a stray honey-colored hair back into her chignon with a set of perfectly manicured fingers.

I yawned and stretched my arms above my head. "That's tomorrow. Remember? On Saturday."

"It *is* Saturday."

With a flippant giggle, I said, "Very funny. That would mean Rick and I have been, uh, in this room for more than twenty-four hours."

Soleil's gracefully arched brows pinched together over her nose. "Exactly. Not only are we going to be late, I need the room."

Sheets clutched to my bosom, I sat up and grabbed my cell off the nightstand to check the time. "Shit!" I repeated the curse as I dispensed with modesty and leapt from the bed in search of my clothes. It was like an Easter egg hunt. My panties were hanging from the corner of the wardrobe. My jeans were in a heap under the legs of a Louis XVI chair. With my bare bum in the air, I bent over to pick them up, then glanced back to see if Soleil was staring.

She giggled, light and clear as silver bells, and averted her eyes.

"Sorry," I said sheepishly.

"This wouldn't be a problem if you allowed enough time for proper wedding preparations," she said between laughs. "A March date is too aggressive. It is already mid-January."

I sighed. "It has to be the afternoon of the spring equinox —Ostara," I said. "On March twentieth, the magic surrounding new beginnings will be at its apex. It is the perfect day to renew our life together and begin a new marriage. A metaphysical phoenix from the flames."

"Sounds superstitious," Soleil said.

Arms filled with clothes, I ducked into the bathroom to

freshen up. Although I closed the door behind me, I could still hear Rick's reply.

"The wedding will come and go; the marriage is what's important. If Grateful wants to start our marriage on the day of new beginnings, so be it. I don't care if she walks down the aisle in jeans and a T-shirt and we eat her blessed Pop-Tarts for dinner."

I grinned. Good man.

"I doubt she would be pleased with such circumstances," Soleil said.

She was right.

"If something is not to her liking, she can change it," Rick said.

"You mean, use magic."

"She's getting stronger. Her power has blossomed and her magic is as good or better than mine," Rick said.

"I thought she was still learning her spells," Soleil said.

"Natural magic. She levitated just a moment ago, and you saw how she called the storm during the solstice. Learning the spells will come with time, but natural magic is more powerful than any potion or incantation." Rick sounded so proud. My heart swelled thinking about how he stuck up for me.

"Well, considering she might have a few things to think about on her wedding day other than magic, let's hope we can make it to the dress shop on time," Soleil quipped.

I bounded from the bathroom, fully dressed and face washed. My hair was a wild mess, but I yanked the blond waves into a bun at the crown of my head. "I'm ready."

"Great. We can still make it." Soleil opened the door for me. "Is Michelle meeting us at the dress shop?"

"Oh no, Michelle!"

* * *

"So, you forgot about me. No big deal. I'm just your matron of honor. There's no legal *requirement* that you invite your matron of honor to help pick out your wedding dress." Michelle crossed her arms over her chest and tapped her index finger on her bicep.

"Again, I am so sorry I didn't call you earlier. I'm just stoked you could make it on short notice," I said.

She gave me a tight smile. "Well, I'm here." She circled her hands in the air as if her presence was evidence enough of my forgiveness.

I sensed she wasn't over it.

"Schall I pull zee selection of dresses for you, Miss Knight?" Gertrude Evenrose, owner and proprietor of Carlton City's premier bridal emporium, Evenrose Bridal, stared at me over her bifocals, clearly perturbed that it was fifteen minutes past our appointment time, and I still hadn't tried on a dress.

"Of course, Gertrude. I apologize for the delay," I said.

"Vell, I haf a feelink you vill decite quickly," she said, a note of insistence in her voice. She took off like a whirlwind, sweeping through the store and selecting various styles from the racks. Her slight four-foot-nine frame was swiftly buried under yards and yards of white fabric.

"Do you need to know my size?" I asked.

"Nein. Zee dresses vill be ehltered to shpecifications post purchase. As you ehr khleerly a size eight, you shoult haf no problem vith zee samples."

"I'm a size six," I corrected.

She finished hanging the dresses on a trio of hooks in the dressing room and then turned to scan me from head to toe. "You ehr not," she said through her teeth. "Now, tryen sie das garment!"

I jumped like a dog at her command and raced into the spacious changing room. Geesh. I'd faced vampires, demons, shifters, and more in my role as Hecate, but Gertrude Even-rose scared the bejeebers out of me. I thumbed through the stack on the wall. Too poofy, too sparkly, too yellow (who wears a yellow wedding dress, anyway?). And then, *hello, gorgeous*.

Slipping the dress off the hanger, I pulled the pearlescent-beaded bodice on and zippered. I didn't need help. The plunging back ended just above my backside. A set of sparkling silver spaghetti straps slithered over my shoulders and crisscrossed just under my shoulder blades. Despite not having a proper back, the stiff boning across my ribs provided ample support for the girls. From the waist down, satin gazar draped to the floor in two layers, like the petals of an opening flower. More pearls were sewn in swirls along the hem and slit.

With a beaming smile, I paraded out of the stall and stepped up on the box in front of a three-way mirror to the *oohs* and *aahs* of my besties. Gertrude took one look at me and grabbed a pearl choker from her jewelry chest. In moments she had the necklace clipped around my neck, its drop pearl resting naturally in the groove between my collarbones.

"You look like a princess," Soleil said.

"A kind and thoughtful princess who would never forget about her best friend, or not tell her best friend important things about her life," Michelle added cheerfully.

I gave her a sharp look, twisting left and then right to get a better look at the plunging back. The dress seemed to defy gravity, like it was holding itself up by magic alone. My smile faded. I stared at my naked scapula in the mirror for a second, then at the pile of discarded clothing next to my purse in the changing room.

"What is wrong, Grateful?" Soleil asked.

"I just realized I can't wear this dress."

"Why?" Soleil pointed a graceful hand in my direction. "It is beautiful."

Lips pressed together, I turned toward them, my eyes filling with tears. "Nightshade. There's nothing on my back to conceal her. I don't want my father to walk me down the aisle knowing I have a sword strapped to my back."

Michelle rolled her eyes. "Don't you think you could go one afternoon without Nightshade? I mean, the wedding will be during the day, right? Rick will be there."

I bit my lip and shook my head.

Soleil tried to back me up. "She can't risk it. Not after what happened with Bathory."

Oh hell. I'd never actually told Michelle about Anna Bathory, the ancient vampire who had almost killed me in order to complete an invincibility spell from *The Book of Flesh and Bone*. The omission was a definite violation of our unwritten best friend agreement.

"What happened with Bathory?" Michelle asked. Her accusing stare darted from me to Soleil with an expression that went from questioning to disappointed pretty damn quick.

I spread my hands. "I'm sorry, Michelle. For your safety—"

"For my safety? For my safety, you didn't tell me what?" Michelle crossed her arms again and glared at me. If looks could kill, I would have burst into flames. Thing is, I still didn't think it was a good idea to tell her I'd almost been sacrificed on a stone altar less than a month ago. Bathory was still out there, along with her leprechaun sidekick, Naill. Neither would hesitate to destroy Michelle to get to me. I would protect her, but knowing she was vulnerable could ruin her life. Sometimes ignorance is bliss.

With a defeated sigh, I met Michelle's eyes but gestured

toward Gertrude, who was busily straightening racks. "Later, okay?"

Michelle gave a curt nod. "Okay."

Contrary to her words, as her best friend, I was certain she was not okay. In fact, she was pissed at me. Pissed to the point of silence for fear speaking even one syllable might release a deluge of pointed criticisms.

"Perhaps you should try another dress," Soleil suggested, attempting to defuse the tension between us.

"Good idea." I jumped at the opportunity to change the subject. I did a quick change into a vintage style that was mostly layers of antique ivory lace with a black lace overlay at the top. It wasn't my favorite but would conceal Night-shade. I returned to the box in front of the three-way mirror. Michelle still looked like she wanted to kill me, and Soleil didn't even humor me with a pity compliment.

"What do you think?" I asked.

"I think the style does not do justice to your curves," Soleil said.

Michelle turned pursed lips toward me. "Beautiful," she spat, crisp and short with no resemblance to its proper meaning. "Hey, speaking of the wedding, have you figured out where you are going to live yet?"

Damn. Buttons successfully pushed. Michelle knew this was a touchy subject with me and no doubt intended the question as verbal retribution. I sidestepped. "I'm going to live in my house."

"No. After you're married. Is Rick going to move in with you? Or are you going to live with him?"

Ah, so she wasn't going to let it go. "It's complicated." My magic was fueled by the element of air, hence the importance of my attic. Rick's was fueled by earth, hence his stone cottage. Our differences made us stronger on the battlefield but made living together problematic.

"Right," Michelle said. "Because you need different things than he does. Funny how I know that because I can be trusted … Because I'm your best friend."

"You are not going to live together?" Soleil interrupted, appalled.

A drum line kicked off in my heart—*lub-dub, lub-dub, lubidy dub*. My hands started to sweat. I didn't want to talk about this. I didn't want to think about this right now.

Michelle didn't quit. She was like a pit bull with her teeth in me. "Are you going to keep your nursing job when you are Mrs. Ordenez? Wait? Will you be Mrs. Ordenez? Are you going to change your name?" Michelle fired off the questions like bullets.

Soleil's gaze bounced between Michelle and me as if she were watching a tennis match.

The room grew hot. I took a deep breath. The walls swayed, and my stomach twisted. Saliva filled my mouth. I swallowed and swallowed again, but it just kept coming.

"Are you going to adopt kids?" Michelle asked.

That did it. I was going to be sick. I raced for the nearest door, one that led to the back alley.

"Nein! You khen not go out of dooers, Miss Knight," Gertrude shrieked, but I was already in the alley, the mid-January cold biting into my skin. I doubled over and heaved toward the pavement. Nothing came out. I hadn't eaten anything all day.

An arm slipped around my shoulders, and Michelle's dark head and concerned face appeared next to mine. "I'm sorry. I'm so sorry, Grateful. I was angry at you, but I didn't mean to make you ill."

"No. I deserved it. I should have told you everything. I just didn't want to burden you. My life is so—"

"Crazy?"

"You have no idea."

"It's okay, all right? You don't have to tell me about what happened with Bathory, and you certainly don't have to decide all that stuff I threw at you today. It's not worth getting sick over."

"You are not the reason I feel sick."

Michelle blinked at me curiously. "Then why are we out here?"

For a long time, I didn't say anything. Thoughts swirled loose and disorganized inside my skull. I leaned my back against the wall near the door, the sound of Soleil arguing with Gertrude reminding me I was on borrowed time. "You know how I told you Rick asked me to marry him at Christmas?"

"Yeah."

"I may have omitted part of the story."

She raised eyebrows at me.

"He actually asked me when he was about to die."

"What?" Michelle wrinkled her nose.

I took a deep breath. How could I explain this to her in a way she would understand? "Before our engagement, before I understood our history, I pushed Rick away. I took him for granted. He'd thought I didn't want him anymore and sought out another witch, like me, for help. She gave him a magic candle that could have broken our connection permanently by making him human. While the candle was burning, Rick sustained injuries that would have resulted in his death. I stopped the candle before it burned all the way down, halting the magic spell and allowing Rick to recover from his temporary humanity. I agreed to marry him on the floor of his stone cottage, amid a broken ring of skulls and magic. My answer in the affirmative was the only way to end the spell and make him immortal again. My 'yes' saved his life."

Michelle's mouth dropped open and a small disgusted

sound came from the back of her throat. "Are you saying he extorted marriage out of you?"

I shook my head. "No. Well … Not exactly."

She narrowed her eyes and tipped her head, her arms crossed defensively across her ample chest.

"I love Rick." I met her eyes and made sure she knew I was serious. "I really love Rick. To my core. And I *want* to marry him. I'm happy about the way things are going."

"But?"

"Have you ever heard the expression, 'I'm not afraid of flying; I'm afraid of crashing'?"

"I love that one. Who's not afraid of crashing?"

"I'm not afraid of marrying Rick. I'm afraid it won't work out. We can't even live in the same *house*, Michelle. How are we going to build a life together?" I stared hopelessly at the snow-covered pavement, the cold seeping through my skin like a poison.

Michelle pondered my words for a minute, then squatted down next to me so her shoulder grazed mine. She nudged me slightly to get my attention. "You'll figure it out. One day at a time, together."

"Did you read that on an embroidered pillow?"

"I'm serious. If you are in love and committed, you will figure it out. People work out all sorts of arrangements. There's a nurse in ICU who works opposite shifts as her husband and only sees him on weekends. They have two kids. They're making it work."

"What if it doesn't?"

"No one promised you easy. Every couple has challenges."

I widened my eyes at her, my jaw dropping.

"I know your challenges are a bit more… unconventional, but you are blessed to be loved, Grateful. Rick's love for you has straddled lifetimes. Never forget that."

With an air of gratitude, I pulled her into a tight hug.

Clangorously, the door behind us opened, and Gertrude berated me in German. I didn't understand her words, but her gestures clearly meant, "Get inside my damn shop." The look on Soleil's face told me she'd done her best to detain Gertrude. I squeezed her shoulder as I re-entered the building to let her know I understood.

Slipping past Gertrude, I ducked into the changing room and checked to ensure the dress I was wearing was clean and dry, apologizing profusely while simultaneously changing out of it. Gertrude's German chastisement rose in intensity. I'm pretty sure the small fireball of a woman was throwing me out. I hung the antique lace number on the hanger, and pressed it onto the too-full hook. The pressure knocked a dress from the back to the floor. As I bent down to pick it up, a tingle ran up my arm. I lifted the dress and turned it this way and that, checking it out in the mirror. Fashion insta-lust swept over me.

"I'll take this one," I said, bounding from the changing room and handing the dress to Gertrude.

"Aren't you going to try it on?" Michelle asked.

"Gertrude will need measurements," Soleil said.

"I'm feeling lucky. I'll try it on at home. If I need any adjustments, I'll call."

Lips pursed, Gertrude shook her head. "No returns," she said, suddenly speaking accent-free English.

I nodded. "I'll take it."

She rang me up in record time and zipped the dress into a vinyl bag. "Six thousand."

"Okay."

The girls looked at me like I was insane, and maybe I was. Who bought a six thousand-dollar wedding dress without trying it on? Me, that's who.

I grabbed my purchase and led the way out the door. If every decision were this easy, this wedding would be a cinch.

We'd just climbed into the back of Soleil's town car when Michelle completely ruined my sense of accomplishment.

"The way you hurled in the alley earlier reminded me of when I had morning sickness with Manny Junior." She snorted. "It's a good thing you know you can't be pregnant."

2

THE TEST

Pregnant. *I could be pregnant.* I trudged into my kitchen with my new dress in one hand and a Red Grove pharmacy bag in the other. The first I hung in the hall closet. The second I stared at blankly while images and incantations swirled through my brain. I attempted to make sense of the emotions brewing within me, but couldn't sort them out.

As I stripped out of my winter clothes, my raven familiar, Poe, swept into the room on wide black wings.

"We need to speak, Witchy Woman," Poe said. He landed on the back of the couch.

"What's up?" I asked absently.

"Only that you have still not retrieved *The Book of Light* from the ghost-man Logan's home. May I remind you once again that the rightful place for your magical grimoire is in your attic?"

"Ugh." I tipped forward, conking my head on the kitchen island. "I know. I know. I know." I banged my head in time with the mantra. "I keep texting him, and he's always busy with the restaurant."

"Perhaps pick up a phone? Get off your spell-casting ass

and take back what is yours? Grow a spine and stop taking 'later' as an answer?"

"It's not that easy. Logan gave me a key. Rick destroyed the key. Then, in the same conversation as I told Logan about the crushed key, I had to tell him I was engaged. I think I broke his heart."

"More than enough reason to demand your book of magic back," Poe insisted.

"I know. I know. I know." *Bang, bang, bang.* "I'm just hoping if I give him enough time, he'll get over it. I miss his friendship." I straightened, scrubbing my face with my hands.

Poe scrutinized me from head to toe. "This isn't just about *The Book of Light*, is it? As the kids say, what is up, buttercup? You have the pale malaise of a human suffering from the dengue."

"I threw up this morning. Still nauseous."

"The flu, perhaps?" Looking bored, he picked at his feathers with his beak.

I toyed with the corner of the bag on the counter. I was late. Not a lot late. Just about a week. "Can I ask you something?"

Poe shrugged his bird shoulders. "You can ask. I can't guarantee an answer."

"Do you think... with the candle Rick used... Do you think he was human? Like entirely human?"

"At the end? When you saved him?" Poe asked.

I nodded.

"As close to human as he could be. He was dying. If you hadn't put out the candle, you'd be up witch creek without a paddle."

The bag rumpled and ripped as I pulled it open and removed the pregnancy test.

"Bloody hell! You think you're pregnant!" Poe covered his beak with one wing.

Mouth gaping like a fish, I tapped the package down on the counter. "I don't know. I mean, I hope not. I haven't been on birth control since Gary, and Rick and I definitely did the sexual healing thing when he was humanlike." I raised both eyebrows. "Plus, I'm late and perpetually nauseous."

"You said it yourself. Humanlike. Not fully human." Poe gave a cynical snort. "The chances are …"

I furrowed my brow as I stripped out of my puffy white parka. "What, Poe? You know nothing about the magic of that candle. Are you going to babble off some made-up statistic about the chances I could be preggers? I'll save you the trouble. It doesn't matter if it's one percent or ninety percent, I'm peeing on this stick."

Smugly, I marched into the guest bathroom. I was in there all of thirty seconds before I realized I never used the guest bathroom and marched back out. No toilet paper. With an indignant swagger, I jogged up the stairs to the bathroom off my bedroom, tearing into the box on the way. I tossed the package in my overflowing trash can.

What if I were pregnant? How could I raise a baby when I couldn't even empty my own trash or keep toilet paper in my guest bathroom? Michelle made her own baby food from organic produce. I could barely make a sandwich.

"Please don't let me be pregnant. Please don't let me be pregnant," I chanted as I took the test. I placed it on the back of the toilet while I washed my hands. Two minutes. Two minutes until I would know for sure if my life was over.

Into my bedroom I paced, heart thumping and mind racing. If I were pregnant, I'd have to keep the baby. This would be my only chance to ever have a child with Rick. Would the kid be normal? I was a witch. I had magic in my blood. What if the baby was born with horn stubs? Would electric lights flicker when it cried?

Poe flapped into the room and landed on my dresser. "By

the goddess, breathe into a bag or something. You're going to give yourself an aneurism."

I laughed and wiped away the tears in residence on my cheeks. "What are you talking about?" Poe couldn't read my mind, but familiars, by nature, were intuitive of their witch's feelings. It bothered me a little that I couldn't hide what a mess I was about this from him.

"Whatever the outcome, it won't help the situation to have a magical meltdown. In the time I've known you, my worrying witch, in this life and the last, you've been uniquely adaptable."

"Adaptable. Not nurturing or intelligent. Not… parental."

"No one is parental until they become parents. But you've become a great witch in just a few weeks. You could become parental if you had to. You are… resourceful."

I plopped down on my bed. "I could learn to cook."

"Or hire a cook," Poe said under his breath.

My line of sight followed the trail of clothes on the floor to the dust on my dresser. "Also, someone to clean." Rick had money thanks to some wise investments in the early 1900s. What better use for it than improving his child's environment?

"Exactly. If by some miracle you are 'preggers,' as you say, you shall overcome." He blinked at me slowly.

I nodded, relaxing a little.

Poe rolled his eyes toward the ceiling. "It would, of course, be helpful if we knew the nature of the candle Rick used. What did he tell you about the source?"

"Nothing. Every time I mention it, he puts me off. On his deathbed he told me it came from Salem's Hecate, but whenever I ask for details, he changes the subject."

"Hmm. I'm afraid Salem's Witch has a reputation that precedes her." Poe narrowed his eyes like he was trying to choose his words carefully.

"Spill it." My demand went unanswered when the timer on my phone chimed. I tapped the screen to stop the alarm. "Hold that thought. Time to learn if I have a bun in the oven."

On shaky legs, I traversed the formidable space between my bed and the toilet. Lifting the test from the porcelain with both hands, my eyes focused on the little round plastic window. One line for not pregnant, two lines for pregnant. Simple. I blinked. Blinked again. Then, I tossed it in the garbage. It rolled off the top of the heap and clanked on the floor.

"Well?" Poe asked.

"You were right. Not preggers. Probably the flu."

"Ah. All is well then." He bobbed his head joyfully.

"Yeah." My spacey gaze found the gnarled branch of the oak tree outside my window. "Hey, Poe, I was up really late last night and I'm still not feeling the best. I think I'm going to lie down. Do you need me to let you out?"

"No. I've been using the flap in the attic window."

I groaned. He'd shattered a glass pane a few weeks ago, and I'd never replaced it. What was the point? He needed a way to go in and out during the day and the flap of plastic worked. I had more important worries, even if it did mean my heating bill was atrocious.

"I'm going to take a nap," I said. I removed my sweater and leaned Nightshade against the corner near my closet.

A raven's eyes are beady and black, but Poe's brimmed with pity. He transformed into a small black dog and curled up on the braided rug in front of my bed. Instinctively, I knew he wouldn't leave until I was asleep. Poe could be a pain in the ass, but he was a good familiar.

As I climbed under my quilt and began to shed new tears, I took comfort in Poe's understanding presence. I'd just lost my last chance at a real family. For as much as I didn't want the test to be positive, at the moment, the negative was far,

far worse. I closed my eyes, and slipped off to sleep, trying my best to forget losing the precious thing I'd never even had.

* * *

"*MI CIELO? MI CIELO?*" RICK'S VOICE BROUGHT ME OUT OF A deep slumber, his hand rubbing my shoulder gently as he perched on the side of my bed. Maybe I was getting sick. Everything felt heavy. My body pressed into the mattress like I'd gained four hundred pounds. I struggled to shake the paralysis of sleep from my limbs.

"Hi." With some effort, I rolled onto my back so I could see him better. Black wavy hair that curled below his ears, gray eyes, full lips. Even exhausted and flu-ridden, the sight of him lit my fire. "What are you doing here?"

"I fixed your window."

"You fixed my window?"

"The one in the attic. I installed a pet door for Poe."

From the direction of the dresser came an offended caw. Poe was bird-shaped again. "Veritably, I am not a pet," he said.

Rick turned toward me so only I could see him roll his eyes. "They were all out of doors specifically for magical familiars," he said under his breath.

"Thank you," I said. "My heating bill has been ridonku-lous lately."

"I began to worry when you did not wake. My work wasn't quiet."

I glanced toward the window. Late afternoon daylight streamed in, casting light against the far wall. I tapped my phone on the nightstand. Four o'clock. "Sorry. I'm not feeling well."

He placed a palm on my forehead, the tips of his fingers

brushing my hair. "Do you need blood?" His wrist hovered in front of my lips.

"No." I threaded my fingers into his and lowered his offered arm to my chest. "Just tired, and I was nauseous this morning. I'm better now though."

"I discovered something on your bathroom floor." From my bedside table, he lifted the pregnancy test. "Can you explain this?" The concern in his voice tugged at my heartstrings. I hadn't intended to tell him about this afternoon, but I felt the truth press against the inside of my teeth, an unrelieved pressure. After all we'd been through, why keep secrets?

"I thought I might be pregnant with your baby," I blurted. The confession slammed awkwardly into the space between us.

The corners of his mouth twitched, and his eyes crinkled at the corners. "*Mi cielo*, I explained to you, I am unable to produce children. Immortals are sterile," he said kindly. He brushed my hair back from my face.

"The candle made you human. Maybe not completely, but I thought, maybe..." The waterworks started again, and I turned my face away.

He placed a finger under my chin and returned my gaze to his. "You *wanted* to be pregnant?"

I sighed. Sitting up, I tried to put it into words. "Not really. Not initially anyway. But then I started to think about it. Now is not the best time, but when is? I just feel like I missed our only chance."

"If it is important to you, we can explore alternatives once we are married. Although, I beseech you to consider the inevitable hardships of raising a human child. We will live forever. Our child will not."

His point wasn't lost on me. Still, I picked at the corner of the quilt. "I was thinking, what if we bought another candle."

I shrugged. "When we are ready, we could try again. We could make you human temporarily. I could use magic to improve our odds."

His face fell. "No."

"Why not?"

"I cannot obtain another." Eyes shifting away from me, he moved to stand.

"Why not?" I demanded.

With a groan, he placed his hands on his hips and shook his head. "Isn't it enough to adopt? Perhaps a supernatural infant?"

I shook my head. "Don't change the subject. Why can't we get another candle?" I gave him my strongest I-will-not-let-this-go look.

He sighed. "Will you walk with me? The story is not a simple one."

I nodded. "Give me a minute."

Ten minutes later, hair and teeth brushed properly for the first time all day, I wrapped myself up in my puffy white snowman parka and followed Rick into the woods across from my house. A thick layer of snow crunched beneath our boots as we wound between the dormant trees. The sky above was gray but bright. I couldn't see the sun behind the clouds.

"I need to tell you about the candle," Rick began. "When I saw you kiss Logan—"

"*He* kissed me," I clarified.

"So I have learned, but at the time, given the circum-stances, I was convinced that you would choose him in my place if given the opportunity."

"I see."

"I visited Salem's Witch, Tabetha. She comforted me."

I stopped abruptly, my women's intuition perking ears at his words. "Define *comforted*."

He sighed, ignoring my request. "I've known her for hundreds of years. She offered to help me. To free me."

"She sold you the candle."

"She made me the candle. There has only ever been one."

Holy shit. This witch made Rick the candle from scratch. A custom spell was a lot of work to do as a favor or at any price. "How close were you two?" Jealousy crept into my voice, and I saw a muscle in Rick's jaw twitch. Oh my God, had he had an affair? "How close, Rick?"

He looked away. I had a feeling he was going to say more, but at that moment, the sound of splintering wood demanded our attention. I squinted, leaning forward to get a better look at the tree nearest us. "Is that—?"

A face formed in the bark, fine boned and feminine. The eyes popped open, sending me jumping back with a yelp. Rick barely flinched.

"She is coming," the bark lips said, and then a shoulder burst from the wood followed by a woman's body.

"Tree sprite," Rick whispered.

"Obviously," I deadpanned.

Once out of her tree, her skin took on the grain of birch wood; her hair, oak bark; and her dress, layers of green leaves. She bolted past us dancing, leaping, and twirling between the branches. She brought company. Sprites hatched all around us, giggling and bounding between the trees.

"She is coming. She is coming," they sang as they flit by.

"Isn't it early for them to awaken?" I asked Rick. It was twenty degrees outside. I wasn't familiar with tree sprites, but I was fairly sure they should be sleeping when the trees were sleeping. In fact, I was almost positive Soleil had told me as much when explaining why her fae cousins hadn't come to our aid during the winter solstice.

Rick didn't answer me. His brows knit, and his head

dropped forward. I followed his line of sight and watched the snow melt beneath our boots.

"What the fuck is going on?" It was like spring was tearing through winter from the inside out.

"She's come," he said.

"Who?"

"Allow me to introduce myself, *sister*."

I turned toward the potent voice. A tall figure in a hooded cloak stood in a warm space of her making. A large scarab brooch fastened the cloth at her neck, the same scarab beetle I'd seen imprinted on the candle Rick was trying to tell me about. Her boots were tall. Her skirt, red leather. A black corset emphasized her sleek figure. As her long, graceful fingers brushed her hood back from her raven-black hair, my mouth fell open. The woman was stunning. She looked like Cleopatra—dramatically dark with flawless olive skin.

Her full red lips completed her introduction. "I am Tabetha."

3

THE DEBT

"What brings you here, Tabetha?" Rick's voice was firm but not threatening. It resonated with professional politeness.

I was too taken aback to speak. Tabetha was everything I wasn't. To my short and curvy, she was tall and lanky, like a ballerina. I was fair; she was dark. In her hand, she cradled a jagged twig that glowed purple at the tip. A wand. She had a magic wand. I didn't have a wand. Why did she get a wand and I didn't?

Pointing the purple glow in Rick's direction, Tabetha stated her purpose in a voice thick with power and lacking the politeness Rick had shown her. "We had an agreement, caretaker. I've come for payment." Her eyes flicked toward me. "When the magic of my candle called to me, I expected you to seek me out, as we agreed. I did not think I'd have to retrieve you."

Rick shifted a fraction of an inch, placing himself between Tabetha and me. "I apologize for the confusion. The spell was not completed. I am as I was before."

Tabetha stepped closer, sending the tree sprites swirling

and leaping in the warm spring air that followed her. "That was not our agreement. Our arrangement was clear: if you used the candle, I would receive payment."

Finally, I found my voice. "What the hell is going on?"

"*Mi cielo*—"

"Sister," Tabetha interrupted, holding her wand hand up to Rick. I cringed at her familial label for me. While it was true the goddess Hecate was the mother of our magical selves, I had a family, and Tabetha was not part of it.

"What do you want here, *sister*?" I said the last through my teeth, like a curse. She didn't seem to notice.

"It is a shame such awkward circumstances have brought about our first meeting, Grateful Knight, but you should know your caretaker promised himself to me in return for the use of my candle, and I am here to collect." Power rolled off her, sending goose bumps marching across my arms.

My insides twisted at her use of my name, again an unearned familiarity in her tone. "What exactly do you mean by 'he promised himself'?" I asked.

"As my caretaker," she said with a throaty laugh. "Once he was human, I planned to claim him as my own."

My jaw dropped. I stared at her, waiting for the punch line. When she didn't say anything else, I turned to Rick.

He lowered his chin and faced her head-on. "You misunderstood. I never promised to be your caretaker. I never promised anything beyond helping you manage your new territory."

"And did you think you would do that as a human?" she snapped, voice rising in pitch.

"Yes," Rick said firmly.

"Well then, we have a problem. I am owed a great debt." Tabetha looked pissed.

"The contract is null, as the spell was not completed. I did not use it as intended," Rick stated.

Tabetha's perfectly shaped red lips pulled into a grimace and ripples of power blasted like sound waves from her body. Crocuses exploded from the ground, growing in fast forward. The atmosphere became warm enough that I was tempted to unzip my coat. But when the goddamn tree branches started to reach for us with their gnarled branch hands, I knew we were in trouble. We'd practically been transported to the dark forest in *Snow White* or the *Wizard of Oz*. It was freaking me out.

"Are you suggesting that I am owed nothing for my effort?" Tabetha seethed. "Are you going back on your word?" Her eyes burned into him. Worse, the look was familiar. Tabetha was a woman scorned. She had feelings for Rick. *Crap.*

"I will return the remaining candle to you," Rick said. This time he looked away from her when he spoke, as if he were ashamed. As if he recognized that he owed her something.

With a wave of her wand, Tabetha made it clear she did not accept his answer. She knocked Rick on his ass. Rick's eyes bled to black, and his beast exploded from his skin. The winged creature Rick shifted into had the scaly body of a dragon with tufts of hair protruding from the points of his ears and between his scales. Shifted, he was big—T-rex big—with jaws that could swallow a human-sized creature whole. His mere presence was foreboding.

I assumed his change would be a conversation ender. I was wrong.

One twist of Tabetha's wrist, and a blast of purple light hit Rick's beast. By force, his beast transformed, his bones bending and snapping painfully until he was human again.

"Rick!" I ran to his side. He'd collapsed to the ground, shocked and disoriented by the quick change. What a bitch! Fine, Tabetha didn't get the payment she expected for her magic, but she didn't need to get violent about it. I stepped in front of Rick and pointed a finger at her. "You say my caretaker made an agreement with you regarding the candle and that the price was himself?"

She nodded. "I have a contract signed in his blood."

Signed in blood! I glared at Rick. I desperately wanted an explanation, but now was not the time. "There's been a mistake," I said. "Rick had no right to make that agreement with you. As my caretaker, his soul is mine and not his to give." I glanced at Rick, who gave me a ghost of a smile. "However, I also understand that you worked hard on the candle's enchantment and deserve some compensation. What price would you consider suitable payment?"

She popped out her hip and shifted her jaw from side to side as she considered me. Finally, she avoided my question altogether. "Are you denying our agreement, Enrique? Are you denying that you begged me for release from your connection to her?" Tabetha's shrill voice made the surrounding tree sprites clutch at the bases of their throats and leer at Rick in silent union.

He looked her directly in the eye. "It was a mistake."

"Mistake or not, you are mine." Power, thick and palpable, rolled off her skin. The trees swayed, reaching for our heads. A gnarled branch gripped my bicep, bark digging in. Another wrapped around Rick's neck and squeezed. The tree sprites growled and closed in, wrestling Rick toward Tabetha. I tried to help him, but the goddamned forest restrained me. Pain tore through my ankle as a thorny vine sprouted from the earth and lassoed my calf.

That was it. This bitch had to go.

I reached for Nightshade with my one free hand. She wasn't there. *Fuck.* I'd forgotten to strap on my blade after my nap. She was still in the corner of my bedroom. "You can't have him," I yelled. "He's still *my* caretaker."

She ignored me. Rick's skin bubbled as the sprites dragged him toward her. Deep grooves formed in the dirt where his heels dug in. But Tabetha's magic was keeping him from shifting, and the sprites overpowered him by sheer numbers.

Without really thinking about it, my fear and adrenaline took over. As it happened on the night of the solstice, when my magic saved me from Bathory's vamps, the power came naturally, without an uttered word or any effort at all. The air sang to me, connecting to my will as if it were an extension of my body. Instinct and intuition took hold.

Wind and ice blew up between Rick and Tabetha, a hurricane of stinging snow and dropping temperatures. The tree sprites dropped Rick and sprinted for their trees, limbs sluggish. Rick staggered back toward me. With a little effort, I directed the storm to form a barrier between the two of us and Tabetha. Snow caked the ground, burying any sign of the warmth Tabetha had brought with her. The reaching limbs of the trees lost their animated properties and recoiled, falling back asleep in the dropping temperature. I rolled my shoulders, relieved to be free of their grip, then yanked my ankle from the dying thorns.

"Storm's a-brewin'," I said.

Tabetha narrowed her eyes at me. "Perhaps, sister, but I never did mind about the weather. You underestimate me, baby witch." She raised her wand. A blast of heat plowed into me, dissolving my storm, the snow, and the cold. I cried out as my power was forced back into my chest. Rick jumped between us again and held up his hands to her, but Tabetha was just getting started.

A new branch of thorns wound up my leg, shredding what was left of my pants. I howled in pain as thorns wrapped around my waist, sliced through my jacket, and scored my skin. When the vine reached my neck, I tried to turn up the volume on my magic to spare my trachea. The winter storm responded but not before the vine took hold. Warm and wet flowed over my throat and down my chest. I reached up and dug my fingers in, gasping for air. The plant tightened.

"Stop," Rick said. His eyes locked onto Tabetha's. I watched something pass between them and my heart broke. The look had meaning. The look had history. "Please."

"Do you give yourself to me?" Tabetha demanded, the power in her voice reverberating.

I strained to tell Rick no, but I couldn't catch my breath. My wheezing gasps had stopped, and nothing but gagging sounds came from my efforts to breathe. Black spots danced in the corners of my vision. My lungs burned. I slumped against the vines, and the thorns dug in.

"Stay with me," Rick said frantically, clawing at the vine around my neck. It was no use. Death was as close as a lover, and my magic was reduced to a faint and useless breeze.

And then, a miracle.

Thunder clapped above us—not my doing—and a sheet of lightning plowed into the ground near my feet. The vine retracted a fraction of an inch, and my lungs worked to pull in a trickle of oxygen. The earth shook violently, echoing the raging storm above and knocking Tabetha backward. Rick grabbed my shoulders to steady me, although he didn't need to, the thorns held me up like barbed wire. With fear in his eyes, he looked at the sky above and the ground below. Rick was rattled. I'd never seen anything shake him like this.

A booming female voice said, "You do not have permission." I could not place the source. It seemed to come from everything, every direction.

The thorny vine withdrew as if my blood were toxic, sinking into the ground from whence it came. I fell forward on hands and knees, wheezing as new air penetrated my pinched throat and filled my lungs. Rick's hands were on me in an instant, his wrist thrust between my teeth. I drank quickly and willingly of his blood. As soon as I was well enough, I got to my feet.

"I am due blood!" Tabetha raged toward the thunderous sky.

Another lightning bolt landed between us.

With a pained sigh, she straightened herself and fixed me with a threatening glare. "It appears Mother wants you alive. Very well. An alternative price for a caretaker requires some thought. It will not be insignificant. Both of you will come to my home when I call you forth. I will tell you my price then."

"Your home? No. A neutral location," I rasped.

Her dark eyes flashed. "Mother may spare your life, but even she will not deny me my due, sister."

I had nothing left. I could barely hold myself up, even after Rick's blood. Tabetha wasn't going to back down.

I nodded my acquiescence.

She sneered at Rick, her mouth twisting in disgust as if he repulsed her. With a flick of her wand, she dissolved into thin air, the overwhelming scent of roses lingering in her wake.

As soon as she was gone, I turned the full force of my stare on Rick. "Start. Talking."

4

TABETHA

"Tabetha came to my aid in your absence. I couldn't have managed our ward for so long on my own without her help," Rick said. The snow began to fall again, this time on its own. My magic was spent, and my chest ached.

"In my absence?"

"After you died but before you returned. Twenty-two years is a long time."

"When you say she *helped you…*" My mind immediately went to sex. Caretakers fed on sex and blood. "You told me you'd never had sex with anyone but me."

He jerked back as if I'd struck him. "I did not have sex with Tabetha."

"Then why did she look at you like that? You obviously have a history. The way she addressed you, it was almost possessive."

"I can explain, but come. You need to sit down." With a sweep of his hand, he suggested we return to my house, and I agreed. The snow descended in earnest, big fluffy flakes that collected on our hair and shoulders. I followed him across the street.

"As I was saying, Tabetha helped in your absence with particularly difficult cases. A caretaker's magic is effective against the supernatural, but things become difficult when humans are involved. Some work requires a witch."

"For example?"

"A demon possession near Manchester around a decade ago. Tabetha had to expel the demon so that my beast could sentence it to hell. I can't separate the natural from the supernatural."

"I see. So Tabetha helped you because, as Salem's Witch, she's the closest Hecate to our ward."

"Not exactly. There was another—Polina, the Smugglers' Notch Witch—but she refused me. She was reclusive and wouldn't leave her ward. More recently, she's gone missing entirely."

"Missing?"

"Tabetha has been covering her territory for months. That was why she said she needed me, to manage Polina's ward. At the time, Tabetha was sure she would be given permanent power over Polina's realm."

"Why permanent? Polina will come back, right? If the Vermont witch is dead, she'll regenerate like I did."

He shook his head, holding my door open for me.

I stripped off my torn winter clothes and flopped down on the floral sofa. I didn't even bother attempting a seated position. I stretched across the cushions ragdoll-limbed and closed my eyes.

"Polina did not have a caretaker, which should have made her immortal, but unfortunately, even immortals can be neutralized."

My eyes popped open. "Wait, wait, wait a minute." I spread my hands in the air above my chest. "Explain. I thought most Hecates had caretakers."

Just then, Poe flapped down the staircase, swooped

around the banister, and landed on the kitchen island. "Caretakers are rare, Witcherella. Very few witches would give up their own immortality for the sake of another."

I paused and let that sink in. During my first lifetime, when I'd put a piece of my soul into Rick, I'd made him immortal, but doing so had meant that my body would suffer death. Why had I done that instead of keeping the immortality for myself? Because I loved Rick and was afraid the angry mob that burned me at the stake would turn on him next. Only now did it occur to me that true love was unusual. Another witch might not split her soul to save her lover. Tabetha and Polina did not have caretakers. They were true immortals. They'd kept all their power for themselves.

"So Tabetha was an old friend and the acting witch of both territories. How does the candle come into play?"

"After I saw you with Logan, I went to see her. The times we'd worked together she proved a uniquely powerful witch. I told her you wished to dissolve your commitment to me. Who could blame you, Grateful? You are a new person. I thought I was doing the right thing by giving you a choice."

As much as I wanted to deny it, I couldn't. It was true. Before the candle, I'd felt trapped by my relationship with Rick. Choosing him in this life had made a difference to me. Still, I was furious. "I did *not* wish to dissolve our commitment," I snapped. "You had no right claiming to know my feelings without talking to me first. Your jealousy almost cost you your soul."

"I'm sorry." Rick turned his head away. "I could not bear to see you in Logan's arms."

I held up my hand. "Do not make this about him or me. You could have faced me. We could have talked out our problems. Instead, you did something incredibly dumb and dangerous."

He met my eyes and nodded his acceptance of my accusation.

"What happened next?"

"She agreed to help me." Again, his eyes shifted. He was keeping something from me.

"It wasn't that simple, was it?" I glanced at Poe, who quickly became obsessed with cleaning his feathers while clearly eavesdropping. Nice.

The muscles in Rick's jaw clenched. "No."

"Just tell me," I said softly. "It's done. All we can do is manage the consequences."

"She kissed me." The words tumbled over his lips all at once, as if he'd released them on one shaky breath. "The terms of her aid were wrapped in a proposition that I join her in Salem after I was free. True, she needed help managing her new territory, but the implication of her lips was that the partnership would go beyond business."

I cupped the base of my head. Where had all the air gone? Each breath stung and my eyes burned with the need to cry.

"You intended to take her up on her offer. You intended to leave me," I stammered.

"Never." He took a step toward me, but I leapt from the sofa and dodged backward, evading his touch.

"Then what *was* your intention, Rick?" I asked through my teeth.

"I intended to die," he said flatly. "Why do you think I lit the candle before our battle with the nekomata and Bathory? I knew what it would do. I battled your demons knowing they would kill me and set both of us free."

My gaze snapped to his. "But ... then you deceived her. Tabetha believed you were giving yourself to her to be her caretaker. You led her on. She was a victim of your vindictive suicide."

All at once his features hardened, and his soul seemed to

leave the room. The man in front of me was an ice sculpture resembling my beloved. "Yes."

Lips trembling, I tried to focus. "Assuming you don't want to give yourself to her now, how do we get you out of this?"

Rick grimaced. His irises had gone black again, the beast coming to the surface. "Of course I do not wish to give myself to her," he spat. "I love you. You must consider the circumstances. Unrequited love is a particularly painful torture, Grateful. You were doling out that cruelty in spades."

"So this is my fault?" I said.

Poe chose that moment to interrupt. "May I propose the two of you focus on the problem at hand? The sun has almost set. Time to punch the clock."

My familiar was right. Rick and I had work to do tonight. "What was in the contract you signed? She said you signed in blood."

"I don't remember. I never thought it would matter."

"Well, it matters now."

The space between us widened into a black hole that sucked the life from the room. I'd thought he'd cheated on me, but in some ways this was worse. His jealousy had put both our lives in jeopardy. I didn't know what Tabetha would ask for to settle the debt, but I was willing to bet it would be no small thing. The worst part was that I couldn't blame her. Rick had used her. She was as much a victim in all this as any of us.

A vibration from my back pocket pulled me out of the tense moment. My phone. I brought it to my ear and tapped the screen to answer the call. "Grateful Knight."

"Grateful, it's Silas."

Silas worked as a detective for the Carlton City PD. He was also a werewolf and dating my fae friend, Soleil. He rarely contacted me to chat though. A call from Silas usually meant a police case involving a missing or dead human by supernatural hands. "Is this call personal or professional?"

"Unfortunately, professional. There's been a murder. I need you and Rick down here right away."

I glanced at Rick and mouthed "Silas" pointing at my phone. "Sure. Hit me with the address," I said.

"You won't need an address. You've been here before and under circumstances I'm sure you'll remember."

"Where?"

"The Thames Theater."

Continue Queen of the Hill…

Award winning and USA Today bestselling author Genevieve Jack writes wild, witty, and wicked-hot paranormal romance and fantasy. Coffee and wine are her biofuel. The love lives of witches, shifters, and vampires are her favorite topic of conversation. She harbors a passion for old cemeteries and ghost tours, thanks to her years attending a high school rumored to be haunted. Her perfect day involves a heavy dose of nature and one crazy dog. Learn more at GenevieveJack.com.

Do you know Jack? Keep in touch to stay in the know about new releases, sales, and giveaways.

Join my VIP reader group
Sign up for my newsletter

facebook.com/AuthorGenevieveJack
twitter.com/genevieve_jack
instagram.com/authorgenevievejack
bookbub.com/authors/genevieve-jack

Virtue, Book 2

Vengeance, Book 3